He was over her, wasn't he?

Scott had been telling himself that Mike's death had changed everything, helped him overcome an unwanted awareness of a woman he had no business being aware of.

He'd been wrong.

But he was surprised. By the way his gut twisted hard. By the way he stood watching her, practically holding his breath, waiting. He had no clue for what. But he did know that the only thing he could control in life were the choices he made. He'd already made this choice. Long ago.

No man he'd want to know would covet a friend's wife. Period.

Riley glanced around and spotted him. "Scott."

Her smile flashed fast and real. She held out her hands and headed toward him.

"Welcome home," was all he had a chance to say before she was taking his hands and leaning up on tiptoes to press a kiss to his cheek.

Dear Reader,

Pleasant Valley, New York, is a very real place that's near and dear to my heart. And while this quaint town has grown up in the years since I spent time there, it's a place filled with warm memories and wonderful people living life to the fullest.

Her Husband's Partner combines my love of action and suspense with the very thing I love best about Harlequin Superromance—falling in love while dealing with the struggles and issues women know intimately. For Riley, returning to Pleasant Valley means facing a devastating loss and finding her footing as a single parent. She accepts those challenges and comes face-to-face with a few others she hadn't anticipated. That's life. Learning to roll with the punches. Riley does and in the process learns to live and love again. Life is too precious to waste a second.

Ordinary women. Extraordinary romance.

I hope you enjoy Riley and Scott's love story. I love hearing from readers so visit me at www.jeanielondon.com.

Peace and blessings,

Jeanie London

Her Husband's Partner
Jeanie London

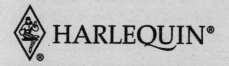

TORONTO • NEW YORK • LONDON
AMSTERDAM • PARIS • SYDNEY • HAMBURG
STOCKHOLM • ATHENS • TOKYO • MILAN • MADRID
PRAGUE • WARSAW • BUDAPEST • AUCKLAND

Recycling programs
for this product may
not exist in your area.

ISBN-13: 978-0-373-71635-7

HER HUSBAND'S PARTNER

Copyright © 2010 by Jeanie LeGendre.

ABOUT THE AUTHOR

Jeanie London writes romance because she believes in happily-ever-afters. Not the "love conquers all" kind, but the "we love each other so we can conquer anything" kind. Which is why she loves Harlequin Superromance—stories about real women tackling real life to fall in love. She makes her home in sunny Florida with her romance-hero husband, their two beautiful and talented daughters and a menagerie of strays.

Books by Jeanie London

HARLEQUIN SUPERROMANCE
1616—FRANKIE'S BACK IN TOWN

HARLEQUIN BLAZE
153—HOT SHEETS*
157—RUN FOR COVERS*
161—PILLOW CHASE*
181—UNDER HIS SKIN
213—RED LETTER NIGHTS
    "Signed, Sealed, Seduced"
231—GOING ALL OUT
248—INTO TEMPTATION
271—IF YOU COULD READ MY MIND

*Falling Inn Bed...

HARLEQUIN SIGNATURE SELECT SPOTLIGHT
IN THE COLD

To the real Camille and Jake,
because I love you both so very much

PROLOGUE

SHE KISSED MIKE GOODBYE, arms still immersed to the elbows in soapy dishwater at the kitchen sink. The twins hopped up from the table, eager to make the daily pilgrimage to the porch to see Daddy off to work. Mike, the twins, even the dogs, clustered around her, surrounding her as if she was the sun in their universe. Seraphic chaos, Mike always called it, and she could practically hear those unspoken words when he handed her the dish towel. A perfect moment.

"Got to run," he said.

Without another word, she herded the troops toward the door. He needed to get out early to make court on time, and the traffic getting into downtown Poughkeepsie could be hellish. Judge Callahan ran an orderly courtroom, and Mike didn't want to be late the day he'd be taking the stand. Not when he and Scott had worked for over a year to collar the gang leader on trial.

"Good luck," she said once they made it to the porch, lifting her face for another quick kiss. "You'll be great."

He met her gaze with a deeply amused look as if he'd known she wouldn't say anything else, and that he appreciated how she always thought he was great. No matter what.

Then he scooped up the twins, one in each arm, because at three they were still small enough for him to do that. She wondered what he'd do when they grew too big. Pick up Camille first because she was the princess and the oldest by twenty-two minutes? Or Jake, his little guy? Knowing Mike, he'd take turns and always manage to remember who went first.

Now they'd never know for sure.

Letting her eyes drift shut, Riley blocked out reality for another desperate instant, clinging to the details of that morning, details that had been looping in her head nonstop until she couldn't sleep, eat, *feel.*

Had it only been days since life had been normal?

"Riley," a voice prompted, forcing her back to reality.

Opening her eyes, she found Chief Levering extending a neatly folded American flag. He didn't offer condolences to the widow. He didn't have the words. She knew it, recognized the grief he bore in the worn lines on his face, the heartbreaking weight of a job that cost more than he had to give.

She wanted to thank him for caring, thank the entire force that had loved and respected Mike. She didn't have the words, either. When she accepted the flag, her hands shook.

The chief stood there a moment longer, finally signaling his men to begin the salute to honor their fallen brother.

A gunshot cracked the silence, then another and another, each exploding before the whine of the previous one had faded. The deafening blasts rattled the morning, should have rattled her. But each came as if from a distance, the volume almost too low to make out.

She was disconnected, numb, the only person left alive on the planet though a thousand people surrounded her, fanned out in every direction from the grave site. But they were just background noise, too. Not one of those people could come between her and the reality of that gaping hole in the ground.

Not one could come between her and the extravagant flower sprays with their blossoms so jarringly alive, the bright colors violent against the misty gray morning.

Not one could come between her and her husband's wooden casket, polished to a high gloss that reflected her image, an image as disjointed as she felt.

Had it been only days since Riley Angelica's dream had become a nightmare?

CHAPTER ONE

Two years later

"DADDY'S HERE?" Camille sounded unsure, so Riley glanced in the rearview mirror to find her daughter peering through the minivan window with a disbelieving expression.

Despite grief counseling, Camille's idea of a cemetery clearly wasn't lining up with the sight of lush forest and crowded gravestones whizzing past.

"Daddy's in heaven," Riley prompted. "Remember what we talked about with Ms. Jo-Ellyn? This is his special place on earth so we can visit him whenever we want."

"Like God at church," Jake explained, the caring brother.

"That's exactly right, sweet pea." Riley caught her son's gaze in the mirror and gave him a smile. "We can always talk to God because He's everywhere, but church is His special place."

Jake nodded slowly, looking so serious that Riley knew he wasn't convinced about this cemetery business, either. Tough little guy was just looking after his "girls." She didn't think he could actually remember when his daddy had charged him with that responsibility....

"You're the man around here while I'm gone," Mike had always said. *"Take care of our girls for me."*

Obviously Jake had been affected on some level. One thing Riley had learned during the past two years of grief counseling was that the human mind had an amazing capacity to cling to long-ago details. She also knew caring for "his girls" was a big responsibility for a five-year-old.

She maneuvered the minivan down one of the narrow paths winding through St. Peter's Cemetery. Left. Left. Right. Left. She made each turn as if she'd just visited the grave site yesterday.

Her mind definitely had an amazing capacity for the past.

In some ways Riley felt as if she'd lived a lifetime since that last time she'd been here. Yet she didn't even have to close her eyes to see the place as it had looked then. Stark during that bleak time of year before spring breathed even a hint of promise. Just mere months after Mike's death, when she'd finally accepted she wasn't going to forge through the healing process like the strong widow.

Riley had intended to deal with grief head-on. She knew it would be hard, the hardest thing she'd ever tackled in her life, but she was practical and had every reason in the world to cope with this unexpected turn their lives had taken.

Two very precious reasons—both securely strapped in the back seat of the van.

Much like Jake felt the responsibility of caring for his girls, Riley's responsibility was to care for the family in Mike's absence, to make their dreams happen even though he wouldn't be with them.

It had never even occurred to her that the healing process wouldn't be hers to manage and control, that the process had a mind and a will all its own.

The Law Enforcement Support Network provided a variety of services for family members who'd lost loved ones in the line of duty. She'd read every word of the literature, followed every counselor's suggestion, listened attentively to other grieving folks in the support group. She'd accepted the help of loving family and friends though her inclination was to put on a determined smile and tell everyone, "I'm good. It's all good."

She hadn't been good at all.

It had taken months to accept that fact, months to realize that her decision to grieve in a healthy fashion for herself and her kids didn't matter. Not when everywhere Riley turned she'd been bombarded by memories of Mike, their wonderful life together and all the dreams they'd made for the future.

Riley could barely stand to be inside the house. She couldn't sleep. She couldn't eat. She couldn't concentrate long enough to write a 1200-word article. No matter how hard she tried, she simply couldn't believe that Mike wasn't coming home. Ever.

Part of the problem, she knew, had been the investigation. While Mike had managed to kill his murderer on the courthouse steps, there'd been other gang members who had organized the shooting behind the scenes, a revenge killing against the cop responsible for building the case that would send one of their own to prison. Mike's partner and the entire police department had been determined to bring down each and every one.

Even if she could have avoided the newspaper headlines and television and radio sound bites, she would have had to burn the city to the ground to avoid the reminders of gang graffiti on street signs and bus stops and the sides of buildings.

Every time Riley drove through downtown Poughkeepsie—and her job as a reporter for the *Mid-Hudson Herald* brought her there often—she'd witness the visible displays of anger and violence that had cost Mike his life.

In that fragile emotional state, she hadn't wanted to make decisions about selling their farmhouse in Pleasant Valley, Mike's twenty-five-acre dream home for the horses he loved.

Fortunately she hadn't had to. Their college-age nephew had become caretaker as a way to move out of his family home since he hadn't earned scholarships for dorm housing.

Riley had made arrangements to stay with her mother and stepfather in Florida. On that long-ago day, she'd come to the cemetery on her way out of town to apologize to Mike for abandoning their life until she could figure out some way to heal and go on. But Florida wasn't meant to be forever, and now she and the kids were coming home.

Steering the van off the path, she came to a stop in the grass so a car could squeeze past if one happened along, not that she could see another living soul around. The place was quiet, but with that lively silence of summer. Birds twittered. Insects chirped. Fat squirrels scampered around trees. Though there wasn't much of a breeze, leaves rustled sharply as a squirrel leaped in a daredevil arc from one branch to another.

These antics of nature were familiar reminders of the life they'd left behind in Florida. A life spent largely outdoors with play group visits to parks and the beach. The twins couldn't remember the reality of an upstate New York winter, and Riley hoped the novelty of snow would ease their transition through the upcoming, and unfamiliar, season changes.

"We're here." She forced a brightness into her voice she didn't quite feel and turned the key in the ignition. "Let's grab the things we made for Daddy."

She'd barely gotten the words out of her mouth before seat belts snapped open, the minivan door rattled on its hinges and sneakers hit the ground, ready to run.

She didn't bother repeating her direction, didn't stand a chance against the twins' curiosity and excitement. She just said, "Hang on," while retrieving the backpack from the floor of the van.

"Where is he?" Camille scanned the sea of gravestones impatiently.

Riley handed her daughter a bouquet of bright tissue-paper flowers and her son the Popsicle-stick frame showcasing him displaying the foot-long bass he'd caught on his latest fishing excursion with Grandpa Joel.

"Follow me." She directed them down a winding path, careful not to tread on other folks' resting places. Her two high-energy little kids grew eerily quiet.

"Here we are," she finally said, placing a hand on each small shoulder as they gathered around Mike's grave.

Riley couldn't bring herself to look down, not yet, so she watched her kids instead, the sun glinting off their pale blond heads as she tried to gauge their reactions.

Jake frowned intently, the spattering of freckles across his nose crinkling with the effort. Camille's crystal-blue eyes took in every detail, and she could barely contain her need to move, a need that had her bouncing up on her tiptoes excitedly.

As fraternal twins, Jake and Camille resembled each other as any brother and sister might, but they were entirely their own little people. While both were towheaded with fair skin that held enough of Mike's Italian heritage to let them tan to a deep golden brown, they had distinctly different features. Jake's eyes were a deep, almost sapphire blue while Camille's were startlingly light, the sparkly blue of ice.

The last time Mike had seen them they'd been adorable three-year-olds. Not quite kids, but no longer babies, either.

Now they were all kid, each with his and her own personality and opinions, both raring to get out into the world, which at this age meant kindergarten—the very reason Riley had decided now was the time to come home and get settled.

Unsurprisingly, Camille was the one to make the first move. She launched forward with a hop-skip and sank down in front of the headstone, propping her bright bouquet against it.

"Hi, Daddy," she said in her singsong lilt. "I made this for you at Chiefie school. Jakie made one, too, but Ryan knocked over his juice bag and grape juice squirted all over it. The flowers melted on the table."

"Ms. Kayleigh said it wasn't my fault so it was okay," Jake added in a hasty defense, taking a few tentative steps toward his sister.

Chiefie school had actually been a child-care class in a public high school. The program was designed to give student teachers hands-on experience in child care while gearing up preschoolers for kindergarten. Since Chamberlain High School's mascot was a Native American chief, the preschoolers had been known as chiefies. With four student teachers caring for each little chiefie, the mornings the twins attended the program had been filled with structured fun and a lot of caring attention.

"Here, Jakie. Give Daddy your present." Camille mothered her twin every step of the way, even reaching out to take the frame he held tightly in both hands. Jake pulled away and held it away from her. Camille just shrugged, familiar with her brother's unwillingness to accept help, and told her daddy, "Jakie made you a frame for his fish picture."

"It was a bass, Camille," Jake corrected, still clearly put out that she'd tried to take his gift. Slanting his gaze toward the headstone, he steeled his nerves and said, "Grandpa

Joel said it was the biggest bass in the lake, and he showed me how to bend the hook so his mouth didn't have a big hole when we threw him back in."

The thought of Mike watching this show from heaven helped Riley shift her gaze down to the headstone, too.

> *Michael Jacob Angelica*
> *Beloved Husband and Father*
> *4/4/1975—2/2/2008*
> *Always in our hearts*

She'd chosen that tombstone for the simple design. Two angels poised on top, wings touching to create an arch over the marble memorial. That was the only ornamentation other than the inscription, and somehow seeing those words brought all the expectation she'd tried not to feel, all the anxiety that had been building to fruition. Riley exhaled a deep sigh.

Mike's place was peaceful.

Taking a step forward, she ran her fingers along the smooth arch of an angel's wing, felt the warm marble beneath her touch. A headstone that marked the resting place of the man she'd loved with all her heart. Then she noticed the bottle of Guinness Stout propped against the side of the headstone.

And smiled.

That would be a gift from Scott Emerson, Mike's partner on the vice squad of the Poughkeepsie Police Department, a longtime friend and drinking buddy. Since the label wasn't weathered, Riley guessed this unusual memento must be a recent addition. Leave it to Scott to continue the friendship despite death. That quiet loyalty had always been a part of her husband's partner and friend.

"Mommy, aren't you going to say hi to Daddy?" Camille asked.

"Hi, Daddy," Riley said softly, brushing aside a cluster of tiny leaves from an angel's wing. "We miss you."

"He knows that, silly." Camille rolled her eyes. "We tell him when we say our good-night prayers."

"So, Camille," Jake shot back. "He still likes to hear it."

"Oh, shut up, Jake."

"Camille," Riley cautioned.

"He's grouchy."

No argument there. Riley shifted her gaze to her son, assessing whether or not the emotional letdown was the cause of this mood swing.

Jake shifted from one foot to the other, clutching his picture frame against his tummy. "I'm starving, Mom. We haven't eaten in forever."

Riley bit back a smile at the exaggeration. Apparently now that his apprehension about the situation had been dealt with, Jake's mind was back on the priorities.

Camille pivoted on her sneakers and raced back to the minivan. "I'll get the cooler. We can have a picnic with Daddy."

That wasn't exactly what Riley had had in mind while making peanut butter and jelly sandwiches in their Maryland hotel room this morning, but a picnic with Daddy sounded like just the thing to kick off their return home. And with the canopy of leaves filtering the sunlight overhead, Mike's grave was the perfect place to take a deep breath before gearing up for the next big challenge.

Facing the house and the memories.

Riley took that deep breath, then sidled close to Jake. He'd inherited her hair color but Mike's cowlicks, and his thick blond hair always wanted to stand up like a rooster's whenever it started to grow out from a cut. She ruffled her fingers through it, making it spike even more.

"Mom," he groused, ducking away.

Riley smiled above his head where he couldn't see her. "Are you going to tell Daddy about your bass? Grandpa Joel was really proud of you. He said you reeled in that big boy like a pro."

Jake frowned down at the headstone, at the bright bouquet there. Riley didn't rush him, just slipped an arm around his shoulders when he glanced down at his photo.

"I miss Grandpa Joel," he said.

"I know, sweet pea. Do you want to call him after we get home? He and Granny want to know that we made it safely."

Jake nodded, still clutched his photo.

Riley's father had been a career naval officer, a larger-than-life man as fast to laugh as he'd been to issue orders. He'd died during Riley's sophomore year in high school, and her mom hadn't remarried until Riley's sophomore year at Vassar College, the year she'd met Mike, who'd been playing rent-a-cop at a campus concert.

Riley's stepfather was an Oklahoma farm boy who was as laid-back as Riley's father had been intense. There was no question why Mom had fallen in love with him. Not only was Joel charming, but as senior VP of international relations for a Fortune 500 company, his travel schedule was more active than Riley's dad's had been. Mom got antsy if she stayed in one place too long.

Riley had no doubt that her military upbringing was the very reason she was so set on rearing her kids in one place. In the States. Overseas. You name it, and if Riley hadn't actually lived there, she'd probably visited at some time or another during her early life.

Grandpa Joel had stepped in as the man in Jake's life

whenever he was in town, inviting her son along in the mornings and evenings to help water the yard. He'd taught Jake how to plant and tend tomatoes, how to fish and how to tell the difference between venomous and friendly snakes.

As if any snake could be friendly.

"Is Grandpa Joe as nice as Grandpa Joel?"

Camille reappeared and plunked down the soft-sided cooler. "Grandpa Joe and Grandpa Joel. That sounds funny."

"It does, doesn't it?" Riley laughed, knelt down and unzipped the cooler. "Camille, would you please grab the beach blanket. Then we can sit and have a real picnic."

Her daughter took off again like a bolt, granting Riley a few private moments to deal exclusively with her son—alone time was always a challenge with twins.

"Don't you remember how much fun we had at the Magic Kingdom when Grandpa Joe and Grandma Rosie came to visit? You liked them both then."

Jake nodded.

"Grandpa Joe was a lot of fun. You told me you liked looking for shells on the beach with him. He was the only one who'd climb up those scary nets with you in the tree house at Busch Gardens."

That got a smile.

"His feet kept poking through the holes."

Oh, Riley remembered, all right. She'd been convinced the next ride they were going to take was in an ambulance on the way to the emergency room because her father-in-law had been determined to keep up with his grandkids.

Joe had wanted to make memories, he'd told her, inadvertently driving home the point that by leaving New York Riley had taken away the only remaining connection to his son. Until then, leaving hadn't felt like running away, only an unavoidable necessity. But her father-in-law's comments made her realize the time had come to decide where she wanted to raise the kids, to get them settled before school started.

In her heart she'd known the time had come to go home. And home was the Mid-Hudson Valley, where Mike had lived his entire life, surrounded by his family and friends.

It was all his children would ever have of him.

Slipping an arm around Jake's shoulders, she squeezed. "Sweet pea, Daddy will understand if you've changed your mind about the picture. A reminder of your big bass would be nice, but he doesn't need it. He already knows you caught the biggest fish in the lake because he's keeping his eyes on us from heaven. I know he's really proud of you."

Jake slanted his gaze her way, indecision written all over his face. He glanced down at the photo then at the head-stone. She knew the instant he'd made his decision because he squared his shoulders and set his mouth in a firm line.

So like his daddy.

"I want Daddy to have this," Jake said. "Then he won't ever forget how big my bass was."

Riley pressed a kiss to the top of his spiky head and said, "Go ahead, then. Give it to him."

She watched him cover the distance in two determined steps and position the photo frame carefully beside the tissue-flower bouquet. Add the beer bottle and Mike's grave made a festive sight. She'd bring along some memen-tos of her own next visit.

"I want the cherry juice bag," Camille shouted on her return, the blanket a haphazard tumble in her arms, ends trailing in a threat to those little feet.

Riley launched forward and hauled the blanket from her arms. "Thanks, little helper girl. I'll spread this out while you get those juice bags, okay?"

Camille obliged while Riley settled the blanket, trying to avoid picnicking on top of Mike or his neighbor. She finally managed an acceptable compromise, and as the kids tussled over who got the only cherry yogurt stick, Riley decided that she'd probably be too busy dealing with life as a single working parent to spend too much time obsessing about the past.

She hoped.

CHAPTER TWO

SCOTT EMERSON PUSHED out from under the pickup, the wheels of the floor dolly grinding over the concrete beneath him. Setting aside the wrench, he wiped sweat from his brow and glanced through the open garage doorway where Brian had gone outside to take a phone call on his cell. Scott didn't blame him. It was hotter than hell in this garage, despite the industrial fans whirring overhead.

He sat up to give his back a break from spending too damn long under the antiquated truck used to transport hay for the horses. Why the kid had waited until the last minute to load the hay was beyond understanding. A few days earlier and a broken pickup wouldn't have been a crisis situation.

Scott squelched his annoyance by taking a cooling swig of water. Brian was a twenty-year-old kid who'd been shouldering a lot of responsibility around the farm since his uncle had died. While both Brian's maturity and foresightedness could use some fine-tuning, he'd been remarkably reliable. And that was saying something. Four horses were a lot of work.

After eavesdropping on half the conversation, Scott wasn't surprised when Brian snapped shut the cell and announced, "Aunt Riley just passed Purple Parlor."

"About ten minutes, then."

Brian nodded, uncharacteristically subdued, and Scott couldn't tell if the kid was relieved to be getting some help around here or depressed not to have the house to himself anymore. At Brian's age it was probably a good measure of both.

Scott motioned toward the truck. "Crank her up. Let's see if we got it."

Brian circled the flatbed with a few easy strides and climbed into the cab. He'd been a kid when first offering to help out at the farm after Mike's death. Two years of tending horses and baling hay, and Scott had to wonder if Riley would even recognize her nephew.

The engine roared to life, growling loudly in the lazy afternoon heat.

"All right, Scott." Brian goosed the accelerator for good measure, sending a blast of heated exhaust from the tailpipe.

Tossing the wrench into the toolbox, Scott got to his feet. "Don't wait until the last minute next time." He tapped on the hood with a palm. "Give this old girl a break. Leave yourself some time in case she's having a bad day."

Brian shut off the engine and stepped out, saying, "I know. I couldn't deal with the hay until I finished cramming for a test in Anthropology."

Yeah, right. Always an excuse. Brian was going to do things his own way because he was twenty and he could.

After hanging the keys on a hook above the workbench, Brian cast a forlorn look at the steps leading to the upstairs apartment.

His new home.

"What do you think about moving into the apartment?" Scott asked. "Beats knocking around that big old house by yourself."

Brian scowled, and Scott guessed nothing could be further from the truth.

"It's a bachelor pad with everything a college guy needs," Scott added. "Kitchen. Heat. Private entrance."

"Aunt Riley watching over me."

True. She could glance out any east window to see what her nephew was up to. And knowing Riley, she would. Often.

"I think your aunt will have her hands full enough with the twins to spend too much time worrying about you."

"You think?"

"The twins are starting school so, yeah, I think."

Brian didn't look reassured, and Scott conceded that the garage apartment was a demotion from having a 150-year-old farmhouse to himself, but he couldn't feel too bad. Lots of kids would think Brian had a sweet setup. College. Tending horses in exchange for room and board. Too many kids of Scott's acquaintance would have given their left nut for a shot at college if it meant hauling ripe trash.

Scott dropped the subject. "You going to tell me when you want the posse to work on the yard or should I ask your aunt?"

"I'll tell you," Brian said quickly. "I don't want her thinking she doesn't need me around anymore."

There was the real trouble. Brian was worried about his meal ticket. Good. Worry might motivate him to get organized. Riley didn't need to add another kid to her brood.

"Let me grab my things and I'm out of here," Scott said. "Just call me if the old girl acts up again."

"You should stay. Don't you want to see Aunt Riley?"

"Your grandmother told me she warned everyone not to bombard Riley until she had a chance to get settled."

"There are only two of us, Scott. That's not bombarding."

The kid wanted backup, plain and simple. "I'll stay long enough to say hi."

"Pound it." Brian raised his fist in the air.

Scott pounded Brian's fist in a familiar salutation just as a white minivan slowed on the road before making the turn into the circular drive.

The Angelica family had come home.

Scott reached for the degreaser and a rag to clean his hands as the minivan doors burst open and kids hopped out.

For a moment, he stared, frozen with the rag trapped between his fingers, surprised by the jolt of emotion he felt. These were not the chubby children who used to trail behind Mike while he performed chores in the barn.

These were kids in every sense of the word, from lanky bodies that appeared to be growing with rapid-fire speed to energetic curiosity that had them taking in everything all at once. If not for the blond hair that was bleached almost white against their Florida tans, they'd be unrecognizable from the toddlers Mike had been so crazy about.

Until Scott took a closer look.

Mike was all over these kids. The boy—Jake—came to a screeching stop the instant he saw Brian. Folding his arms over his chest, he gazed out of Mike's eyes with a thin-lipped expression Scott had seen too many times not to recognize. The kid took in the lay of the land with the same deliberation that had made his father such a good cop and trusted partner. Mike had never missed a beat, which was why no one but he and the shooter had died in front of the courthouse that day.

Camille, on the other hand, clearly the more social twin, propelled herself forward on sneakers with wheeled soles, riding to a smooth stop in front of Brian. "Are you my cousin who takes care of Daddy's horses?"

"Yeah," Brian said. "You remember how to ride them?"

Camille might look more like Riley with her delicate features and light eyes, but the look she shot her cousin was pure Mike. "I don't turn six for two months."

She held up two fingers to emphasize her words in case Brian was too thick to understand what she meant. Scott was definitely too thick to understand.

Maybe she was too young to remember living here?

"I'll teach you." Brian seemed to get it. "On Baby. She's the sweetest."

Camille squealed excitedly, while her brother noticed Scott inside the garage. Jake narrowed his gaze and stood his ground, glancing at his sister to make sure she didn't need help.

Scott tossed aside the rag, about to join the party, when the driver door opened and Riley emerged from the van. Mike used to joke that the day he'd met Riley was the day he'd figured out dreams really did come true. It was one of those statements that could have sounded so corny but never did.

Because Mike meant what he'd said.

Scott, and anyone who'd ever been around Mike and Riley together, had understood Riley was the kind of woman to stand beside a man and help him make his dreams come true. And Mike was the kind of guy who appreciated a wife who believed in him.

Sure, it hadn't hurt that she was drop-dead gorgeous, too, long and lean with a head full of wild blond hair.

"You know my wife, Riley," Mike used to say. *"The one with hair bigger than she is."*

Ironically her hair did seem bigger than she did right now. Dressed casually in long shorts and a short-sleeved blouse, she didn't appear to notice any of them while pausing with her hand on the door as if she needed to hang on for support. She stared at the house, looking lost in her memories.

Scott could only stand there, galvanized by the sight of her. The monthly phone conversations they'd had during the past two years hadn't prepared him for seeing her again.

Or for feeling this forgotten but all-too-familiar awareness.

Scott had been telling himself that Mike's death had changed everything, helped him overcome an unwanted desire for a woman he had no business having.

He'd been wrong.

Riley's voice coming at him over a bouncing satellite signal had only placed distance between them, and distance only masked the symptom. The problem was still there. He supposed that shouldn't surprise him, given who he was.

But he was surprised. The moment stretched forever. He practically held his breath, waiting. He had no clue for what, but he did know that the only thing he could control in life was the choices he made. A valuable and hard-won lesson. He'd already made this choice. Long ago.

No man he'd want to know would covet a friend's wife. Period. The words echoed from a barely remembered youth, when he'd had someone who'd cared enough to point out the differences between right and wrong.

A young voice blessedly shattered the stillness. "Mommy, can my cousin teach me to ride Baby?"

Riley turned to her daughter. "We'll see, sweetie." She moved away from the van, all smiles for her nephew. "Brian, ohmigosh, what happened? You're all grown-up."

Before the kid could get away, he was wrapped in his aunt's arms and hugged exuberantly.

Scott found himself breathing a little easier as Brian mumbled some incoherent greeting and started to blush.

Riley and the twins looked as if they'd been on an

extended vacation with their tans and summer clothing, but Scott knew these past two years hadn't been any kind of holiday for Riley. Their phone conversations had revealed how hard she'd been struggling after Mike's death. He could see evidence of that struggle etched behind her smile now. She was thinner. And that tan didn't hide the shadowed circles around her eyes.

Why had she come home to face the past instead of starting fresh somewhere new? And a town where the sun shone most of the year sounded perfect. He knew firsthand time couldn't erase the stink from some places, which was why he'd put New Jersey behind him.

Poughkeepsie had once been his fresh start.

"Come here, Jake." Riley finally let up her death grip on her nephew. "Come meet your cousin Brian."

Jake dutifully stepped forward and extended a gentlemanly hand. "I'm Jake."

Brian shook, looking amused.

"Where are the ducks, Mommy?" Camille wanted to know. "You said there were ducks. Can I go see them?"

"I'll take you down to the pond in a minute." Riley glanced around and spotted him. "Scott."

She hadn't expected to see him, he could tell, but her smile flashed fast and real. He shook off the last thought of anything that was unworthy of a man greeting his friend's long-absent wife and met her halfway.

"Welcome home" was all he had a chance to say before she was taking his hands and leaning up on tiptoes to press a kiss to his cheek.

"What are you doing here?" she asked.

He inclined his head toward the garage. "Pickup decided not to show up for work today. I dropped by to give Brian a hand."

"Come here, kids. Come meet…" She hesitated, shooting him a quirky look, then said, "Uncle Scott."

Scott managed a smile. Uncle worked for him. Gave him a proper place in their lives, a place with clear-cut boundaries. His own upbringing hadn't prepared him for the reality of loving families, so he learned on the fly.

"Hey, you guys have grown up since the last time I saw you. At first I thought you were Brian's friends from college."

That scored him a few points, with Camille, at least. She giggled, gifting him with a beaming smile before bolting away to see what was around the side of the house. Jake hung close to Riley and eyed him warily. Or protectively, Scott decided.

"There's a problem with the truck?" Riley asked.

"Don't worry, Aunt Riley," Brian said quickly. "Scott fixed it, and I was just headed down to load the hay."

Riley didn't blink, but Scott got the impression she caught pretty much everything Brian hadn't said. Giving Scott's hands a squeeze, she released her grip and mouthed the words *Thank you* while turning toward Brian.

"Get going, then," she told her nephew. "Don't let us keep you. We're going to take our time unloading our stuff and getting settled."

Brian looked ready to bolt, but before he could manage a getaway, Riley asked, "Where are you staying?"

"I moved my stuff over the garage."

She nodded thoughtfully, not bothering to hide a wistful smile. "My best arguments didn't change your mind, hmm?"

The kid didn't meet her gaze. "Well, you know… It's your house and all."

Riley chuckled. Stepping forward, she gave him another quick hug. "I do know. You're older now, and you like your independence. Just promise me you'll pop in now and then."

Brian nodded, and Scott guessed the kid would be showing up whenever he got hungry.

"You want some help?" Brian asked.

Riley shook her head. "Thanks, but no thanks. If you've got to get hay, then the horses win. We don't have too much to unload. Just enough to keep us going until the moving company drops off our boxes. There weren't too many of those, either. The Angelica family travels light."

She sounded all breezy, but Scott didn't miss the subtext that seemed to suggest that traveling from her home was a skill she could have lived without.

"Hey, can the kids come?" Brian asked. "We can get some corn to feed the ducks after I'm done with the hay."

"You're just loading?" Riley asked.

"Please, Mommy." Camille circled Riley on those wheeled sneakers before Brian even got a chance to reply. "I want to feed the ducks with my cousin."

"Your cousin's name is Brian."

"I want to go with Brian. Jakie, you want to go, too, don't you?" Camille gave her brother a sly look, trying to implicate him in her efforts.

This twin was a total live wire, Scott decided, and for a moment, he thought her brother might resist on principle. But Jake finally nodded, a willing accomplice.

"I'm just loading," Brian said. "They can help me bale."

"Okay, but you two ride in the cab and share the seat belt. Got that?" Riley knelt down so she was eye level with her twins. "You won't be going out on the road, but it gets bumpy riding down to the barn. It's really important that you listen to what Brian says and don't wander off. Okay?"

Both kids nodded. Riley gave them each a quick kiss, then said to Brian, "They haven't had being-around-horses 101 yet. They can help you bale, but that's it." She patted the cell phone attached to her waist. "Any problems and you call. I'll come down and get them. Got it?"

Brian placed a hand on each twin's shoulder, clearly eager to prove his trustworthiness. "No problem, Aunt Riley."

She said, "Have fun, then, and no fighting," but the words were barely out of her mouth before the twins were chasing Brian to the garage.

Riley watched thoughtfully as they clambered into the cab, and Brian made a dramatic display of strapping in the kids. Then he fired up the engine and drove out of the garage, him and his excited passengers waving as they passed.

Riley chuckled. "That poor kid doesn't have a clue what he's in for. The top of his head's going to blow off. Camille never stops talking."

"They're a handful." That wasn't a question.

She rolled her eyes. "High energy. I don't know who they take after."

She looked serious, and Scott bit back a smile. He knew exactly who those kids took after. He'd never seen Riley do anything at less than sixty miles an hour.

"Brian can handle it," he said. "He's looking for ways to impress you so you'll know how much you still need him."

"Is he, now?"

Scott nodded.

"That's pretty ironic considering I couldn't have done the past two years without him." She stared after the pickup as it made its way down the dirt drive toward the barn. "I'm impressed by how responsible he's been. I'd have had to sell the place or…"

Come home.

She didn't have to finish that thought.

"You're ready to be back now?" The question was out

of his mouth before he had a chance to assess whether or not he was getting too personal. He was. This wasn't his best buddy, Mike, but Mike's wife. And she looked so vulnerable standing there.

He knew the look, just as he knew the struggle to master unwanted feelings and take a step forward. He hadn't missed how she didn't seem too eager to get inside the house.

"You've been helping out Brian a lot?" she asked.

"Here and there. When he comes up against something unexpected."

She didn't believe him. Scott wasn't sure if his training as a vice cop gave him the edge, or if listening to Mike talk about her all these years gave him an advantage, but he didn't have any trouble reading her.

"It's mutual," he reassured her. "Brian always helps me out when I need him at Renaissance. He gets the volunteer hours for school, so it's win-win. I mentioned that I've had a crew of the Renaissance kids dealing with the yard. They appreciate a steady landscaping gig."

She nodded, sending glossy blond curls tumbling over her shoulders. "The place looks great."

Scott glanced around the yard of the farmhouse, which was situated at the very front end of twenty-five acres, close to the road. Riley was right. The hedges around the house and two-story garage were neatly trimmed, and bright annuals lined the circular drive. The place could have been professionally landscaped, and Scott felt pride. Not of himself but of the street kids who'd earned a place on the landscaping crew.

"Yeah, it does, doesn't it?"

Riley nodded. "I know Brian appreciates the help, too. Dealing with the yard during the summer is a lot to ask on top of the horses."

Scott didn't contradict her, although he knew Brian hadn't ever taken summer classes so the additional work-load wouldn't have killed him and would have saved Riley some money. But Scott had been happy to put together a crew that had earned the trust and privilege of being employed for fair wages.

Those opportunities didn't come along easily for former gang members.

Renaissance was a fresh-start program designed to keep inner-city teens off the streets. It began as a Poughkeepsie Police Department program over ten years ago, and Scott had been on board ever since, helping at-risk kids break away from gangs or avoid them altogether. The programs offered kids more productive things to do like getting through school and earning wages for hard work. Things that helped kids build self-esteem and earn the respect of the community.

The program volunteers provided encouraging role models and helped these kids realize they could live the kind of lives that didn't involve gangs, drugs and prison.

Scott thought Riley had been particularly decent to allow the Renaissance kids to come and work on the farm, considering Mike had been killed for his work against a local gang....

"So tell me what's new with you?" she asked.

"Nothing much since we talked, but thanks for asking."

"Nothing at all?"

Scott knew exactly what Riley was avoiding so he obliged. "Chief Levering got another civic award. They had a luncheon to roast him."

"Oh, how nice."

The chief hadn't thought so, but Scott kept that to himself. "And we got a local cosmetic surgeon to sit on the

Renaissance board of trustees. He's been offering free tattoo removal services to the kids."

"Wow. Good for you. That's quite a coup."

Scott nodded. "Rosie warned everyone not to bombard you until you got settled in."

"Did she? Probably afraid they'll scare us off."

"Probably. She and Joe have missed you."

"I know," Riley said softly.

"And the pickup broke down, but we got it running."

She finally met his gaze, laughter sparkling in her eyes. "That's it?"

"That's it."

"I hoped to keep you talking so I could avoid unpacking."

"Figured that part out."

She gave an exaggerated sigh. "It was worth a shot."

Scott gave an equally exaggerated sigh, and she laughed, a sound that rippled through the sunny quiet like bells in the wind. Riley was easy to be around. He'd always loved—*no*, liked that about her.

"Want some help unloading your things?" he asked.

"Only if it's no trouble. There's not really that much."

Scott stared down at her, recognized the strong woman who'd picked up the pieces and returned home to get on with life. But he also glimpsed so much vulnerability in the shadows beneath her eyes, the unaccustomed fragility. He had the wild urge to be the guy to step in and take away her burden, let her rest her head on his shoulder. So not appropriate.

Long before Mike's death, Scott had made a promise to watch over Mike's family if anything ever went south on the streets.

It had been the promise of one partner to another.

It had been the promise of a friend.

Helping Riley and the kids had been easy when they were in Florida. Keeping an eye on the farm. Giving Brian a hand. But now they were home. Scott would have to figure out how best to keep his promise without losing his head. He wouldn't do that to Mike.

With a newfound resolve, Scott anchored himself to his purpose. This was a job he was trained for, and he kept that thought in mind as he held her sparkling gaze.

"No," he said, and he meant it. "It's no trouble at all."

CHAPTER THREE

RILEY CRADLED THE PHONE against her shoulder and cast a panicked glance at the kitchen table, where bread crusts, half-eaten carrots and browning apple slices still graced the kids' lunch plates. The past weeks since arriving back in Pleasant Valley had been hectic to say the least. "I can be there in forty minutes, Max. Will that work?"

"If that's the best you got, darling," Max shot back. "This is about to go down, so get moving or you'll miss the action."

"On my way." Riley disconnected and waited impatiently for a dial tone. Then she called her mother-in-law, hoping— no, praying—Rosie would be available to watch the kids.

"Of course, dear. No problem," Rosie said.

"You're a lifesaver." Riley hung up, taking her first real breath.

She still cradled the receiver against her shoulder while snatching plates from the table. Tipping the remains into the trash, she put the plates in the dishwasher and called, "Code Tasmanian Devil. Use the bathroom and grab your things. Pronto."

Code Tasmanian Devil relayed that Mommy had been called into work, and they all needed to be out the door with fire-drill speed.

Excited shouts echoed from the farthest reaches of the

house, and Riley plunked down the telephone receiver in its base, grateful the kids were still young enough to view rushing out the door as an adventure.

She wanted to brush her teeth, but decided not to take the time; gum would have to suffice. Sailing into the foyer, she snatched up the briefcase she kept beneath the antique bench for such speedy exits.

Recorder?

Check.

Camera?

Check.

Laptop?

Check.

Everything a reporter needed to get the scoop on breaking news. If she got out the door and to Hazard Creek in time.

"How are you guys coming?" she asked as Camille wheeled around the corner, backpack hanging from one shoulder.

Riley pressed a quick kiss to the top of her silky head, smiling at the haphazard ponytail.

"Good girl. Your hair looks lovely. Is that what you were doing in your room?"

Camille nodded, clearly pleased by the praise. "I'm going to do my nails at Grandma and Grandpa's."

"Oh, a manicure. Can't wait to see. Jake, where are you?"

"Coming." He appeared in the hallway in front of his room, hanging on to a CD and looking surly.

This one obviously missed the memo about the adventure and had decided he didn't want to be rushed today. Or maybe he just wasn't in the mood to cooperate. Riley didn't know yet.

"Where's your backpack?"

"In my room."

"Go get it, Jake. Camille's already in the car."

Their lives had degenerated into bags packed and ready for action. Hers with everything she needed to cover a story, the kids' with activities for Grandma's house, along with spare clothes, CDs and DVDs. Fishing bag and tackle box. Dance bag with ballet slippers, acro shoes and leotard. T-ball bag with Jake's uniform, helmet and glove. And she hadn't even packed the schoolbags yet.

That would be next week's project.

Time. There simply wasn't enough of it nowadays.

If Riley could have turned back the clock, she'd have had Mike beside her, running through the checklists. There'd have been no need to rush the kids out the door. She'd always tried to work her schedule around Mike's shifts.

For one striking instant an intense physical feeling of longing swept through her. She missed him so much. She always would. That was the reality. She'd expected to feel this way again, being back home, but to Riley's credit and surprise, she hadn't felt it all that often in the weeks since they'd been home. She was living in the present. She'd come a long way in the two years since his death. Further than she'd thought.

Jake reappeared, and Riley herded him out the door onto the front porch to the tune of: "Go, go, go."

After activating the security system, she made her way to the minivan, where she found her daughter already buckled in and her son hard at work with the CD player.

"Jake." She exhaled his name on one long, exasperated breath. "I'll put in your CD after we get going. Get your seat belt on."

He finally got settled, and Riley glanced at the digital display while cranking up the van.

"Great job, guys. We were out the door in less than five minutes. That's a record."

"Will you buy us Popsicles for our reward?" Jake asked.

Riley slipped on sunglasses and glanced over her shoulder, considering. "If you have any room left in your tummy after Grandma Rosie gets hold of you. If not, we can buy snow cones at the summer festival this weekend."

"Yay." Camille clapped.

That seemed to content her son, too, who quickly moved on to the next order of business. "Turn on the music."

"Please," Riley prompted, looking both ways down Traver Road before pulling out of their driveway.

"Please," he said.

She depressed the power button. The noise that blared from the speakers at an insane volume shot her blood pressure—which was already pretty up there—skyrocketing.

In the time it took to turn down the volume, Riley's head pounded with gravelly rap vocals so hard and raw she hadn't been able to make out a word, just the pulse-pounding beat that threatened to blow off the top of her head.

"What on earth is this?" she asked.

"It's Daddy's."

Riley frowned. "Where did you get it?"

"Daddy's office."

"Not in the case where the others CDs are?" She caught Jake's gaze in the rearview mirror.

He shook his head, and Riley didn't see anything about his freckled face that made her think he wasn't telling the truth.

She cranked up the volume again, enough to make out the words. She'd heard rap music before, but never like this. Crude. Vulgar. Unpolished. As if someone had recorded it in a basement rather than a studio. Definitely not the sort of music appropriate for her almost six-year-old.

In a few measures she heard lyrics she could barely understand. But she got the gist. Criminal activities made to sound cool.

Was it Mike's? More likely Brian's. And hopefully not from anyone he was hanging out with. She couldn't even imagine what her sister-in-law would say. Or worse yet, her brother-in-law, a strict Italian dad in every way. Riley made a mental note to ask Brian about it.

"Why don't we listen to Radio Disney?"

Camille's approval drowned out Jake's complaints, and Riley flipped over to the AM radio station.

"Thanks for compromising, Jake." Grudging though that compliance was. "Mommy's got to work, and I need to collect my thoughts before I get there."

Only her second week back and already she was scrambling to keep up. Thank God they'd come home before school started to settle in. Not that she felt settled yet. Not even close.

She glanced in the rearview mirror again at those sweet faces that meant more to her than anything in the world. They were all rolling with the punches. Trying to, anyway. She needed to take her own advice and work on her spirit of adventure.

Mike's folks didn't live far away, and their house happened to be located in the very direction she needed to go today—the Taconic Parkway. She caught the light at the end of her road and made it to her in-laws' place in less than five minutes. Now if she could just get in and out quickly, she might actually get to Hazard Creek in time to get the story.

"We're here, guys." Riley brought the van to a stop but left the engine idling, hoping to save time. "I know you'll both be good for Grandma and Grandpa."

"Can we call you?" Jake popped open the seat belt and leaned into the front seat to retrieve his CD. He made a last-ditch grab, but Riley stopped him.

"Play your other CDs for Grandma Rosie." Grandma Rosie couldn't watch the kids again if she died of a heart attack from listening to *someone's* idea of music. "You can call me if you need me, sweet pea, but I won't be long. We'll be home in time for dinner."

"Pizza?" Camille asked hopefully.

"Tacos." Healthy ones with beans and lettuce. Riley kept that part to herself.

Camille gave a good-natured shrug and hopped out of the minivan. Riley followed with Jake in her wake just as the front door opened and Rosie appeared.

"Hugs, please. I want hugs from my beautiful family." She extended her arms and wouldn't let the kids pass until they'd been greeted in proper Rosie fashion.

Riley's mother-in-law was a woman who knew what it was to love and to lose what she loved. That experience was etched in the lines on her face, in her warm hugs and in the hope that seemed to glow from the inside out. She was determined to wring every moment of joy from every day, to savor every second as if it was a gift. She'd been that way ever since Riley had met her. She was still that way today. It was a quality Riley had always liked, but one she'd grown truly to admire since Mike's death.

"Give me kisses before you go, guys. I'm not coming in." Riley knelt and gave each kid a big squeezy hug. "Love you bunches. Give Grandpa Joe a kiss for me."

"Grandpa Joe is in the kitchen." Rosie stepped out onto the portico to let the kids pass into the house. "Why don't you go find him then we'll decide what we want to do for fun."

The kids didn't need to be asked twice and disappeared without a backward glance.

"Big assignment?" Rosie asked.

"A scoop that the DEA and HCPD are going in on a crack cookhouse."

Rosie scowled. "I thought you weren't covering this sort of stuff anymore."

"Max's making a spot for me on staff, Rosie. I can't turn down hard news."

"I can't believe he wants you covering that sort of stuff."

Max Downey was an Angelica family friend whose family owned the *Mid-Hudson Herald*.

"I appreciate your concern, Rosie, but I need this job."

Rosie narrowed her gaze but didn't say another word. They both knew jobs weren't so easy to come by in this economy. And as both Rosie and Joe had helped Riley manage Mike's death benefits, they knew better than anyone that Riley's days as a stay-at-home mom in Florida had been numbered.

She gave Rosie a hug. "I can't tell you how much I appreciate your help. Please thank Joe for me."

"I will. But it's our pleasure. You know that."

Riley gave her another squeeze. "Oh, and before I forget, Camille has nail polish in her bag. She's planning a manicure."

Rosie nodded knowingly. "Thank you, dear. I'm on it."

Riley checked off that worry from her mental list. Rosie wouldn't want Kiss Me Pink all over her tile or, heaven forbid, the furniture.

Then Riley took off, grateful she didn't have to angst about the kids being in good hands. Driving toward the Taconic Parkway, she tried not to speed, though her impulse was to put the pedal to the metal. She did not want to explain to her boss, family friend or not, that she'd arrived on the tail end of the action because she'd been pulled over by a state trooper, leaving the *Mid-Hudson Herald* to parrot the reports of the other local news services.

No, Max had gotten the scoop about the bust, which meant if Riley did her job—and he was counting on her to do that—they'd break the news online first. One part of her was pleased he had so much faith in her work. The other part had to question whether his faith was well-placed. Once, she'd been on top of her game, but she'd been off her beat for a while now. No one knew that better than Max Downey, managing editor of the paper.

She'd interned under Max during the summer between her junior and senior years at Vassar. That internship had been the opportunity of a lifetime, and she'd jumped all over it. He'd hired her straight out of college, and she'd worked her way up the rungs at the paper, establishing her reputation and finding an unexpected and very dear friend in Max.

That was why he'd rolled with her during pregnancy and motherhood, allowing her to scale back her assignments to accommodate her family. That was why he was taking her back after a two-year leave in a down economy when the Internet was making print media scramble to stay relevant.

Riley had to earn her place on the paper again, and that meant getting to Hazard Creek and covering this breaking news. Fortunately luck was with her, and in less than twenty minutes from the time she'd taken Max's call, she was following GPS directions through the streets of an older residential community on the outskirts of the township.

Max's source had come through big because Riley spotted several cruisers from Hazard Creek's PD and a truck that must belong to the DEA. She was surprised the sheriff's department wasn't here, too. A cluster of spectators—most likely folks evacuated from the surrounding homes—stood beyond the perimeter beneath the watchful gaze of the HCPD that had parked a cruiser to block access to the neighborhood.

Riley circled the minivan around before getting caught up in the roadblock. After glancing at the GPS, she cut down a side street that brought her around to the other end of Alban Lane, where she hoped to get a better view of the house.

She'd no sooner brought the minivan to a stop against the curb when she heard shouts. Crackling radios. The screech of tires over the road. Grabbing her gear, she slid from the minivan and cut across someone's front yard to get close to the officer manning this side of the street.

To get closer to the action.

After flashing her press pass, she nodded when the officer told her to keep behind the caution tape. She slid down to the very end where the tape hung from a wooden blockade that had been set up to cut off access to the sidewalk. Aiming the digital camcorder at the house where DEA agents and police officers garbed in Kevlar swarmed the yard, she started to record, already deciding to pull stills from the footage for her story.

If she could catch anything on video, *Herald Online* would run it. That would make Max happy. Especially since she saw no other media personnel. Heck, she'd barely made it.

But as she watched the agents swarm the house, Riley knew something was wrong. Those in the doorway disappeared inside, but those on the lawn seemed to freeze, as if someone had pressed the pause button on a video.

Anxiety crawled uncomfortably at the base of her neck, but she had no time to question the sense of premonition, no time to make sense of what she was seeing in the view screen of the camcorder before the sound of locked brakes shrieked, and the grind of tires screamed over the street, way too close.

Snapping her gaze to the direction of the sound, she froze, unable to register the sight before her. All she could see was the face of a teen, a boy who could be no older than Brian, his expression pure determination as he clung to the steering wheel of a car…

And headed toward her.

Riley could only react, twisting around to get out of the way, lurching into motion so fast that her knees almost buckled beneath her. She staggered for an instant but managed to make it onto the curb just as she heard the wooden barricade shatter behind her. She heard shouting, too, but couldn't make out who or what. All she heard was the solid thunk of a groaning axle as the car jumped the curb.

Run, run, run.

The random thought that she should have worn sneakers popped into her head, followed by the sounds of Camille and Jake's sweet voices crying out in time with the pulsing throb of her heartbeat.

"Mommy died. Mommy died like Daddy."

CHAPTER FOUR

"THE CHIEF WANTS TO SEE YOU," the desk sergeant said, and Scott only nodded as he and Kevin Rush exchanged an uncomfortable glance.

His partner was a decent enough guy, a good cop with a feel for vice that not all cops had. It wasn't entirely Kevin's fault they'd spent the morning chasing their tails, but a more seasoned cop would have recognized that the prostitute they interviewed had been lying through her teeth. She'd claimed to have witnessed a direct purchase between a known street peddler and a suspected head of a drug supply ring.

Her story had been fiction. She was a hooker with a vendetta, Scott had quickly decided, but Kevin believed there was something in her story, something worth their morning. It had taken him hours to admit he'd been duped. Literally. A more experienced cop would have known that shooting in the dark was all part of the game. Sometimes it made more sense to back up and admit a wrong turn rather than barrel ahead.

Scott needed to rein in his irritation because the chief was guaranteed to notice. Then he'd start up with the twenty questions about how Scott was adjusting to his new partner.

There was no way in hell he was going there again. Not when the past two years had been an exercise in humility, starting with the day the chief had paired Scott with an older vice cop who'd known what it was like to lose a partner.

When that match had proven *not* to be made in heaven, the chief had tossed another partner Scott's way. Kevin was a few years younger and had just earned his promotion to detective.

The chief had been giving Scott a vote of confidence by assigning him someone fresh, someone to train into the kind of partner Scott wanted to work with. Turned out he wasn't really in the mood to train. Just as he hadn't been in the mood to change the way he did things to fit in with a hardheaded cop with an eye on retirement.

Scott wanted to work, to immerse himself in his cases and do his bit to clean up the streets. That was what he did, what gave him a sense of purpose.

Kevin had potential, no question, but he got distracted too easily by nonsense—tripping over his own ego for one. The wasted morning wasn't such a big deal. Scott had spent his fair share of mornings going around in circles. Still, he hadn't exactly come away empty-handed today. No, he had an attitude he couldn't shake and a truth he didn't want to admit.

Kevin's biggest offense was that he wasn't Mike.

But that was an old problem that would have to wait for another day. They arrived at the chief's office, and right now Scott had to contend with the expectations of a boss who wanted him to accomplish the sort of miracles that he and Mike had in their heyday. Figuring out why he couldn't settle in with a new partner when even Riley was managing to get on with life would require more time and energy than Scott had right now.

Kevin didn't say a word as he knocked and pushed open the door. In all fairness to the guy, he wasn't the only one feeling the weight of the chief's expectations.

"What did you come up with?" Chief Levering glanced up expectantly from the report he held.

Scott stood there silent, keeping his face carefully blank. He'd give Kevin the chance to spin this however he thought best.

"Nothing," Kevin said. "Dead end. She didn't have anything except a grudge against our guy."

The chief glanced at the clock. "You went in at nine?"

"Yes, sir."

To Scott's surprise the chief just nodded. "Kev, you can go. I need to talk with Scott."

Kevin narrowed his gaze, clearly concerned whether this dismissal boded ill for him, then headed out the door. Scott knew better than to ask the chief what was up. He waited.

Chief Levering was generational law enforcement. He'd worked his way up the ranks from homicide, the son of a son of a son, and someone with a foot still on the streets while hanging on to the oh-shit handle with city bureaucrats.

The chief inspired an insane amount of loyalty from his men, probably because he was insanely loyal himself. He was the kind of cop to take a bullet as quickly as chew out a cop for doing the same. The chief wasn't afraid to get his hands dirty. His men respected that.

He also didn't miss a trick. "Kevin thought something was there and you didn't."

Scott shook his head.

"You tell him?"

"Yes."

The chief eyed him appraisingly with a look Scott knew all too well, and he expected the chief's next words to start up an interrogation about how the two were gelling as partners.

Interestingly the chief only nodded and said, "DEA went in on a crack operation in Hazard Creek."

Since Hazard Creek was a township southeast of Poughkeepsie and out of their jurisdiction, Scott knew there must be a point to this news. "Hadn't heard anything over the radio."

"They just went in."

"How'd it go down?"

The chief scowled. "Not like they hoped, I'm sure. Place was completely cleaned out. Neighbors said the renters scattered like roaches not an hour before the cops showed up."

"Who tipped them off?"

"No clue, but the Narcotics Commission has had a team working on this bust for months."

The Narcotics Commission was big news in the Mid-Hudson Valley. The task force had been instituted by the governor a handful of years ago, a coalition of police agencies charged to stop drug trafficking into Dutchess County. The governor had appointed Jason Kenney, police chief of Hazard Creek, as the most recent commanding officer.

It was a nice nod, no question, even though it was a lot more work on top of an already demanding job. But Jason Kenney thrived under a spotlight, so Scott was sure he'd grabbed the reins of the Narcotics Commission with both hands.

Jason had once been on the force with Scott. He'd been a good cop, instrumental in cracking a few highly visible cases, which had shot him to the forefront of the local media. Jason liked seeing his face on the front pages of the *Mid-Hudson Herald* and *Poughkeepsie Journal,* so he'd accepted the position of police chief with the village of Hazard Creek.

The department might have been smaller than the

Poughkeepsie PD, but Jason also liked being a big fish in a little pond. Scott considered him somewhat of a fame whore, but Mike, who'd known the guy for years, had always taken a lighter view. Every time Jason opened his mouth in front of television cameras, Mike would just roll his eyes and say, "You know Jason."

Scott hadn't known Jason, but knew enough to guess that their limited past history didn't explain why he should care about a bust going south in Hazard Creek.

"Why are you telling me this, Chief?"

Beneath a heavy brow, the chief leveled a stoic gaze, and Scott braced himself. "Whatever went down didn't filter through the drug operation. Some mules arrived for a pickup and found the place shut down by the law. They tried to run for it, and Riley got in their way."

Scott just stared. "She okay?"

"From what I hear. DEA's still got the scene locked down."

Scott was already to the door before the chief said, "Don't kill yourself getting there."

Scott didn't have to. He shoved the light on the dash of his unmarked cruiser, turned on the siren and made Hazard Creek before the HCPD had finished taking witness statements.

He didn't understand why Riley had been at the scene. He was going to kill Max, who should be assigning her city council stories or entertainment reviews. Not drug busts, which around here had everything to do with gangs.

But there she was, sitting in the open doorway of the emergency vehicle, talking to Jason and another man, some fed wearing Kevlar and a vest with the stenciled bold letters: *DEA*.

Scott shut off the siren, swerved the cruiser against a curb and jumped out, taking in the scene as he made his way to the emergency vehicle. Skid marks had left rubber on the asphalt. Deep tire gouges on a lawn where the runaway car had jumped the curb. Not one but two wooden barriers splintered over the street. Scott flashed his badge at the uniform who made a move in his direction.

"Jason," Scott said as he approached, eyeing the DEA agent.

Jason performed the introductions, and Scott gave a barely civil nod to Agent Barry Mannis before kneeling in front of Riley. He took her hands and asked, "How are you?"

She shook her head. "Okay. All good."

She didn't look okay. *Not okay* was all over her face, from the tight set of her mouth to the way she avoided directly meeting his gaze. There were grass stains on her khaki slacks and a tear that revealed white bandages below. Bandages that matched the ones on her arm. Likely where she'd fallen.

Her hands were cold, delicate, fitting in his so neatly, silky skin against skin. He squeezed slightly to reassure her.

"Riley," he said, a whisper between them.

She finally met his gaze, and Scott saw so much in her eyes, in her expression. She was rattled. And relieved to see him. *That* got a reaction deep in his gut, and he tried not to notice how smooth her skin was against his, telling himself she'd have been glad to see any familiar face right now.

But it was *his* face she stared into, *his* hands she clung to, and rationalizing her response didn't stop his pulse from lurching expectantly, didn't stop him from hanging on to her as if magnetized.

And for a stunning few heartbeats the world seemed to disappear, just completely vanish, leaving nothing but him and Riley connected by a touch and a glance.

"Damned hoods freaked when they saw the roadblock." Jason's voice shattered the moment like a gunshot. "Riley had to make a quick exit."

Their gazes broke away to find Jason staring uncomfortably at the remains of the wooden blockade that littered the street.

Riley slid her hands from his as a paramedic reappeared from inside the vehicle.

"Ma'am, I need to—"

"We're done," she said, clearly bristling. "I'm good."

Jason cast an annoyed look at Scott that translated into *Will you deal with her? I've got my hands full.*

Scott glanced between the expectant paramedic and Agent Mannis, and managed to squelch his own annoyance at Jason's lack of concern. This was *Riley,* not some random pain-in-the-ass reporter. Then again, Scott wouldn't want to be in Jason's shoes right now. Bust going balls-up on the DEA's time. No wonder Hazard Creek's normally imperturbable police chief looked perturbed.

Deciding to cut the guy some slack, Scott inclined his head in another silent communication. *Got her.*

Jason nodded, looking relieved as he escorted the DEA agent away from the ambulance to where the HCPD was mirandizing a group of kids handcuffed against two cruisers.

Scott shifted back, and Riley popped to her feet as if detonated. "I need to go home."

She still didn't sound like herself, and Scott raked another gaze over her tight expression. He couldn't miss her agitation or pallor.

"No problem, Riley. Let me wrap things up with these guys." He turned to the paramedic. "Where are we? Did you get everything you need from her?"

The guy seemed to understand that Scott was asking whether or not his resistant patient was in shock. "Vitals are good. Cleaned up the surface scratches. She has some bruising."

Not so bad considering she'd outrun a car full of panicked drug dealers. Scott glanced back to where the HCPD were loading the last of the young hoods into separate cruisers. Scott didn't recognize any of them. That at least was good.

He spotted a brightly colored tote bag sitting inside the ambulance. "This yours?"

She nodded.

Grabbing the bag, he placed a hand on her uninjured elbow, steering her away from the ambulance and toward their cars.

"Did you get your story?" He needed to get her talking.

"The little there was."

"I'll bet this wasn't the outcome Jason was looking for."

She nodded, then reached for her bag. He handed it over, frowning as she plunged a hand inside and fumbled around. He heard the rattle of keys.

If Riley thought she'd be driving herself home, she'd need to rethink her plan. He didn't care what the paramedic said.

"Come on, ride back to town with me," he said.

She stopped short and glanced up at him with a frown. "I have to pick up the kids at Rosie and Joe's."

"No problem. I'll take you."

"My van."

"I'll make the trip back to pick it up with Kevin."

She shook her head and inhaled deeply, visibly steeling herself. "Thank you, Scott, but no. I'm fine."

He didn't believe her. She knew he didn't but wasn't backing down. Had she always been so stubborn? He looked into her clear blue eyes, sparkly eyes that couldn't hide how rattled she was no matter what she said. How would Mike have handled his willful wife?

"How about if I follow you back?" Scott suggested a compromise. "Just to make sure you get there okay. My day will be shot if I'm worried about you making it home in one piece."

She held his gaze for another moment, and her expression eased up. "Fine. I promised the kids I'd get them before dinner. We're having tacos."

He wasn't sure why she was sharing the menu and considered this another good reason why she shouldn't get behind the wheel. He was about to have another go at persuading her to let him play chauffeur when Jason showed up.

"You okay?" he asked Riley, earning back a few points in Scott's book. The guy wasn't always a jerk. Nice to know.

"Yes." She lifted up on tiptoe and pressed a kiss to Jason's cheek. "Sorry things didn't work out as you'd hoped."

Jason flashed the smile that folks on both sides of the Hudson River were familiar with, a smile as fake as if it had been carved on a Halloween pumpkin. "Just remember we go way back when you write your article. I really don't want to see my face all over the front page associated with this mess."

Riley gave a weak smile while depressing her key fob. She reached for the handle as the lock on the van door clicked, but Jason got it first, making her wait.

"How'd you hear about the bust, anyway?" he asked.

"Max. He didn't share his source."

Jason frowned, but Scott was frowning even harder by now. He'd thought the guy would be too busy with the feds, who were swarming the HCPD cruisers almost ready to leave the scene, to be playing twenty questions with Riley.

Jason glanced Scott's way, then pulled open the door. Riley slipped inside.

"Sorry we had to meet up again like this, Riley," Jason said, leaning on the open door. "Welcome back."

"Thanks," she said.

Jason blinked hard, then he eased shut the door before asking through the open window, "Are you all right to drive back?"

"I'm following her," Scott said. "Pull over if you need to stop, Riley. And don't lose me in that hot rod, okay?"

She rolled her eyes. Scott headed toward his car, not really good with letting her drive but unsure what the hell else he could do. Short of handcuffing her, anyway.

CHAPTER FIVE

JASON KENNEY BACKED AWAY from the van while Riley cranked the engine. He came to a dead stop as a roar of sound blasted from the stereo. Riley jerked back in her seat, and for a stunned instant Jason froze as raw rap music rocked the suburban quiet.

A string of words that had no business pouring from any young mother's minivan.

Words from the streets.

Riley slammed her palm against the steering wheel to shut down the noise.

"Too much convenience isn't always a good thing," she said wearily while popping out a CD from the stereo. She tossed it onto the passenger seat with a muttered, "That kid."

Jason didn't ask what she was talking about. He didn't need to know. He only needed to know why she had that CD.

And did Scott know?

Casting a quick glance at the unmarked cruiser, Jason found Scott inside the car with the door shut.

Was this some sort of setup? What else could it be?

"Take care, Jason," Riley said, and he stepped away from the door automatically to allow her to pull out.

The gleam of red taillights flashed as Scott followed her, and Jason remained immobilized by indecision. About the only thing he knew right now was that he had no time to figure out what to do and how it would to come back to bite him in the ass. And it would. That much he knew. Lately everything he did circled around like a damned concrete boomerang ready to smash him in the face.

He could feel Barry's gaze burning a hole through him from across the street. The DEA agent from hell wanted answers. Jason stubbornly decided to let him wait and buy himself a few extra seconds to think.

He couldn't be mistaken. No. He hadn't heard much of the poison blasting from Riley's van before she'd stopped the show, but he'd recognized what he'd heard.

Veteranos got it down. Ace cool in the game. The Busters hooked up. For a piece of curb service.

The lyrics of that pounding rap beat were a language all their own. The language of the streets. And Jason was well versed in what those lyrics meant.

Cops had backed up veteran gang members during a drug delivery, protecting the criminals and their cut of the action from drugs that would be sold on the streets.

Jason couldn't be sure without listening to the complete track but guessed the lyrics would provide details about the specific crime. And specific cops.

HCPD.

In a perfect world, the idea of any law-enforcement officer getting into bed with the hoods would have made him see red.

But this wasn't a perfect world, and the cops perpetrating illegal acts weren't always corrupt. Sometimes they were simply following orders. Bad orders, maybe, but orders nevertheless.

Homemade CDs like the one Riley had came from gangs who circulated them on the streets to boast of their exploits. A gang friendly with local law had a built-in safe-guard against other gangs that might want to intrude on their operations.

Those CDs were also insurance policies. Bad cops might be in on the street action, but when push came to shove, they also had the power. Gang members didn't trust cops—particularly ones who betrayed the law they'd sworn to uphold—when those same cops could send them before a judge. Gangs understood loyalty. Sometimes Jason thought that was all they understood.

So what was Riley doing with that CD on the day she'd turned up at a bogus bust?

Jason was sure Scott hadn't heard, and that might be Jason's only decent luck lately. Scott would have known what was on that CD. He worked knee-deep in gangs. Hell, he even dealt with them for fun with that volunteer group Chief Levering had started when Jason had been with the PPD.

Or was this whole thing a setup? Had Scott given the CD to Riley? Had she played it to get a reaction from Jason? Did they suspect what was going down in Hazard Creek?

No, Jason decided. That was paranoia, plain and simple. How could they have possibly known he'd show up at Riley's van?

Then again, they shouldn't have known about this bust. But Scott had only arrived after Riley had gotten hurt, and Jason seriously doubted Riley would have put herself in harm's way for any reason. Not after what had happened to Mike.

But someone had spilled something to the *Mid-Hudson Herald* and Riley had that CD...

Damn it. This situation was a mess.

"How did they know about this hit?" Barry Mannis aka Agent Asshole asked from a distance, barreling across the street like an out-of-control semi, which was what the

DEA agent looked like. Short. Thick. Muscular build making up for what he lacked in height. Fast, though, as if he rolled along on eighteen wheels.

Agent Asshole couldn't wait for answers, so Jason was out of time. He shrugged. "Editor at the paper got an anonymous tip and sent a reporter."

"You know her." It wasn't a question.

"Not really. I worked with her husband back in my PPD days. Haven't seen her in years."

"What about the cop with her? He PPD, too?"

Jason nodded.

"Let me get this straight. Not only do we have the media showing up at what was supposed to be a surprise hit, but now we've got Poughkeepsie's department involved, too."

What was Jason supposed to say? He'd cast his vote that this was a stupid move. Insane. Agent Asshole hadn't wanted to hear it. Not when he was getting pushed around by DEA brass and needed to look as if he was doing some honest work around here.

Pumping drugs into the area wasn't honest work.

But Agent Asshole didn't care who he risked. Why should he? It wasn't his team that would look stupid when they came up empty.

Jason took a step forward, forcing the DEA agent to sink back on his heels to maintain eye contact. And though he couldn't see the man's eyes through the polarized aviator shades, the reminder of how short he was would irritate the hell out of him. Jason knew Agent Asshole always stood at a distance because he didn't like looking up to anyone.

Petty, maybe, but it was all Jason had right now.

So he stared down at the thickset man, absolute loathing burning through him like battery acid. How had he ever thought this man might be a useful contact? How had he missed that nothing in life, especially appointments to high-profile commissions, would ever come free?

"So who tipped off the media? One of yours?" Mannis held his ground and looked pissed about it.

"Not one of mine," Jason retorted. "You're the one who set up the bust, then tipped off the hoods. My men aren't in the loop. I told you that. Not one of them."

That was the only thing that let Jason look in the mirror at night. He might have gotten sucked in with the wrong bunch of high-powered pricks, but he wouldn't implicate his men. If anything went wrong—and with his luck it was only a matter of time—then his men could honestly stand before Internal Affairs and say they weren't involved.

Jason had a responsibility to the good, loyal men serving Hazard Creek. He wasn't going to drag them down until he could figure out some way to make this nightmare go away.

Until then he had no choice but to play the game.

"You better hope like hell you're right, Kenney," Mannis finally said, and Jason could almost see the agent's eyes narrowing behind the dark lenses. "I don't want to call in an anonymous tip of my own. Got some shots from Atlantic City that would make a much better story than what happened here today. That streaming video of you with those pretty *cholas* would make you really popular on YouTube. You'd be a cyber-celebrity."

The blood drained from Jason's head and, for one blind instant, all he could see was himself surrounded by a bunch of naked young women. Prostitutes, most likely. Jason couldn't be sure. He'd been so stoned on ecstasy at the time he'd thought he'd stepped into a friggin' wet dream.

He shut his eyes against the sight, against the vision of what *that* night would look like immortalized on video and playing in a courtroom, and in that moment, he would have given his reputation, his job and every man on his squad to unload his service weapon in Agent Asshole's face.

But until Mannis wound up the victim of a public service murder—and he most definitely would if there was a God—Jason had to deal with damage control. At least until he could figure out how to safeguard the incriminating evidence he'd unwittingly given this man to use against him.

"I'll find what went down," he said flatly.

"Get on it," Mannis said. "I don't want trouble right now."

No damn doubt. Jason hadn't been trusted with all the details of the seven-hundred-and-fifty-thousand-dollar shipment coming into their area, but he knew the operation had been in the works too long to screw up at the finish line.

"Keep me informed," Mannis repeated when some of his agents emerged from the abandoned cookhouse.

Jason collected himself as he headed back to the crime scene, snapping at Hank Llewellyn as he passed. "Get those blockades out of the street."

His department would look stupid enough without his office being flooded with complaints about trashing the neighborhood.

The HCPD would certainly get real estate in the news. Some talking head would tell the world about how the Narcotics Commission had let a drug manufacturing ring slip through its fingers. Then the governor would be calling for an explanation.

Jason didn't know how this day could have turned into any more of a nightmare than it already had. But he had figured out one thing—he wasn't sharing the bit about the CD. Nothing else was getting out of his control if he could help it.

He didn't know what the hell was going on with Riley and Scott, but he was going to find out. Riley had gotten that CD somewhere. Its contents would tell him exactly what he was up against. If Scott and the PPD were involved…

CHAPTER SIX

ABOUT THE SAME TIME Riley had taken the phone call from Max, drug dealers had been clearing out their operation in an older residential neighborhood and driving away. She might have even passed them on the Taconic Parkway in her rush to Hazard Creek.

All that scrambling around to catch the action, stressing the kids out as she hurried them out the door… For what?

Mommy died. Mommy died like Daddy.

Her eyes fluttered shut as she endured yet another blast of anxiety so physical it rushed through her like a cold wave.

Maybe she needed a new career. She'd come home to start a new life. *Her* life. She could be a teacher. Journalism or maybe English. Better yet, she could work in an elementary school. Then she and the kids could be together in the same place all day, have the same schedules. A career where she wouldn't get in the way of law-enforcement officers doing their jobs and drug dealers doing theirs…

Riley couldn't shake the memory of scrambling to get away from that out-of-control car. The details had etched themselves in her head. Always too many details.

The scooter carelessly discarded on the front porch as if a child had dropped it without a thought.

The baskets hanging from the gables, filled to overflowing with cheery summer blooms.

The violent ruts in the carefully tended grass where car tires had dredged deep into the dirt.

That drug operation had been hidden in a neighborhood where folks reared families and moms walked the streets with strollers and kids riding scooters.

How did such a dichotomy exist in one place? Families living alongside drug dealers? Such a wholesome environment coexisting with a destructive one?

Riley felt the same incomprehension she'd faced with the reality that her husband, such a vital and loving man, could be there one day and be gone forever the next.

Merging with traffic on the Taconic, she glanced in her rearview mirror to see Scott's unmarked car stuck like glue to her bumper. She couldn't see him, of course, with all the tinted glass, but felt such a profound wave of relief that the feeling came as another shock, so wildly out of proportion to what she should have felt.

Scott had been Mike's partner and friend, but in this moment, when she felt so off center and anxious and unsure, she knew he was more.

Riley glanced again in the rearview mirror, the relief still so completely there red flags were flying. When had Scott become *her* friend, a part of her life? When he'd made it clear he'd intended to keep his eyes on his best friend's family? By regularly calling her in Florida? By listening to her unload about the details—big and small—of her days? By helping Brian around the farm?

Or maybe this relief was simply a side effect of the anxiety she felt right now. Though she'd covered her fair share of drug busts, even had a few run-ins where she'd been in the way, she'd never been this rattled. She couldn't cover breaking news without getting into the thick of things, and breaking news had been all she covered in her prekid life. But now…

Mommy died. Mommy died like Daddy.

Sometimes the voice was Camille's, sometimes Jake's. And the only thing that helped Riley get a grip on her emotions was knowing that the man in the vehicle behind her had cared enough to drive to Hazard Creek to make sure she was okay. Him, and deciding to spend the night researching the requirements to become a teacher in Dutchess County. She had a master's degree, after all. Shouldn't it be a matter of getting some sort of teaching certificate?

But her anxiety melted away the instant she pulled into her in-laws' driveway. The front door swung wide and her kids burst out at a run.

"Mommy, Mommy! Are you all right?" Camille called out, ponytail bouncing as she clomped down the porch steps in sandals not meant for breakneck speed.

Jake, in sneakers, raced ahead, eyeing Riley with such a look of worry that her heart ached. He made it to the driveway so fast Riley had to shoo him back to get her door open.

"I'm good, guys. How was your afternoon?"

"Grandma said you got boo-boos. Where?" Camille caught up and gazed at Riley, who tugged her ponytail in greeting.

Hiding what had happened hadn't been an option. Not while adorned with gauze and grass stains. Still, she didn't want to make a big deal and worry the kids.

Reaching for Riley's hand, Camille urged her to her knees. The adhesive pulled painfully against her skin, tugging the raw flesh along her thigh, but Riley schooled her expression to meet two worried gazes.

"Not big boo-boos." She lifted her elbow to reveal the gauze bandage. "Just some scratches."

Camille pressed a careful kiss to the wound. "There, all better."

Jake didn't say a word, just rubbed her shoulders, comforting her in a way that would have comforted him.

"Were you worried?" she asked him.

He gave a stoic nod.

"Mommy's fine." She gave him a smile then pressed a kiss to Camille's hand where the tiny nails had been polished a blinding shade of pink. "Your nails look lovely."

Camille lifted a sandaled foot and wiggled her toes. "Look, my toes match."

"Beautiful." She glanced up as Rosie appeared in the doorway with Joe behind her.

Riley waved and gave them a reassuring smile just as Scott joined her.

"Are you okay?" Joe huffed to a stop as he joined the small party congregating beside the minivan.

Mike's dad looked a lot like Riley imagined Mike would have looked at the same age. Tall and fit even well into his sixties. His northern Italian heritage was all over the gray hair that had once been a tawny blond, the warm eyes and sturdy olive skin that did a lot to conceal his true age.

"I'm fine," she said. "But how did you know?"

"Scott called." Joe nodded toward the man in question.

Again, that feeling of relief. Riley kept the smile on her face. She guessed Scott had wanted to reassure everyone. Of course, no one would have known what had happened had he not given them a heads-up. But knowing Scott had her back, that he'd stepped in to calm the people she loved…

"Appreciated you getting over there." Joe clasped his hand and thanked him for the call.

Scott waved off the gratitude with a grimace.

Riley seized the chance to distract her father-in-law from the discussion she sensed forthcoming. A conversation that made Scott seem uncomfortable.

"Come on, kiddos," she said. "Collect your things so Grandma and Grandpa can have their day back. What's left of it."

"Oh, no, dear." Rosie looked aghast from her perch on the front steps. "You're staying for dinner. Ground beef's all thawed and Camille's been helping me cut up the veggies. The kids told me we're having tacos."

Okay. Riley was not up for a party at the moment. All she really wanted to do was get home and surround herself with normalcy. But what could she say? Everyone wanted to help, so she kept her mouth shut and followed the group as they headed toward the front steps.

"Scott, you'll stay, too," Rosie said then frowned. "Unless you have to get back to the station. Got twenty minutes or so? That should be enough to get things together."

"You know I'd never turn down food in your house, Rosie," he delighted her by saying. "I don't think the chief will mind me taking a break."

Rosie laughed, giving Scott a hug when he reached the top step. "Not unless he wants to answer to me."

As it was just past four in the afternoon, this break qualified as less a late lunch than an early dinner. But Riley took each of the kids' hands and led them inside, unable to help noticing the way Scott preceded Rosie into the heart of the Angelica home well familiar with the way.

Rosie immediately began issuing orders.

"Camille, you help Grandma Rosie get everything on platters. Jake and Grandpa, you get the table set. Oh, and make sure you put out extra napkins. Riley and Scott, you two wash up for dinner."

"Yes, ma'am." Scott spun on his heels and disappeared down the hallway where the guest bathroom was.

Riley stood for a moment, watching all the activity,

feeling disconnected, as if she was an outsider looking in on this warm family scene.

While Rosie and Joe had always had an open-door policy, Riley had never known Scott to be one who readily accepted social invites or dropped in anywhere for casual visits. But he seemed more at home than she could ever recall seeing him.

When Mike had been alive he'd regularly had his buddies over for barbecues, dinners and whatever game was on TV. Their house had often been pleasantly full with friends and family. Scott certainly had been a guest, but now that she thought about it, she realized he'd rarely been there on his own—instead being one of many visitors. And until she'd moved to Florida, she could easily count on one hand the number of times she'd had a private conversation with him.

So why this connection now? Why was he the one to help her get her equilibrium? And why did she *want* him to be the one she could turn to? Why did it seem so natural for him to be here, at the Angelicas', with her?

No, wait. He wasn't *with* her. No. He was simply looking out for her and the kids. Fulfilling some promise made between friends and partners. That's all this was.

Still, when he brushed past her to enter the kitchen, the brief physical connection felt intense and far from casual. It felt strong, intimate…a man-woman touch rather than a friend's touch. That surprised her.

Because she wasn't sure when she started noticing Scott as anything more than Mike's partner.

CHAPTER SEVEN

"YO, BIG HOME," General E. called to Scott while launching himself into the air to sink an easy basket.

Groans erupted from the nearly half-dozen teens with chests bared beneath the blistering afternoon sun swarming the court. General E.'s team wore T-shirts. A few players cheered.

It didn't take long for Scott to decide where he was needed. Yanking off his T-shirt, he tossed it onto a bench.

"Hey, homie. Hey, homie." The acknowledgment went up among the "skins," and Scott laughed, pounding a few fists before Mateo passed him the ball.

Throwing himself into the game, Scott was grateful for the activity and some downtime for a brain that had been steeping in frustration from one too many stalled cases.

And too many thoughts of the woman he shouldn't be thinking about.

A hard-nosed game of basketball would be just the ticket, and these guys were hard-nosed about everything. Everyone always wanted to come out on top. But all things considered, this was a good group of kids, which was a break for Renaissance. All too often the tough job of turning around inner-city kids was made even tougher by past history on the streets.

Scott and the other volunteers who kept the program

going tried to create an environment that didn't invite gang
rivalries inside the walls of the leased warehouse that
housed the program. The Center, as it was known, was a
place filled with counseling rooms for support groups and
classrooms for tutoring programs that helped kids get
through school or earn their general education diplomas.

The Center had even carved out a few niches for spe-
cialty interests. A local artist volunteered time to teaching younger kids how to paint. A martial artist taught tae
kwon do. A nurse-practitioner not only performed triage
on kids without access to reliable health care but taught
parenting classes to kids who had kids themselves.

Renaissance was a safe haven for anyone who didn't
want to die behind bars or from drugs or in a gang war. In
a perfect world, it would be Poughkeepsie's equivalent of
Manchester Bidwell, a social program that had originated
in Pittsburgh decades ago and still boasted a mind-blowing
success rate.

Funding didn't allow Renaissance to compete on the
same scale as Manchester Bidwell, but Scott and the
other volunteers didn't need money to adopt the concept.
So they raised their expectations for the kids who found
themselves here, sometimes without being able to
explain why they'd come. Those expectations were high,
because the simple fact was, when the volunteers
believed in these kids, the kids learned to believe in
themselves.

The results got better and better each year.

Of course, Scott got older and older each year, too, which
meant he was sweating a lot more than these kids by the
time General E. sank the basket that irrevocably widened
the point gap. But age and experience wasn't always a
negative. It helped him recognize the instant the tenor of the

cheering changed. He was already wiping the sweat from his eyes with his T-shirt by the time the snarling started.

Sure enough, General E. was in Cakes's face. Instinct took over, and in the blink of an eye, team members were taking sides.

"Don't make me start breaking heads." Scott grabbed a fistful of General E.'s collar and hauled the big teen backward.

"What you gonna do, Big Home?" General E. tried to pull away, hostility a few steps ahead of rational thought. "Kick me to the pavement?"

"Hell to the no." Twisting the kid's collar tighter, Scott forced him around until they could make eye contact. "I'm going to pull my service piece and shoot off your ear. The one with the gauge."

It stung Scott's pride to acknowledge that might have been the easiest way for him to take down this kid, who had a good four inches and fifteen pounds on him. General E., whose real name was Eric, stood six foot four with a build that had made him a natural in command, hence the nickname. He'd been on his way to senior status in 16 Squared, the gang that owned 16th Street around town square, before a judge had sent him to Renaissance for his one and only chance to straighten up.

"Get a grip, Eric." Scott held his gaze.

With any luck, General E. would funnel all this natural talent for leadership in a productive direction. If these kids could get a break, a decent job or enroll in community college, they usually created new identities for themselves and fit back into their real names again. Not all kids did, but General E. looked as though he might make it as he sucked in a deep breath.

"You breaking your own rules, Big Home?" General E. sounded genuinely shocked. "You brought a piece into the Center?"

"Not hardly." Scott twisted his collar harder for good measure. "I wouldn't bring a gun around you thugs. Wouldn't trust you not to steal it and blow off your damn feet."

That got a round of laughter and made General E. growl out, "What? You going to take me down with your busted self, old man? Like your boys shut down that cookhouse in H Creek."

Cakes threw down his arms and backed off, shaking his head. "Hell with you, chump."

So word had gotten around the streets about Jason Kenney's nightmare bust. That got Scott's attention.

"You go, Cakes." He released his grip on General E.'s collar, and backed up enough for the kid to straighten up.

Cakes raised a fist and said, "Pound it."

Scott connected fists and didn't have to say another word. Renaissance was all about teaching these kids to expect more from themselves than society did. Cakes had every right to feel good right now. It was too easy for them to get sucked into not-so-old habits.

General E. was still visibly wrestling with his pride, but Scott let him be, content when the other kids started breaking away, grabbing shirts that littered the perimeter of the court. The pack mentality evaporated as fast as it started. Good. Scott wasn't in the mood today to deal with this crew out of control.

Pulling his shirt over his head, he turned toward the sound of wolf whistles and found a group clustering around the fence as two girls walked by. "Dudes, you really need to act like gentlemen in front of the ladies."

"Man, who are you calling ladies?" Mateo yelled out, loud enough for the girls to hear.

One of the girls flicked him off, and a bunch of the guys hooted with laughter.

"I think you're pretty, ladies," Do-Wap said. "So does Big Home here. Forget those losers."

"You need a life, Do," Cakes called out.

Cakes's real name was William Brown, and Scott had never understood the nickname. Some handles made sense. Devonte "Do-Wap" Smith was from Wappinger Falls. Easy for his "busted old self" to figure out. But all Scott had heard about Cakes was that he was a world-class liar who could cover up anything. Like icing covered a cake?

Scott had no clue.

"You need a life, too, Big Home." Cakes fell into step beside him as the guys started filing inside the Center.

Scott, of course, was Big Home. He couldn't remember who'd started calling him that because it had been so long ago, but he answered to Big Home. Kept him one of the crowd.

"What, you're tired of seeing my smiling face around here?" he asked. "I'm hurt."

"Dude, you called Shae Cherry a *lady*."

"Do-Wap seems to think she—"

"Do-Wap's the only one in town who hasn't tapped it." Cakes shook his braided black head sadly. "Do-Wap and you, looks like. He's angling, but you need to hook up with someone who can show you the difference between a lady and a ho."

"That's harsh." Scott motioned to the hallway filled with teens coming in from the court and emerging from a tutoring session. "Exactly when do I have time to *hook up?* If you hoodlums aren't keeping me busy running the streets, you're wearing me out on the basketball court."

"You need to chill with your lady, dude." Cakes's eyes widened in horror. "You do have a lady? You know what I mean...*tending the farm.*"

"Don't you worry about *the farm*." Scott wasn't having any part of this conversation.

The only woman in his life right now was the one he couldn't think about. Big difference between feeling and *acting on* a feeling, exactly what he preached to these kids. He knew firsthand because he hadn't been any different than they were before learning that he had control of his life, that he could turn things around with the choices he made.

He'd chosen not to think about Riley. He valued looking himself in the mirror more than letting his feelings get control of him.

"The cows are mooing, man, so let it rest." A lie. "General E. mentioned H Creek. Lot of talk?"

Cakes eyed him narrowly as if he suspected the motive behind Scott's change of subject. "Word's out the busters screwed up."

"Suppose that's one way to call it."

"Sheeeet. What else do you call Drano in your cop shop?"

"It's not *my* cop shop," Scott clarified. "And that's what you're hearing—a leak?"

"H Creek ain't Mexico," Mateo added, obviously keeping up with the conversation. "You all brothaz in blue."

Scott had no problem discussing gang-related activities if these kids needed to talk. Not only was a leak in the Hazard Creek bust news to Scott, but his senses were tingling.

Mateo was right about one thing—law around here was tight. No surprise when Hazard Creek, Hyde Park and Pleasant Valley orbited like satellites around Poughkeepsie.

Then there was Riley. She might only have been in the wrong place at the wrong time, but in his mind she was now involved. Any word on the streets that might impact her was his business.

"Who's talking leak?" Scott asked.

Cakes gave him a sidelong glance.

"Why you scared, Angel Food?" Mateo demanded with a laugh then turned to Scott. "Everything is everything. You know talk's out about how the chefs in that cookhouse did a ghost."

"Who heard they were tipped off?" Scott asked.

"Some peripheral was running her mouth about how she'd hooked up with a prince from Big House. She was way fine, too."

Do-Wap gave a low whistle, another eavesdropper to the conversation. "I'd buy anything that sweet piece was selling."

Cakes snorted. "You'd sell your mama for a piece o' anything."

Do-Wap elbowed him, and Cakes sidestepped the blow, nearly taking Scott down in the process.

He scowled. A girl who hung in the periphery of any gang wasn't likely to have a bead on the inner workings, even if she was sleeping with a senior member. "A peripheral? You think there's something to that?"

Mateo shrugged. "The Big House brothaz all up in H Creek's grill, Big Home. Everyone knows that."

Not everyone. Big House operated on Scott's beat, and this was the first he'd heard about any connection to Hazard Creek. If the gang was operating out of Poughkeepsie proper, there had to be some solid link to the area.

The link wasn't likely to be a bunch of similar-minded drug dealers, otherwise Scott would have heard. Any connection between Poughkeepsie inner city and H Creek had to be one that could enable these thugs to branch out operations into new turf without a lot of press. That meant only the most senior gang members were in on the operation.

Had these kids heard right? Could there be a leak in one of the departments?

CHAPTER EIGHT

THROUGH TEARY EYES, Riley stared in the rearview mirror, her stomach sick.

Just four days ago, Mrs. House, with her kind smiles and soft voice, had seemed to be the most perfect kindergarten teacher in the world. Today, she seemed more prison warden while leading Jake through the car-rider line execution style.

"Mrs. Angelica," she'd said oh-so diplomatically on the telephone last night. "I think it might be better if you drop Jake off at school. Camille and I will get him to class, and he'll have a little time to adjust before we get inside."

All the excitement of kindergarten had disintegrated into a raging case of separation anxiety for her son. Riley assumed he'd feel better when he had a clearer idea of what to expect. But the situation wasn't working out that way, despite Riley's best efforts at reassurance. She'd given Jake checkpoints to look forward to during the long day.

Smiley-face notes in his lunch box.

One of Daddy's handkerchiefs in his pocket.

Unfortunately, after three days of panicked tears at the door, the teacher had decided to assume control.

In her heart, Riley knew Mrs. House was right. Camille, who was genuinely excited about school, became worried and sad whenever Jake melted down. Then there were the other twenty-five little kids in class to consider. This wasn't the best start to anyone's day, nor did Riley want Jake labeled a problem this early in his school career.

So last night she'd spent the night prepping him for today's change of routine. She'd placed her picture in his pocket so he could pull it out whenever he missed Mommy. Then she'd bypassed the parking lot and headed for the car-riders' line, where Mrs. House stood waiting as promised. Riley had given each kid a kiss and hug. Camille had jumped out of the minivan eagerly. Riley had nearly had to throw Jake out.

This was not how life was supposed to be. Riley should be walking her kids to class, then hanging around to help out as homeroom mom whenever she didn't have an early assignment. *She* should be comforting her son, not relying on a kindhearted but all-too-busy teacher to do the job.

An impatient horn sounded behind her, and she dragged her gaze away from the kids and quickly glanced at her blind spot before pulling away from the curb.

That sick feeling in her stomach intensified at the stop sign. Her own separation anxiety spiked as she faced the decision to drive home or wait at the nearby coffee shop until she knew for certain Jake had calmed down. Did she want to be too far away if she had to pick him up?

Uncertainty echoed in her head, and the horn beeped again, impatient, forcing her to make a choice she didn't want to make.

Riley wheeled the minivan into the flow of traffic.

Of course Jake would calm down, she told herself, physically willing herself to drive past the coffee shop. He had to make peace with school, and Mrs. House was trained to help him. She also understood the unique aspects of the situation, and the factors that made leaving mommy difficult. And Jake wasn't alone; Camille was in the same class. Thank goodness Riley had kept them together instead of separating them as so many parenting guides suggested.

No. She'd go home. She'd hope for the best, and if she was needed, she'd only be fifteen minutes away.

The best obviously wasn't on the schedule today, though, because as she rounded the last bend before her house, she was greeted by the police.

Cruisers parked haphazardly in her driveway, on the street, on the lawn between, as if the entire police force had been dispatched to her place. For one breathless instant, her memory flashed back to the day Chief Levering had shown up to tell her about Mike....

Had something happened to Brian?

Her heart pounded out an uncomfortable rhythm. She couldn't remember if she'd seen her nephew's car in the driveway this morning.

One of the uniformed officers recognized her and flagged her to a place on that semicircle of grass between the driveway and street. He was at her door by the time she'd set the emergency brake.

"Riley, it's good to see you again." He was smiling. That took her by surprise.

"Charlie, what happened—"

"Everything's okay," he reassured her. "459a came through dispatch." He glanced around and gave a sheepish shrug. "Everyone recognized your address."

"My alarm went off? Why didn't the security company call?" She slid a hand automatically to her waist to check her cell phone, then realized it wasn't there. In the turmoil of the morning's anxiety, she must have forgotten it.

Charlie frowned. "Intruder attempted to gain entry

through a bathroom window—the one over the basement door. Looks like the alarm scared him off."

"A burglary?"

Charlie nodded. "Got through the window on that overhang. Don't worry. We don't think he got into the house."

Don't worry? That was the twins' bathroom.

She had to stop her imagination from leaping straight to the worst possible scenario, to an image of Camille or Jake walking in on an intruder.

But they were safe at school, settling in for the day, or trying to in Jake's case. No worries.

"Riley?" Charlie asked. "You okay?"

She forced herself to move past the fear, forced herself to reply, "The point of entry makes sense."

Charlie nodded. "No question. No one's getting in around back without a ladder."

The house was situated on a descending slope that left the front porch ground level and the back of the house a full story higher with a magnificent view of the duck pond and the surrounding acreage. Since the front of the house was visible from the street, the bathroom window provided some cover.

"Have there been burglaries in the neighborhood, Charlie?" She didn't want to overreact, but the idea of someone inside the house… "I need to call Brian and make sure he's okay. May I go inside and get my phone?"

Charlie didn't get a chance to reply because just then another uniformed officer—Janet DiBenedetto—noticed Riley and called out, "She's here, guys. Riley's here."

That began an avalanche of greetings. Riley had never seen so many of Mike's former coworkers together at one time except at police functions. And his funeral.

They welcomed her home and sought to reassure her

they'd be working double-time, no *triple*-time, to keep watch on her place after this break-in so often that she couldn't help but be overwhelmed.

She felt as if she was repeating the same words over and over. But "thank you" wasn't nearly good enough in the face of so much support, and just as the lump in her throat grew almost impossible to talk around, she spotted Scott circling the side of the house.

He came to an abrupt stop when he saw her, and their gazes met across the distance. One brief instant and the crowd seemed to vanish. All the greetings and laughter faded to white noise. From where Riley stood his eyes seemed almost black, but she knew they were really deep, deep brown. He searched her face, assessing, and he was relieved by what he saw, the look in his espresso-colored eyes somehow liquid.

She knew how relieved he was. Though his expression never changed. Though the sharp lines of his face might have been chiseled from stone.

As though held by some bodily connection, she just stood there, trapped by his gaze, feeling so aware of him, so glad he was here.

She could barely acknowledge that this wasn't the first time she'd felt so *relieved* to see him. So grateful he kept showing up exactly when she needed him. How, Riley couldn't say, but he seemed to know with an uncanny knack because he headed straight toward her. Suddenly he was at her side, assuming a quiet control over the well-meaning chaos simply by inserting himself into the conversation.

He complimented Janet on her suggestion to notify the neighborhood crime watch for some extra eyes. He thanked Roger, who offered to have his son, a friend of Brian's, spend a few nights. He ragged on Charlie for offering to drive by Riley's place at three in the morning when he was coming off duty. And his good-natured presence gave Riley time to catch her breath before she had to deal with the matter at hand.

The *matters* at hand.

Someone had broken into her home.

And she was far too grateful to have Scott beside her.

Charlie's waist crackled a static interruption, and he withdrew from the group, taking the transmission where he was out of earshot.

Scott glanced down, his dark eyes looking over her, not assessing but gently, as if they stood alone. "You okay?"

Two simple words, but somehow they were a caress, no different than his gaze. She found her voice. "I need to call Brian, but my cell phone is in the house. May I use yours?"

Scott nodded, adding, "I spoke to him already. He's been on campus since the crack of dawn. Doesn't have a clue what went down. He tried calling you. He was worried."

Again she felt that sense of appreciation. For Scott. For his becoming a part of her life. "Oh, thank goodness he's okay. And thank you for checking on him."

"Called you first. When I couldn't get you, *I* got worried."

Riley didn't get a chance to reply, didn't get to dwell on the fact that Scott so obviously cared, when Charlie circled the cruiser again. "Neighbor reported seeing a motorcycle tear-assing toward Route 55 not long after dispatch got the alarm."

"Motorcycle?" Janet narrowed her gaze. "What makes you think it's our perp and not some kid out for a joyride?"

"The neighbor said she didn't hear the bike coming

down the road. It sounded as if it pulled out from somewhere right before the bend. That would be Riley's place."

Riley guessed the neighbor must be Peg Haslam, the widow who'd parceled off some of her own land after her husband's death to add to Mike's acreage.

"Sal." Charlie radioed the officer investigating the shoulder of the road leading away from the house. "That fresh rubber look like a motorcycle to you?"

"You betcha," the voice transmitted. "Our intruder must not have been looking to score stuff he could hock."

"Money or jewelry, then," Charlie said. "That would be easy to carry."

Janet nodded. "Jewelry's an easy enough pawn."

Scott frowned. "He obviously didn't know the security system routes a silent alarm to the precinct. A normal system would have given a burglar a good five or six minutes before the security company dispatched the police. Time enough for Riley to get a call and confirm whether or not this was a false alarm."

"I didn't get that call, either," she admitted, frustrated by her own absentmindedness. Leave it to her to forget her phone the day she actually needed it. She had so much on her mind that things were slipping through the cracks. "But I don't know anything about a silent alarm. What are you talking about?"

Scott met her gaze. "The chief authorized it as a precaution after Mike. Until we figured out exactly what went down and who was involved, we didn't want to take chances."

"It's active?" She wasn't the only one looking at Scott.

"We talked about disconnecting after we closed the investigation, but you were gone, and Brian was alone in the house." He shrugged. "Seemed a good idea to leave it.

"Which raises a question." Scott leaned against the

cruiser and folded his arms across his chest, looking strong and capable, a man in control. "So as far as the perp knew, he should have had time to get in and out. But if that was the case, we'd have caught him. So why'd this guy run?"

"Petty hood got spooked?" Sal offered as he joined them.

"By what?" Janet asked.

"Or he knew the cops were on the way," Scott said.

Sal frowned. "You thinking he had a radio?"

Scott nodded.

"He must have been looking to make a fast getaway," Charlie said. "Why else the bike?"

Scott usually wore a poker face, but right now Riley could see through his intensity. She wasn't sure why. Perhaps only because she was getting to know the nuances of this man who was becoming her friend, establishing his own place in her life. He wasn't going to let this go until he had answers.

And knowing that reassured her. So much.

"It's not possible to predict your work schedule, Riley," he said, his gaze holding hers. "You don't always know when you're heading out on assignment. So how long have the kids been in school—a couple of days now?"

"Since Monday." Four days that had passed in a blur.

"So whoever tried to break in didn't know about the silent alarm, but he knew the exact time you'd be gone. How long does it take you to drop the kids off and get back?"

"Thirty minutes round-trip give or take."

That got everyone's attention. Riley could see it in the way everyone focused on her. Even the latest arrival, a man appearing from around the garage, wore a frown. A detective, judging by his casual dress.

"That's not a very large window," Scott said. "And not a very established routine."

Riley thought she understood what was troubling him. "Brian only takes early classes on Tuesday and Thursday mornings."

"And the semester started last week."

She nodded, feeling her heart rate speeding up again.

The new guy extended his hand to Riley. "Kevin Rush," he said. "Scott's partner. Pleased to meet you."

Riley introduced herself. Mike had been Scott's partner for as long as she'd known them. She'd never thought to ask how his new partner was working out, hadn't thought of Scott in any role other than the one he'd always played— as Mike's friend.

But now she wondered how this man compared. How did their work measure up? How did Scott pass his days now—with camaraderie or stoic professionalism?

Then Kevin said, "Whoever this guy was, he had a pretty tight bead on your schedule."

"That's what I'm thinking." Scott reached for Riley's elbow as if he knew she was putting two and two together and didn't want her to worry. "Come on, Riley. Let's unlock the house. We need to do a walk-through."

"You said he didn't get past the bathroom."

He squeezed her elbow, a gentle touch. "He didn't. Barely had time to break the window let alone get inside. It's a precaution."

"We're the best. You know that." Janet laughed. "We want to be thorough."

"The chief'll fry our asses if we're not," Sal added. "You don't want to make us deal with him, do you? We'll wind up in front of the review board."

"Or suspended without pay," Charlie added. "Can you imagine what Sarah-Lynn would have to say about that?"

Riley smiled, knowing the performances were for her

benefit. Charlie's wife would be as bad as the chief, she knew. Maybe even worse since Charlie actually lived with her.

"Come on." Scott guided her to the front porch door. "I want you to check your messages."

That snapped Riley back to her right mind. "Ohmigosh. My phone. What if Mrs. House tried to call me? Who has the time?"

"Eight twenty-four," Janet offered, clearly puzzled.

But Riley didn't bother to explain, just grabbed her keys off her belt and headed toward the front porch. She'd left school nearly thirty minutes ago. What if Jake hadn't settled down? What if Mrs. House had been trying to reach her?

She was yanked from her thoughts when Scott plucked the keys from her hand.

"If you don't mind." He didn't give her a choice as he unlocked the door.

Suddenly she found herself flanked by a personal security force made up of Poughkeepsie's finest. They kept her from entering until assured the coast was clear.

Riley finally entered and beelined straight for her cell phone charger, which she kept on her bedside table. The phone read Charge Complete on the display. She cleared the screen and, sure enough, found her missed calls.

Home security.

Scott.

Brian.

No calls from the school. She exhaled a pent-up breath.

"Everything okay?" Scott asked, startling her.

She hadn't heard him approach and turned to find him framed in the doorway, his broad shoulders filling the opening, that serious expression hinting at how much he cared.

"Jake had a rough morning. I was afraid the teacher might have called."

"She didn't?"

Riley shook her head, appreciating his concern.

Scott didn't move. He didn't quite meet her eyes, either, as if there was some invisible line that kept him from even glancing inside the private domain of her bedroom. He shifted from foot to foot, looking so uncomfortable that Riley keenly felt the distance between them, the way he no longer seemed like Scott, who'd been around forever. Her husband's partner. His friend. Scott had been many things through the years. A handsome, sometimes somber man, who wore his loyalty to those he loved on his sleeve. But he'd never been *her* friend.

He'd always kept his distance. She didn't know why. Yet now, as Riley watched him, she knew things were changing between them. And she was very, very aware of those changes.

CHAPTER NINE

WHAT IN HELL was wrong with him?

Scott didn't have a ready answer, but he stood at the threshold of Riley's bedroom, more physically affected by the sight of her than he should have been. Way more.

She glanced down at the display again, scrolling through her telephone messages. Her wildly curly hair fell forward, covering much of her face. Still, he could see the tight set of her jaw, the delicate profile set in anxious lines.

In that moment there should have been only the two of them. There should have been only relief that the perp hadn't broken into the house, hadn't harmed her or given her anything else to worry about. She was already struggling to settle in.

She hadn't said anything, not to him or Rosie or Joe as far as Scott knew, but tension was all over her. In the way she had to work for smiles that used to come so fast and easy. In the way so much attention from overzealous and well-meaning cops seemed to swallow her up. In the way she looked fragile right now, as if she stood there holding her breath just waiting for something else horrible to come at her.

So what was wrong with him that he was standing here, almost painfully aware of the neatly made bed, the silky blouse hanging from a bedpost, the toiletries scattered over the dresser that seemed so much more personal than if they'd been on a grocer's shelf?

And why in holy hell was he suddenly hearing the words *tending the farm?*

Damned kids.

Scott shook his head to clear it. But he didn't move from that doorway as he swallowed past the lump in his throat and tried to ignore those words.

What was wrong with him? He needed to back up and get out of this room. But he was still standing there when Riley glanced up again, curls tumbling over her shoulders, the tight lines of her face relaxing as sunlight spilled through the window, bathing her in a glow that made her tanned skin seemed cast in gold.

Their gazes met, and a frown tugged at the corners of her mouth. His gut gave a hard twist.

"Scott?"

"Yeah," he forced out.

"Is anything wrong?"

"No. Just need you for the walk-through." Stupid ass he was. Doing exactly what he didn't want to do—worry her.

"Of course. I'm sorry."

He was pushing too hard. "No hurry. No one's going anywhere."

A small smile. "No real crime to fight out there, hmm?"

He could only snort.

Her smile widened. "I appreciate everyone responding the way they did. Please tell the chief. I can't tell you how much better I feel knowing everyone's got their eyes on us. I mean really, Scott."

"Everyone's glad you're back." He responded on auto-pilot. "But seriously, you should take a few extra precautions. Let Roger's son stay with Brian a few nights. Brian will go along. Do whatever you can to shake up your routine."

The smile vanished as fast as it had appeared. She sank down onto the side of the bed, a boneless motion that made her look tired. "You're worried."

"I'm always worried."

She lifted her gaze, and those crystal-blue eyes weren't sparkling. "I mean more than your normal worrying. Things aren't adding up. I know the look."

No doubt. "We should pay attention."

"What else can I do?"

"You know the drill. I'll have a unit assigned to patrol your place. No problems there. Vary your routine and keep the security system armed even when you're at home. Any chance of getting your dogs back?"

She gave a wry chuckle that didn't reach her expression. "Not hardly. Caroline thrives on playing big sister. Her 'babysitting' turned into a little more than I expected. Hershel and Oodles Marie are hers now. I wanted to bring them down to Florida once I knew we'd be staying, but she insisted they wouldn't like the heat." Riley shrugged. "They're her only connection left to Mike. I'm trying to be gracious. So, no watchdogs. I can't handle puppies."

"Can't blame you there. I don't want you to worry, though." He'd be worrying enough for them both. "PPD's got your back."

He sounded a lot more assured than he felt, but his words had the desired effect. Riley visibly relaxed. With a graceful motion, she straightened and stood.

"Thank you," she said earnestly, an appreciation he didn't deserve. "I feel a lot better. And that's saying something. It's been a rough week."

"Jake going to be okay?"

She cocked a hip against her dresser and clipped the cell phone to her jeans. "Yeah. He just takes a little more time to settle in than Camille. And I'm never sure if I'm doing everything I should be to help him along."

Scott wasn't sure how to respond to that. He had about zero experience with little kids, although he was pretty savvy about the older ones. But when she folded her arms across her chest and took a deep breath, Riley gave the impression she just needed to talk. Sure enough…

"Camille's really excited, you know. She loves school. But when Jake gets upset, she feels bad, like she shouldn't be so happy about something that bothers him. She doesn't understand the problem even though I talk with her about it. They're so different that a lot of the time what works with one doesn't work with the other, and it's hard to get any alone time with either of them." She lifted a hand and rubbed her temples. "My impulse is to fix things, but I can't always do that. I have to help them learn to cope. But it breaks my heart watching Jake struggle so much."

Scott nodded. He thought he understood. She was a good mom. She even shoved aside her own feelings to teach her kids. Sure, it might be easier for her if she fixed the situation, but in the long run, Jake wouldn't have the skills necessary to handle the things that came up in life.

That was exactly what Scott dealt with at Renaissance. Kids whose parents hadn't prepared them to deal successfully with the world. Sometimes parents died or took off, or their own addictions got in the way of their responsibilities. Sometimes they were still around, but didn't know any better. Whatever the reason, the result was the same—kids fighting to cope with life and making a lot of wrong choices along the way.

He'd been a kid like that himself once.

Life had taken away all the people who mattered and left him with a family that had been the antithesis of Mike and Riley's. Scott might have lost a parent—a mother in his case—but the father who'd been left behind hadn't been the least interested in parenting.

But Scott had been one of the lucky ones—he'd had a decent enough start to realize that he wanted more for himself. He'd been smart enough to figure out how to get it. That hadn't happened without a fair amount of good people to help him along the way. People like the chief, Mike and, in her way, Riley. He'd been Mike's friend, never hers. How could he when he'd always been so aware of her, and so ashamed of feeling that way? But he'd made the choice to keep his distance from her long ago, and while Riley might not have known how he felt, she'd always welcomed him unconditionally, always respected the distance he'd kept between them, accepted what he'd had to offer.

"You're doing your best, Riley." That much he did know. "What more can you do?"

She shrugged. "It always feels like I could be doing more, like I'm missing something."

"Trust me on this," he said softly, denying the urge to share details about his own upbringing to convince her. "Jake and Camille are two cool little people. That speaks for itself. You're raising good kids."

She gave a rather lopsided smile, looking sheepish. He wasn't sure why. Maybe because she'd needed reassurance. Or maybe because they were talking about personal things in a way they never had before.

Either way, Scott knew she'd not only lost her husband when Mike had died, but her best friend. Sure, she had other friends, but most had taken off after college, heading back home or launching careers elsewhere. Pleasant Valley had been Mike's town, not Riley's.

She eyed him thoughtfully. "You know, maybe I should ask Rosie to help me arrange some alone time to spend with each of them. I'm sure she'll help out."

"No question there. She'd probably jump at the chance." As Riley had said, the Angelica family didn't have many connections left to Mike.

"Hey, man," Kevin called from down the hallway. "We ready to get this show on the road?"

The moment was over. Pushing away from the dresser, Riley gave a light laugh. "You're so sweet. Thanks for listening."

"I'm here, Riley." It was all he could think to say.

But Scott wasn't thinking, that much was obvious when he stepped forward and reached for her hand, gave it a reassuring squeeze. Her fingers felt lightweight and warm against his, so alive. So Riley. Had Scott been thinking, he'd have remembered he had no business touching her, not even casually.

He couldn't be casual with Riley.

"You ready yet?" Kevin asked when he appeared in the doorway.

Scott slipped his hand from Riley's and turned. "Yeah. Let's do it."

"What do I need to do?" Riley asked.

"Give us the ten-dollar tour." Kevin seized the chance to take control, even going so far as to loop his arm through Riley's. "You can double-check that nothing looks disturbed while I get to know you better. It's a pleasure to finally meet you. I've heard a lot about your family."

"Good, I hope," she said.

"Naturally." Kevin flashed a blinding smile that gave

Scott the sudden, and unexpected, impulse to plant a fist in his cosmetically perfect teeth.

Kevin led Riley through the door, forcing Scott to fall in step behind them. This wasn't going to work.

"Riley, want me to get a jump on the broken glass?" He reached for his cell phone. "I'll give Tony at Father and Son Glass a call. He'll send someone out. I don't want you home alone with that window out."

She glanced over her shoulder, a smile plastered on her face. A forced one, Scott was pleased to note. She wasn't stupid enough to fall for Kevin. "I'd appreciate it very much."

"Done." He made his way to the foyer to place the call.

By the time he reconvened with Riley and Kevin, he had a glass guy on the way.

"They didn't make it inside," Kevin informed him.

"No surprises there." Scott met Riley's gaze, found her looking drained. "Not the best way to start the day."

She only gave a wan smile before accompanying them onto the front porch. She thanked everyone who hadn't taken off yet and waited inside the open doorway as her driveway cleared. Scott wished she would go inside and lock up, so he would at least know she was safe. But he couldn't think of any way to tell her to get inside without looking like an overprotective jerk. An overly possessive one, anyway.

So he slipped into his car, barely giving Kevin a chance to get in before he gunned the engine and took off, watching Riley recede in his rearview mirror.

Kevin sank back in the seat and gave a low whistle. "Wow. The widow is everything I heard and a bag of chips."

Scott shot Kevin a look, not a little surprised he was heading down this road. "You're an idiot."

Kevin's turn to look surprised.

Scott relented. "What'd you hear?"

"That Mike was a seriously lucky man. I didn't know the dude. Not really. Seen him around the station, but I was new with the department. You two were legendary."

Scott snorted.

"No, really, man. You two came and went as you pleased, and always had the chief on your side. Looked pretty good from where I was standing."

What did he even say to that? "Yeah, well, what it looked like and what it was were two different things."

"Maybe, but not with the widow." Kevin closed his eyes. "Heard she was a stunner. I'd say so."

This wasn't news. Not to anyone who knew Riley. Everyone in the PPD had known Mike was a lucky bastard. They'd ragged him about it endlessly. Mike had always told everyone to take a damn hike. He knew they were jealous.

But not Scott.

He might have had unwanted feelings for Riley, but what kind of person would be jealous of a friend? Especially a friend like Mike.

"So you've been keeping your eyes on her," Kevin said. Not a question. "That's decent. Not like you'll go blind, though."

Another image flashed of what Kevin would look like with a few broken teeth. Scott blinked a few times to erase the vision. The rational part of his brain knew Kevin meant nothing more than to pay Riley a compliment. But that rational part got its ass stomped by the irrational part, which didn't want to face the fact that Kevin was all too right.

Watching over Riley wasn't hard. It was easy. Too damned easy.

"WHAT DO YOU THINK, Chief?" Hank Llewellyn emerged from the questioning room wearing a scowl.

"I think you're up against a player," Jason said. "The guy told us he didn't know a thing about guns the first time we questioned him, and he not only hunts but has an NRA membership. Give me a break."

Hank nodded. "I'm booking him."

Jason was about to reply when message traffic over the police radio caught his attention.

10-17.

29 Traver Road, Pleasant Valley.

Attempted burglary. Suspect fled the scene.

Jason's heartbeat upped a notch, though if Hank noticed the frequency for Pleasant Valley's patrol zone, he gave no clue.

Jason might be looking at Hank, but didn't hear a word his officer was saying as the radio relayed details of the call.

10-17. PPD had responded to a suspected prowler.

Jason had been monitoring the sheriff's band, but supposed he shouldn't be surprised the PPD had taken the call. All it would take was one cop to recognize Mike Angelica's address. Half the force had probably shown up before the sheriff had gotten there.

Not all towns in the Mid-Hudson Valley had their own police forces. Smaller townships, such as Pleasant Valley and LaGrange, relied upon the County Sheriff's Department, the state troopers and neighboring departments to serve them.

Jason had been hoping for a little luck today. He'd hoped that when the security company called Riley, she'd assume a false alarm and give her code word. Still, there should be time for Tyrese to find what he was looking for inside the house. *"Attempted burglary. Suspect fled the scene."*

"Damn it," he ground out.

"Chief?" Hank frowned. "You're not okay with that?"

Jason stared, so wrapped up in his own thoughts that he had to shake his head before seeing Hank again, who was looking at him from not two feet away. He shook off his distraction. "No. It's all good. You got it, Hank. Good work."

Jason had no clue what he'd just signed on for, but had to trust Hank's discretion. The fact that Hank looked pleased by the praise only served to ramp up Jason's anxiety. Friggin' domino effect. This grief was taking over his whole life.

He issued a few more statements to get Hank out of his face. Sure enough, no sooner had the door to the questioning room closed when the disposable cell phone in Jason's pocket rang.

Retrieving the phone, he headed into his office and shut the door. "Give me good news, man."

"You want good news?" the voice said, gruff and annoyed. "Then you came to the wrong place."

Tyrese Griffey had been one of the few surprises in Jason's law-enforcement career. He was old-time 16 Squared—a peewee since long before his voice had changed. Few gang members ever lived to see the opposite side of twenty, especially one like Tyrese with a rap sheet as long as his arm before he'd been old enough to get a driving permit.

The various law agencies around the area had collared him so many times he practically had his own police ten-code. His young age would put him right back on the streets again.

Then, during one night in the Hazard Creek lockup, not long after Jason had become chief, Tyrese claimed to have had a divine visitation. He began to witness salvation on street corners, declaring the love of Christ Jesus for all mankind, and becoming another sort of nuisance entirely.

So when he showed up for his day in court, Jason convinced the judge to give him a shot at redemption with the Renaissance program. Chief Levering knew Tyrese personally and didn't want any part of this serial offender, but Jason had managed to convince him to take a chance.

Tyrese had surprised them all. He hooked up with a church that seemed to appreciate his enthusiasm and abilities. They put him to work as groundskeeper and handyman, a sort of living testimonial to the love of Christ. Tyrese had been doing what he could to improve the world ever since.

Until the night some neighborhood thug had raped his baby sister and beat her within an inch of her life. He'd gone to preach mercy and forgiveness and wound up killing the guy.

Tyrese had freaked and called Jason. And when Jason had weighed all the good Tyrese had been doing against this thug from Big House…well, Jason wasn't God or anything, but he thought Tyrese had done the world a public service by taking out one of the bad guys. So he'd given the kid a second chance and helped him make the whole situation vanish.

It had never occurred to Jason that he'd call in the favor.

But now he half sat on the edge of his desk, feeling sick. "What happened?"

"Wasn't any problem getting the place empty," Tyrese said. "Broke a window and had cops breathing down my neck before I'd gotten inside. Good thing I had the radio."

Under any other circumstances, Jason might have complimented the foresight, but not now. Not when he was in way over his head. He needed to know what was on that

CD and if it implicated him. He needed to know if Riley knew what was on it.

"Must have had a silent alarm wired straight to PPD dispatch," Jason said. "It would explain why the cops responded as fast as they did."

But it didn't explain why the house was wired. Jason could understand the PPD adding the precaution while investigating Mike's death, but that had been over two years ago. Why now?

Maybe he was just being paranoid or maybe someone was worried about Riley's safety because she was investigating stories that put her at risk.

"Yeah, I figured that part out for myself." Tyrese sucked in a deep breath. "Listen, Chief. I've got a shot at a life here, a real one. I'm not going down for you."

"You got a shot because I gave it to you."

There was silence on the other end. Jason could practically hear Tyrese's divinity warring with his worldly self. But Tyrese couldn't hang up. Jason needed him. Tyrese was *his*. Not someone Agent Asshole could blackmail or buy off. It didn't matter that he was one more on the growing list of people whose lives Jason was screwing up because *he'd* screwed up.

Callie. The kids. His parents.

So he said the only thing he could think of that might convince Tyrese not to hang up the phone.

"I'm in trouble, Tyrese."

CHAPTER TEN

RILEY HAD ALWAYS LOVED the chaos of Angelica family get-togethers. This Labor Day celebration was no different, if for an unexpected reason. Once upon a time, she'd enjoyed being with immediate and extended family because she'd loved the camaraderie, a welcome change from her solitary and mobile upbringing as an only child in a military family.

And while she still enjoyed that camaraderie with people she'd come to love dearly, today she also appreciated how the chaos distracted her from thinking—about Jake's difficult first week of kindergarten, about available career choices, about how different this gathering felt without Mike.

Different yet somehow the same. As if she still belonged here. That was a good feeling, a hopeful feeling, as if the future would sort itself out as long as she kept putting one foot in front of the other.

"Aunt Riley, I thought you said these kids went to school in Florida," Brian called out from the pool.

"They did." She smiled as Brian hefted Jake into the air and flipped him head over heels into the water.

Her son's laughter rang out, ending as quickly as it began when he landed with a splash. Water exploded onto the deck. Groans and growls erupted from the group playing pinochle not far from the splash zone.

Brian propped himself up on the side of the pool. "I don't think these kids did anything but swim. They're kicking our butts at water tag."

Riley laughed. "It's summer all the time down there, Brian. They went to school and swam pretty much every day."

"Oh, man. That's just wrong."

"My turn." Camille launched herself onto her cousin's back and tried to drag him underwater. "Throw me."

Brian good-naturedly went under, coming up with dramatic sputters that made Camille squeal.

Riley covered her ears. "Dunk her, Brian. Before she does permanent damage."

Brian obliged, and they got a split second of blessed silence before one of the cousins, who'd been congregating at the opposite end of the pool, declared the break over.

"Jake and Camille are it." The cry rang out as energetic swimmers propelled themselves into the water, starting the mayhem again.

Riley plunked down into an Adirondack chair to watch the carnage, hanging on to a glass of water she wasn't drinking.

Camille and Jake had the obvious advantage. They dove in and around their older cousins like little piranhas, delighting everyone—particularly themselves—with their speed and prowess.

"You can't catch me," Camille shrieked when her head broke the surface, clearly wanting her big cousins to do exactly that.

Jake was so much more subtle. He was on the warpath and out for blood.

"Don't you know how to swim, dude?" he taunted Brian, then dove underwater, only coming up for air when he was clear on the opposite end of the pool.

Her kids got their time to shine, their time to connect

with cousins they couldn't remember and, in the process, earn a place for themselves. They had a big Italian family to love them. And Joe and Rosie's family was definitely big. They'd had five kids total. Mike and his twin, Lily Susan, had been surprise blessings, as Rosie always referred to them, twins who were eight years behind the pack. Everyone lived close by with the exception of Lily Susan, whose destination-wedding business was based out of Manhattan.

"Mind if I join you?" Caroline appeared at her side, collapsed into a nearby chair.

"Game over?"

Caroline scowled. "So it would seem."

Riley glanced up in time to see Caroline's husband, Alex, storming into the house, leaving behind a picnic table with various in-laws staring after him, still holding cards.

"Everything okay?"

"Fine, thanks. But I would caution your kids about choosing their life mates at the tender young age of sixteen."

Riley only gave a slow nod, knowing better than to comment. Caroline had met Alex Bosse during her sophomore year in high school. Alex had been a junior at the time, and they'd gotten married not long after Caroline's graduation, so she could go off to college to live with him.

"Then may I say thanks again for lending me Brian?" Riley said to break the silence and distract her sister-in-law from what appeared to have been an unpleasant scene. "He's been a treasure. I couldn't have done the past two years without him."

"He feels the same about you, Riley. Taking care of the horses is a small price to pay for his independence, don't kid yourself. He has a sweet deal and he knows it."

Riley smiled. "A mutually beneficial arrangement. Can't ask for more than that."

"No, I suppose not."

"Do you see him much?"

Caroline scowled harder. "Sunday dinners here unless he needs something. I should be grateful. I'd barely see him at all if he'd have gone away to college."

Which Riley could see invited mixed emotions, and she could certainly understand. Her kids weren't close to college yet, but she filed the information away and hoped to remember a few years from now. Enjoy the moment. It would all too soon be over.

Or all too unexpectedly.

That was a lesson she'd learned well.

"It's good that he's keeping close with Rosie and Joe."

"Yeah. But I wish he would spend more time with us." Caroline shifted her gaze to the patio doors where her husband had disappeared. "Then again, I guess I can't really blame him. No one wants to be home much anymore."

There was so much in that statement. Riley eyed her sister-in-law closely, wishing she could read her mind. "Want to talk?"

"Thanks, but no thanks." Caroline's golden-brown eyes narrowed. "Same shit, different day."

She reached out and grabbed Caroline's well-manicured hand and gave a squeeze. "Well, I'm around if you change your mind."

But Riley knew Caroline wouldn't call. They were fond of each other and had been close before Mike's death. Maybe the years of distance had taken their toll. Maybe Caroline thought Riley had her hands too full to add anything else to the mix. She was thoughtful that way. Or maybe Caroline simply didn't want to talk. Whatever the reason, it served as another reminder of how quickly life marched on. The twins weren't the only ones who needed to reestablish places within the family.

"I'll sit in with pinochle," Riley said lightly. "If you'll teach me how to play."

That got a better response. Caroline's warm eyes crinkled around the edges in real amusement. "I can't teach you during a game. We'll be too busy playing."

An old problem. "What about Max or Rosie?"

"Max isn't coming because Madeleine has a tummy bug," she replied, referring to Max's young daughter. "And forget about Mom. She won't leave the kitchen until dinner is on the table. Speaking of…" Caroline glanced at her watch. "She's running late. She's probably stalling because of Scott. He's late."

"Scott's coming for dinner?"

"Yeah. He usually calls if he's not going to make it, but I don't think he called."

"How'd you all manage to get him here?"

"Dad caught him helping Brian out at your place one Sunday. You know Dad." She rolled her eyes. "He made Scott come with Brian under threat of death. Scott humored him, but he's been coming around more and more. Dad's pretty pleased with himself."

No doubt. Riley had tried for years to get Scott to feel as welcome in her home was Mike's other friends. But Scott had never dropped by without a formal invitation. He'd been prone to waiting in the cruiser outside rather than coming in to pick up Mike before a shift no matter how often Riley invited him in for coffee.

Water sluiced over the side of the pool followed by gales of laughter, and both Riley and Caroline lifted their feet to avoid the flood streaming beneath their chairs.

"Leave some water in the pool, guys," Caroline told them.

Riley only smiled, mulling what her sister-in-law had said about Scott. Was that what she'd noticed the night they'd eaten tacos after the Hazard Creek debacle? That sense of Scott being comfortable in the house, familiar with the dinner routine. She'd been right.

"Exactly how much has he been helping Brian out around the farm?" Riley asked. "I'm getting the sense it's a lot more than I realized."

Caroline met her gaze with that honest stare that reminded Riley so much of Mike. Like her brother, Caroline didn't pull any punches. "Nothing ridiculous or I'd have stepped in. Trust me. But the bottom line…well, Brian's a kid. There's a lot of stuff he doesn't know even though he'd never admit that."

"Oh, Caroline, I knew he was taking on a lot. If it was too much I'd have made other arrangements. You've been telling me everything is fine."

"I've been telling you everything's been fine because everything has been fine." Caroline leaned forward with a conspiratorial glance at the pool. "My son wants to be independent. He was leaving the day he turned eighteen no matter what. That left him with taking care of the farm or moving out with one of his buddies and killing himself to pay rent."

She shrugged. "At least when he's working for you, he's got boundaries. You flat-out told him he has to stay in school or the deal was off. Every last person in this family will narc on him if he screws up, and he won't get any mercy if he kills one of Uncle Mike's horses because he's lazy."

"That's awfully heavy for a kid…." Riley let her words trail off when Caroline shook her head.

"He's learning responsibility. That's a good thing. One of his parents spoiled him." She had the grace to look abashed but quickly added. "Cut me a break. He was my first. Besides, when he gets stuck, he calls Scott. At least he's calling someone to help and not toughing it out on his own. We really would end up with dead horses then."

"Remind me when my time comes, okay?"

"I will. Though I might not get the chance to boss you around." Caroline smiled. "Well, to be honest, I hoped you'd never come back so I wouldn't have to tell you that Hershel and Oodles Marie are mine now. We've bonded. You'll scar them for life if you take them away."

Riley sighed. "I made peace with your betrayal a while ago. But for the record you were only supposed to be babysitting while I got settled at my mother's. It was only a few weeks."

"What can I say? I'm hard to resist."

"You are that, which must be why I'm here now. I do appreciate everything you and your son have done for us. And Scott's really good with young people, so I'm not surprised Brian likes him so much. The feeling seemed mutual."

Caroline sank back in the chair and tipped her face toward the sun. "No question. That's all he has—work and those kids."

Riley shouldn't ask. From the depths of her soul, she knew she shouldn't ask. But she couldn't resist. She wanted to know, plain and simple. "Not involved with anyone at the moment?"

Caroline waved an impatient hand. "Not that I've heard, and I'd have heard."

"Can't say I'm surprised. He was always a dating junkie. Never knew who he'd bring to police events. Hard to keep up."

"I have no clue what his deal is," Caroline admitted. "He's dated some nice women, but I don't think he's been doing much lately. Not since Mike…"

"It's been rough on him?"

"He's on his second partner."

"Oh" was all Riley could think to say. She'd asked Scott how he was doing, of course. Every time they'd spoken on the telephone for the past two years, but he always said he was okay, never went into any specifics. She'd let it go at that. It just wasn't that way between them. He'd been Mike's friend.

Now she wanted to know why he dated but never seemed to have relationships.

"I really wish he'd get more balance in his life," Caroline said thoughtfully. "And that's not gossip, by the way. I've said as much to him."

"Really?"

"Really. Come on, Riley. He's a good-looking guy. Hardworking. He's a volunteer, for God's sake. A guy with a social conscience. But he's never been married. Doesn't have kids. We're the only family he has, and we only see him on Sundays. Doesn't that make you wonder?"

"When you put it like that."

"Commitment issues, do you think?"

"I don't see it. He's committed to so many things—the department, Renaissance, his friendships. Doesn't seem to have trouble to me." So what, then? Riley was surprised by how much she wanted to know. "But what do you mean he doesn't have any family? I knew he didn't have anyone around here. Mike said as much, but he doesn't have any family anywhere?"

"That's what he said. His mom died when he was five, and he lived with his grandmother until she passed away.

Then he came to Poughkeepsie. Been with the department ever since."

Wow. "I've known Scott since I met Mike, and I've never heard one word of that. He told you?"

"Heck no. But you know Mom. When she wants to know how smother someone, she's relentless."

"You mean *mother* someone, don't you?"

"Oh, yeah, right." Caroline cracked a grin, and Riley was about to ask for more details, unable to resist the temptation of getting to know more about this man she was befriending, but the patio door slid open and the man himself came through as if on cue, wielding a bouquet of summer flowers.

"Hey, everyone. Sorry I'm late."

"Should have brought flowers for us, detective," Joey, Rosie and Joe's eldest son, said. "Mama's starving us so we can wait on you."

"That's why she's waiting on him." Caroline smirked. "*Because* he brings her flowers. You're an ungrateful mooch. You should at least bring a bottle of wine or something."

"What in hell are you talking about?" Joey scowled. "I brought the sausage. Freaking *ten pounds* of it. From Bastian's Road House no less."

"Be patient, Joey," Rosie told her son. "You won't starve."

Joey's wife made a show of patting his stomach, which was hanging somewhat over his belt. "No, he won't starve."

Laughter tittered around the table, and Joey scowled. Scott, Riley noticed, had the good sense to keep his mouth shut. Instead, he gave Rosie a hug and presented her the flowers.

"Sorry I'm late. You should eat and not worry about me."

Rosie accepted the bouquet and gazed up at him fondly. "But I do worry. Everything all right?"

"One of the kids let his pride get in the way of his good sense. Now he's in trouble with the law." Scott shook his head. "Needed a character reference."

Rosie reached up and patted his cheek. "You're a good boy."

"And you're turning my stomach here, Ma," Joey complained.

More laughter. Then Rosie asked, "Any hope for this one?"

Scott shrugged. "Maybe. He's got a shot, but you know how it goes. You can lead a horse to water…"

"Good luck with that," Joey said.

Rosie nodded. "I'll hold a good thought."

"Thanks."

"Well, come on, then." Cradling the bouquet in her arms, Rosie headed back toward the patio doors. "Get the kids out of the pool and washed up. Everything's ready, but I could use some help getting it out on the table. We're going buffet today."

"I'll help, Mom." Caroline pushed herself up out of the chair with effort.

"Want some—"

"Don't worry about it, Riley. You take care of the twins."

Caroline sidestepped the patio, reaching up on tiptoe to kiss Scott's cheek. "Glad you made it. You'll sit in for pinochle after dinner?"

"Didn't see Alex inside. He being…difficult?"

"Got your gun?"

Scott laughed. "Locked in the car. And, no, you can't have my keys."

"Not helpful, Scott. *Not* helpful." Caroline gave a laugh and headed inside.

Riley got to her feet, dragging the beach towels from the back of the chair so she could corral her kids.

Catching Scott's gaze as she turned, she smiled a greeting. "Nice to see you."

"You, too," he said.

Then silence engulfed them, the rowdy laughter from the pool fading from her awareness. It was a striking moment, a weird moment, filled with the past and the present. Scott must have been as struck by the weirdness as she was because they just stood there staring at each other. He seemed equally at a loss for words.

Riley wasn't sure why, but all the easy chitchat that had carried them through the years didn't seem to be working now. Not with a man who knew more about what was happening in Caroline and Alex's marriage than Riley did. Not with a man who'd stood in her bedroom and let her share her worries.

Not with this man who stared down at her with eyes so dark and serious that she barely recognized him. Definitely didn't recognize how he'd opened up to the family in the years she'd been away. He seemed comfortable around everyone, well liked and respected.

That part at least shouldn't come as a surprise. Scott was good people. She's always known that. No, the surprise was the way he was inserting himself into her life, becoming more than Mike's friend. She liked the man she was getting to know and couldn't help but wonder what he'd think if he could read her thoughts right now.

CHAPTER ELEVEN

SCOTT HATED STAKEOUTS for a variety of reasons. Topping the list was the fact that he didn't like to sit still for extended periods of time, so cramped in the front seat of his cruiser translated into the worst form of physical torture. Added to the physical torture was a mental one—stakeouts meant maintaining an alertness that was impossible to achieve without moving around to keep the blood flowing.

As such, he was forced to drink copious amounts of coffee to avoid slipping into a coma, but then he wanted to relieve himself way more than was convenient for sitting on a side street trying to look inconspicuous.

Then there was his partner.

Mike had understood the finer points of a stakeout. Even Roger, with his barely-two-years-until-retirement mentality, had understood that spending the night jammed in the front seat of a cruiser waiting for something to happen was a delicate balance of tolerance, patience and not doing anything to make an already bad situation worse.

Kevin hadn't figured that out yet. Scott wasn't sure he ever would. Kevin viewed the stakeout as the land of opportunity. Time to talk shop. Time to brainstorm stalled cases. Time to "bond"—whatever the hell that meant. They hadn't been sitting in front of the hardware store they suspected of being used as a drug drop for an hour before Scott was itching to point his service weapon at his new partner with the directive to shut up or be shut up.

Scott had tried to be reasonable. He understood Kevin was young and didn't seem to sit still any better than Scott did. Then there was the fact that Kevin was new to vice and wanted to impress the chief. One way to do that was to fit in, which Scott guessed had led to the whole "bonding" thing.

He tried to make a game out of it: *How many ways could he convey to Kevin that he didn't want to talk without actually saying the words?*

He'd lost count somewhere around midnight. Kevin refused to get the message. By 3:00 a.m., Scott had dispensed with the subtleties and flat-out said, "Will you shut up, man? You're too busy talking and not busy enough doing the surveillance. A damn cow could stroll by ringing a bell and you wouldn't hear it."

Kevin had just laughed and shut up for a grand total of ten minutes. And Scott knew that Mike was up *there* somewhere, laughing his fool head off.

Maybe that was why Scott had Riley and the kids on his mind after finally dropping Kevin off at the precinct a few hours later. Scott decided to cruise by Riley's place to reassure himself all was well at the farm, even though Pleasant Valley wasn't remotely close to his place out on Salt Point. But he had gallons of Starbucks Sumatra blend pumping through him, so he wouldn't be sleeping anytime soon, especially now that the sun was up and most of the world was starting the new day.

Scott wasn't sure what he'd expected to be going on at the crack of dawn, but it definitely wasn't finding the mini-van doors flung wide and Jake loading up the back seat with pillows, blankets and a bucket. Brian's car was nowhere to be seen.

Scott had planned to drive by, but a little kid with pillows and a bucket invited a visit.

Slowing as he cruised into the driveway, Scott lowered the tinted window so Jake could see him.

"Hey, kiddo," he said. "What are you up to?"

Jake hopped out of the minivan, surprise melting into recognition on his face. "Oh, hi, Uncle Scott. I'm making a nest for Camille. She's sick."

"That doesn't sound good."

Jake shook his head solemnly, expression set in a grimace. "She has a headache. They make her puke."

That explained the bucket. "Brian's not around?"

"Mommy said he had a cook-off at college. He's gonna bring us leftovers."

Scott nodded. "Where's your mom—"

"Jake, where are you?" Riley's voice interrupted him from inside the house.

There was no missing the frantic edge to her voice. Jake didn't miss it, either, because he didn't say another word, just dumped the things he held inside the van and spun on his heels.

Scott slipped the car into Park and got out. He heard Jake announcing him when he got to the door and held the porch door wide, "Hey, Riley. I know it's a bad time—"

"No. No, it's not. Come on in."

He found her in the living room, with the shutters closed and the lights off. She knelt beside Camille, who was curled up in a tiny ball on the couch, a pitiful bundle of bright pajamas, colorful quilts and seemingly well-loved stuffed animals. She had a wet washcloth over her eyes and a bucket within easy reach. Her little mouth was drawn and pale even in the darkness.

Riley was smoothing hair away from her daughter's

forehead, and though she was playing the part of "mom" with her gentle touch and frazzled expression, she certainly wasn't dressed the part. The business suit she wore neatly hugged her curves and left the long expanse of her legs bare. She'd pulled her hair back, exposing her features in a way that normally got lost beneath all the hair. High cheekbones. Graceful curve of her jaw. Slender lines of her throat. Lots of smooth skin.

"She okay?" he asked, a distraction.

Riley glanced up. "Migraine."

"Isn't she a little young?"

"Don't I wish." Riley rearranged the stuffed animals on her daughter's pillow. "Try to sleep, sweetie. The medicine will start to work soon, I promise."

Camille barely managed a weak groan, and Scott just stood there, surveying the scene, not a part of it, but from the outside. He watched Riley rearrange the stuffed animals again, recognized the action as busywork for hands that wanted to be doing more.

"Mom, I'm gonna be late." Jake's urgency seemed to be apace of Riley's, and Scott remembered Riley's words about Jake's tough week at school. Walking in at this hour probably wouldn't do much for morale at this stage of the game. Moving Camille didn't look like such a hot idea, either.

"I'll take Jake to school," Scott offered. "If it'll help."

She glanced up at him, and there was so much in her expression, too much to make out. But Scott made his career out of reading people. She was overwhelmed.

And in that moment she was no longer the Riley he'd always known—laughing, genuine, competent, crazy in love with her husband. Right now she was a woman with responsibilities and a lot of people depending on her.

She was a woman he wanted to help.

"Sweet pea, we'll leave in a minute," she told Jake, standing with an agitated burst of energy. "No worries. Will you sit with Camille for a second while I talk with Uncle Scott?"

Jake plopped down beside the sofa with a huff.

Riley led Scott to her bedroom and motioned him inside. He stood on the brink of a room he didn't want to enter, a room that encouraged thoughts of Riley that he couldn't allow himself to think. But Scott's best interests weren't the priority right now, so he braced himself and stepped inside. The door had barely closed behind him before she erupted.

"Oh, Scott, thank you so much. I'd love to take you up on your offer, but I'm not sure it'll help," she said on one pent-up breath. "Jake gets so worked up. Maybe being with you will distract him. But getting him to school isn't the problem. The county head of criminal justice is giving a press conference in an hour. He's addressing the charges of accepting a bribe to push that food contract through his department. Have you heard about it?"

Scott barely nodded before she forged ahead.

"I've got to get into town before eight, and I was already pushing it with a side trip to school. Then Camille woke up with a migraine. She's so sick, and I've called everyone I can think of to watch her. Rosie and Joe are in Atlantic City. Caroline's hosting a pharmaceutical company brunch at the hospital for Alex. The aunties are at work and the kids are in school. Brian's not even around. I don't want to take Camille to work with me, but what else can I do? I can't leave her."

She exhaled an exasperated groan. "I hate this! What kind of mother leaves her little sickie? But I can't leave Max hanging. He won't be able to get anyone to cover the press conference with this short of notice, and I can't be in three places at one time—"

"Riley." Scott stepped forward and clamped both hands over her shoulders to brace her.

His touch seemed to startle her. It startled him. The feel of her beneath his hands, solid, warm and so completely real.

"Riley," he repeated, trying to block out the way his hands molded easily over her shoulders. A perfect fit. "Take a deep breath."

She lifted her gaze to his.

He met the worry in her expression and found his own breath coming with effort. "Let me help. Does Camille need to go to the doctor?"

She shook her head, finally coming around. He forced himself to let her go, to let his hands slip away.

"No. She needs to sleep. She's had migraines before. I'm pretty sure she's through the worst of it."

"Would you like me to stay with her?"

She narrowed her gaze, a look that, at the same time, was hopeful and suspicious. "Don't you have to work?"

"All-night stakeout" was all he said. "I'm too wired to even think about sleep, so I decided to play patrol and make sure all my favorite people were okay."

Her eyes closed, black lashes shuttering those sparkling eyes for the briefest of instants. A look of such relief crossed her face, as if his action was so much more than a simple offer to help out, as if *he* was so much more than he was.

"Would you, Scott? I can't leave her with just anyone, but she trusts you. *I* trust you. And I won't be long. I swear. Just a few questions after the press conference, and I'll come straight home."

But he wasn't anything more than a friend who'd driven by at the right time. "No problem. Do what you need to do. If the little sickie just needs some sleep, that's easy."

"I have my cell. Call me if—"

"We'll be okay. What's the worst-case scenario?" he asked. "I call 9-1-1. I might not know much about little kids, but I do know everyone at emergency dispatch. They'll fix me up."

That had the desired effect. Riley visibly relaxed and gave a smile, a blinding one that made her seem to glow from the inside out. "You're an answer to a prayer."

Scott didn't know what to say to that, so he pulled open the door and stepped aside. He wanted out of this bedroom. He wanted away from any reminder of Riley as a woman, and that big bed only made his thoughts travel in places they had no business traveling. She was a worried mom, and only a depraved jerk would be pumping his ego up at her expense right now.

Thoughts about riding in to save the day were the stuff of eight-year-old fantasies. He was an adult who'd made a promise to a friend. One he intended to keep. Period.

But Scott couldn't deny the wave of pleasure he felt when she hurried past, the smile still on her face and relief fueling her with purpose as her heels tapped sharply over the wood-beamed floors.

"Okay, kiddos." She reentered the living room with a take-charge stride, her control no longer just a facade for her kids' benefits. "We're back in action."

One fluid motion and she was on her knees beside Camille again, peering cautiously under the washcloth. "Sweetie, how's your head? Any better at all?"

Scott couldn't be sure, but he thought he saw Camille's eyes squeeze tighter against the light.

He resisted the urge to do the same, to block out the sight of Riley, all lean curves and bare legs.

"Uncle Scott is going to stay with you for a little while. Just till Mommy gets back, okay?"

Camille managed a weak nod.

"I have my cell, so you call me if you need me, okay? Uncle Scott will get you whatever you need, but your medicine should kick in soon, so you'll probably sleep." Riley pressed her lips to Camille's hand. "I love you. I'll be back as fast as I can." She kissed that pale little hand again, then tucked it beneath the quilt.

"C'mon, Jake. If we hurry, we'll make it." She rose to her feet, glancing around at Scott. "Please, make yourself at home. There's plenty of food if you're hungry. If she wants something to drink there's Gatorade in the pantry. Not cold. She likes the berry kind. The red stuff."

He nodded. "Got it. I'll call if I have any questions."

She gave him another one of *those* smiles.

"You really are a godsend, Scott. Thank you." She disappeared out the door, leaving Scott standing in the foyer, fighting so hard not to be impressed with himself for making her smile that way.

He was still staring at the door when the minivan ground out of the driveway and took off down the road.

And a huge part of him felt relieved that she was gone, relieved for the chance to get a lid on reactions that were so unworthy of Riley and himself. Of the man he'd chosen to be.

Pulling the door shut, Scott sucked in a deep breath to regain his focus, to release the conflict and send unwanted thoughts on their way.

Okay, so here he was…*babysitting*.

He could handle this. Riley would never have left Camille with him if she hadn't been sure he could handle the job.

Of course, Riley had been desperate.

An answer to a prayer.

Mike—wherever he might be—would be getting a lot

of laughs at Scott's expense today. No question. As long as he couldn't read minds.

Scott definitely needed to get a grip. So he locked the front door, armed the security system with the motion detectors disabled and went to check on his patient.

The little sickie was exactly where her mommy had left her, and he sank to his knees, made sure she was still comfortable. Hard to tell. She was so tiny in that massive bundle of quilts and stuffed animals....

"Uncle Scott?" Her voice was as tiny as she was, a throaty croak in the early-morning stillness.

"Hey, kiddo. How're you feeling?"

She pulled a face, barely discernible except for the effort it took.

"Can I get you something? How about some red Gatorade?"

A few pale blond hairs moved over the pillow as she shifted her head. "Lie down."

"You want me to lie down?"

The living room had been arranged with comfort in mind, and two plush couches created an L-shaped grouping against one wall. Camille lay on the couch facing the fireplace. Scott decided he could stretch out on the other couch and still face her.

"How about over there?" He pointed to the other couch.

"In a nest."

Scott frowned. "A nest?"

With a weak hand, she pushed aside the washcloth and tried to open her eyes. "Mommy has blankets in the closet."

Her voice was a throaty croak, and he knew he was making her work too hard to explain what she wanted. What in hell was a nest? Should he call Riley? Blankets in the closet… Then it clicked. Jake had been making a nest in the van. Little kid wrapped like a mummy in blankets.

A nest.

"I'll be back."

It took three tries to find the right closet, but he soon returned with an armful of blankets. Camille had turned her head to the side to watch him, so pitifully still, as if just the effort of observing sapped her strength.

He spread out the largest blanket, tossed a few throw pillows on one side, kicked off his shoes and lay down. Then he pulled the other blankets over him. "How's this?"

She gave a wan smile. Then she let her eyes close again.

Scott lay there and watched her as the light beyond the shutters brightened the room in slow degrees. But Camille seemed to be resting comfortably. Surprisingly, lying down in the warm comfort of his "nest" was also having an effect on him. He didn't think it was a good idea to sleep, in case the patient needed him. He could last a few more hours. But only if he got up and moved around.

He would. In a minute. Right now, he was struck by the silent familiarity of the dim room. It seemed like a lifetime ago that he and Mike had sat in here with the chief, watching the NFL draft or the play-offs while anyone who wasn't on duty dropped by to catch updates on the game.

Riley would keep the kids occupied or be in the kitchen cooking or brewing coffee, always in the background during those visits, always there making sure Mike's guests had what they needed for a good time.

He watched Camille sleep, knew she had no clue about how lucky she was to have a mom who loved her. But Scott knew. He knew from dealing with the kids at Renaissance. He knew firsthand from his own upbringing. And along the way he'd formulated his own ideas about families, about

the way they should be. Mike and Riley had created the sort
of family he admired. They'd wanted their kids to grow up
in the comfort and security of a home that offered unconditional love and support.

Riley was carrying the torch now.

Scott hated seeing her so upset this morning, guilt
tugging at her from all directions. She was an amazing
mom, the best, but she hadn't felt that way. He was so
damned glad he'd dropped by. But he wasn't Riley's
answer to a prayer.

He was someone who had no business being here.

This was Mike's life, and Mike should be living it. Then
Riley wouldn't be torn between a job she needed and her
sick kid. She wouldn't always have that haunted look
behind her expression, as if she hadn't figured out how to
be happy again.

Scott didn't have a death wish by any stretch, but he'd
worked on that case with Mike...and he hadn't had anything more to lose than his life. Literally. He didn't have a
wife and kids who were crazy about him, who waited for
him to come home after a shift, who depended on him.

And that had never felt as empty as it did right now.

Because he wanted someone to care about him?

Throwing his arm over his face, Scott tried to block out
his thoughts. But the trouble wasn't something he could
shut out by closing his eyes.

Had he envied Mike? The loving wife. The cute kids.
The whole crazy package including extended Italian family. Or was it that seeing Mike's life up close and personal
had been working him over subconsciously, making him
rethink choices he'd made long ago? He dated his fair
share of women, but always kept it simple. He didn't get
involved. Scott had reasons for handling life the way he did.

He came from bad blood. While he'd grown far from his roots, he didn't trust himself. Couldn't. Any man who could covet a friend's wife… While Scott would never act on his feelings, the fact that he felt the way he did proved him untrustworthy.

And maybe that was the real trouble. Riley wasn't married anymore. She was just a woman. And one he cared about.

So much more than he should.

CHAPTER TWELVE

RILEY FINALLY GOT Jake to school, and he'd pulled through when she'd needed him to tough out the situation. Not only had he been worried about Camille, but he'd known Riley was upset. She hadn't said a word, but he'd known.

So, her tough little guy had given her an extra big squeezy hug before getting out of the minivan. He hadn't uttered one word of complaint. It was as if the separation anxiety he'd felt last week had never been.

Riley never failed to be amazed by how many emotions she could feel at once. Pride that her son had found his courage. Gut-wrenching worry about her darling girl at home. Appreciation that Scott had blown in to save the day.

And guilt, guilt, *guilt* for leaving.

She had no clue whether or not Camille was finally asleep or if her head was still throbbing hard enough to make her tummy sick. Riley hadn't hung around long enough to know whether her daughter had managed to keep the medicine down. If not, Scott was likely now holding the bucket, treated to a gritty reality of parenthood no serial single man should have to face.

Serial single.

The phrase popped into her head from nowhere, maybe some unmemorable article or bit of research. But it described Scott. She recalled her conversation with Caroline, but couldn't reconcile the Scott she knew with a man who had trouble committing—not given the relationships he had in his life. He was a solid, loyal man who was in for the long haul. That much he'd proven over and over again. His dedication to the PPD. To the kids at Renaissance. In his friendship with Mike and his continuing and evolving friendship with her.

Then again, Riley reminded herself, Scott had always been a closed book. She couldn't assume anything about him or about life. She'd learned that firsthand. She'd never imagined choosing a press conference over her sick child, yet here she was. The past two years had been nothing if not an exercise in recognizing that life wasn't obliged to follow her plans.

But despite the unexpected start to the morning, she managed to make the press conference. Of course, she had to bypass municipal parking for a place on a side street, but she scooted through the door seconds before the executive director took his place in front of the podium.

Then she put everything from her head and worked.

The executive director—former director, now that the man had surprised everyone by resigning his appointment—fielded too many questions about the charges of contractual corruption. But Riley lucked out and was called upon several times. And she got answers that would enable her to pull together an article that should make Max happy.

She slipped out a side door as the press conference wound down, hoping to avoid both the departing rush and a parking ticket on her windshield. What she found was a puddle of glass on the ground behind her minivan.

For an instant she stood there, unable to do anything but stare at the wreckage of her back window in disbelief. Who would break into a white minivan that looked like a giant refrigerator on wheels?

There was nothing of any value inside that would attract a thief…. Except her work bag, which contained everything she hadn't taken inside the conference center. And since all she'd needed was her handheld recorder that left her laptop and camera. If the alarm had sounded, it had long since stopped. Obviously no one had bothered to call the police.

She stared at the broken back window, wondering if she should scream now or save the meltdown until later.

Every shred of her wanted to hop inside the van and head home, but after checking inside to find—no surprise here—her work bag missing, she had to call the police and report the incident. Not that she thought they stood any hope of retrieving her equipment, but she would need the incident report for the insurance company.

Reaching for her cell, she snapped it open and scrolled through her contacts.

"Poughkeepsie Police Department nonemergency line," the perfunctory voice answered on the first ring.

Riley explained the situation, still trying to understand this turn of events. All her work…research for the articles she was working on. Had she backed up everything to her briefcase on the *Herald*'s server last night? She couldn't remember. If not, how much would she lose? And what about the photos she'd taken of the kids' first day at school? Were they still on the memory stick?

How could she have been so careless?

The answer to that question wasn't hard to figure—she was doing too much and not giving her best to anything. Riley was trying to decide how best to fix that problem when a unit arrived to take her report. Janet DiBenedetto.

"I couldn't believe it when I heard your name." Janet gave Riley a quick hug. "You okay?"

"Fine. Just not my week, I guess." Not her two years by the looks of it. "I left my daughter at home sick."

Janet smiled, a mom herself. "Don't worry. We'll make this quick."

And she did. Riley was on the road within ten minutes, a copy of the report on the passenger seat beside her and Janet's promise to question some people in the area to see if anyone had seen anything.

Riley didn't have much hope, and as the sounds of traffic echoed with the rush of wind through the smashed back window, she reminded herself that the situation could have been a lot worse. She and the kids could have been in the car. She had everything in the world to be thankful for.

Two beautiful, healthy kids. A home. A job. A wonderful family. Scott, who hadn't jumped ship but had been making an effort to segue into her life as a single parent. A caring person like Janet, who went out of her way to help out.

Riley had no business feeling as if the whole world was against her because of a broken window and stolen electronic equipment. If she hadn't taken the time to back up her work, she had nobody to blame but herself. She knew better. And she still had her handheld recorder. She could write today's article if she pulled research from other news services.

She'd managed to talk herself into a better frame of mind by the time she pulled into the driveway to find Scott waiting for her, the cell phone cradled against his shoulder, looking sleep ruffled with his dark hair listing to one side.

He snapped the phone shut as she parked the van. Then he was there, opening the door. "You okay?"

"Janet called."

He only nodded, glancing at the broken window, the worry in his gaze at odds with the pillow creases on his cheek.

"You got some sleep," she said softly.

Running long fingers through his hair, he made the whole glossy mess stand up even more. "Camille had me make a nest. Mistake. The minute I sat, I was down for the count. But she's okay. Still sleeping."

Riley could see her sweet little girl, even in the throes of a debilitating headache, turning the moment into a game.

A nest.

Riley wasn't sure what it was about Camille wanting Scott to have a nest that unglued her, but suddenly, tears prickled at her lids. The distress she'd been staving off in degrees all day formed like a wave from so deep inside. But she wasn't going to cry, refused to give in to the urge. She might be overwhelmed and having the run of luck from hell, but she was blessed. *Blessed.*

She inhaled raggedly, waved her hands as if she could physically fight off the tears.

Who cared about a stupid back window, anyway?

But her struggle must have been evident because for one stricken instant, Scott, a man with no clue what to do for a woman on the verge of melting down, stared at her. A small part of her mind, a rational part that managed to stand back from the encroaching tidal wave, chided her for being so weak. She had no right to burden him with her weakness.

But as quickly as Riley recognized that, as fast as she decided she would absolutely not burden this poor man any more today, he had her wrapped in his arms, cradling her against his warm, hard chest.

"It's okay, Riley," he crooned in a low voice.

He stroked her hair, and she felt the uncertainty of his touch. A friend. He wanted to comfort her, and the feel of his strong embrace was exactly what she needed to fight back. She melted against him, powerless to resist his solid strength, though she had no right to depend on him.

But in his arms, Riley wasn't thinking about right and wrong. She was thinking about him.

Slowly the emotion subsided, the anxiety quieted, smothered by her conflict over burdening Scott. But if he felt burdened, he certainly didn't show it. He held her close, creating a warm shelter with his embrace as one hand lightly stroked her back, as if he wasn't entirely convinced that touching her was the right thing to do.

But standing in his arms felt right. More right than she could have imagined. She was so aware of the unfamiliar feel of his hard body against hers. And she was so aware. Of how tall he was, taller than even Mike had been. Her heels brought her just high enough for him to rest his cheek easily on the top of her head. Her face rested on his shoulder, and she could feel the warmth of him radiating against her skin, feel the steady rise and fall of his chest.

Riley should step out of his arms, offer him a smiling thanks to transition through this intimate moment. She should cut the guy some slack so they could segue back to normal again.

But she didn't move, didn't speak, didn't want to do anything to ruin this moment, a moment where she felt as if she wasn't all alone for the first time in such a long time.

Reality finally intruded. The sound of a passing car. A horse neighing in the distance. Worry about Camille. And Jake. How was he surviving the day? Guilt because she was being so weak and selfish, because Scott had been working all night, and she'd sucked him into her chaos. The guy had only meant to cruise past the house to check on them.

"Thank you," she finally said. "You've been really sweet."

He chuckled, a throaty sound that rumbled deep in his chest. "I'm not so sweet. Nests are...comfortable."

That was even sweeter. "I'm beginning to think I should never have come back."

She tried to smile, but he must have known it was an act. Hooking a finger beneath her chin, he tipped her face up until she met his gaze. Those dark eyes were so still, so serious, a caress. "No," he crooned, still comforting her. "Everything will be all right. Trust me."

She did trust him. Too much. He'd been Mike's friend. While he was bridging the distance he'd always kept between them, he was still just a friend. She needed to keep that straight in her head.

She managed a small smile this time, one she hoped would reassure him. But Riley didn't trust herself to reply. Not when she wanted to tell him how much she appreciated his friendship, how much she liked the caring and strong man she was getting to know. Not when one simple admission would cross the boundaries of friendship and change things between them.

CHAPTER THIRTEEN

"DIDN'T YOU BLOW OUT of here about seven this morning?" Chief Levering asked. "What are you doing back?"

Scott lifted his head from the files scattered over the desk in front of him. Sleep hadn't been possible after leaving Riley's, so he'd headed to the precinct to burn off his surplus energy. "Looking over some recent B and E's and auto thefts."

The chief's eyebrows rose halfway up his forehead. "You don't have enough on your desk keeping you busy already?"

"You're kidding, right? That's why I'm here on my day off."

Scott braced himself for the reprimand he knew would come. An ongoing argument about too much time at the station and not enough living a life outside of work. An ongoing, *old* argument.

The chief surprised him. Glancing down at the files, he frowned and said, "You're worried about Riley?"

"Something's not right."

"Any ideas?"

Scott shoved the files away from him, disgusted. "Nothing but this knot in my gut."

Pulling the door to Scott's office shut, the chief dragged a chair around the side of the desk, then lowered himself so slowly Scott expected to hear creaking joints.

"You need something?" Scott asked.

"I'm a longtime fan of your gut, so why don't you pass a few of those folders this way?"

The chief was full of surprises today. "Don't you have somewhere to be? Busy police chief and all that."

"Got all kinds of time to burn today. Go figure. Now pass me some of those reports."

Scott shoved over a stack with the warning: "I have no clue what I'm looking for."

"Me, either. I'll fit right in."

Scott opened the next folder and scanned the details of the report. The chief did the same. They worked in silence for about five minutes.

"I wasn't okay with the break-in," Scott said suddenly, interrupting the quiet.

"No?" The chief didn't bother looking up. He didn't sound surprised, either.

"The window of opportunity was too narrow. It's not like Riley's routine is written in stone. The kids haven't settled into school yet. Brian, either. That means the perp had to be watching her closely."

"Not if he saw school-aged kids at the house. Doesn't take much of a leap since district elementary schools all start at the same time."

"He would have had to know they didn't take a bus."

"True." The chief inserted a report back in its sleeve, then reached for another. "Did you consider that it might have been random? The perp lucked out and came across the house when it was empty, took a chance, then got spooked. It's a nice place. It would be attractive to someone looking for fast cash."

"No way," Scott scoffed. "The perp went through all that trouble to break a window where he wouldn't be easily seen. He could have gotten in but took off before we got there." Scott shook his head decidedly. "He knew we were on the way."

"Okay. I buy that. Most kids looking for drug cash aren't so prepared."

Scott snorted. He didn't have to point out that most kids looking for drug cash usually kicked in the front door and stuffed whatever they got their hands on in grocery bags.

"Okay, so you got a perp who avoided our silent alarm," the chief said. "Did I mention I'm glad you talked me into keeping the place hardwired to the precinct?"

"You're welcome." Scott skimmed through another report, looking for any similarity to the attempted break-in at Riley's. "So, the question is—what was the perp looking for?"

"What'd he get from the car again?"

"Laptop and camera."

"Purse?"

Scott shook his head.

"He didn't need her identification, so he obviously knew who he was going after. Didn't take any money or credit cards?"

"No. Janet said it looked like he went in the back and didn't bother with anything else. Probably was long gone before her car alarm stopped blaring." Scott leaned back in the chair and met the chief's gaze. "That's what's bugging me. Riley said she normally keeps her laptop bag up front with her. She pushes it under the passenger seat, and there's usually so much of the kids' stuff around that she hides whatever's left sticking out. But she parked on the street this morning because she was running late. That's the only reason she moved her equipment into the back. It's the only place in the van where it's really hidden."

"And the only way the perp would have known that is if he watched her put it there."

"You got it." That knot in Scott's stomach clenched like a fist.

The chief frowned. "You don't expect to find anything in these reports."

"No. But I didn't want to overlook anything before I start interrogating Riley. She's pretty shaken up already."

"The break-ins?"

He shrugged, feigning a casualness he didn't feel, but he wasn't going into details with the chief. Not when they would force him to think about this morning, when he'd been trying all day to stop thinking about it. What had gotten into him? He'd crossed all the lines by touching her. She might think he wanted to console her, but he was a selfish bastard who'd wanted to touch her and hadn't been able to resist. Now that Mike wasn't around, Scott was chafing at the boundaries he'd set.

"Not entirely," he admitted. "But you know Riley. Truth is she's got her hands full with the kids and work. It was tough enough coming back to town without all this added aggravation."

The chief let the folder he held fall to the desk and sank back in the chair. It was one of those moments where he looked the part of aging police chief who'd been worn down by his years on the force and the constant demands.

"Let's come up with something." He massaged his temples. "Unless you've got some ideas you haven't shared with me yet."

Suddenly Scott knew exactly why the chief had sat down in the first place. He knew better than anyone how Scott worked and had wanted to give him someone he felt comfortable to bounce ideas with. So much for thinking he'd been keeping anything from the chief about his work with Kevin.

"You weren't just burning time." Not a question.

"Blew off the mayor for you." The chief glanced at his watch. "Figure he gave up on me about five minutes ago."

"I didn't need any help."

"Didn't say you did." The chief cracked a smile. "That's the best part of working with you. I never actually have to do any work."

"I have a partner. If I wanted him here, I'd have called him."

"I don't think so. Not when it has to do with Riley."

The hairs on the back of Scott's neck stood on end. "What in hell does that mean?"

The chief shrugged, making light of an assessment that felt too much like an accusation. "It means I've noticed how you've made it your new quest in life to watch over her and the kids."

"How is that any different from what the rest of us are doing? Half the department showed up on her doorstep when that alarm went off."

The chief chuckled. "Heard all about it."

"Then what's your point? I promised Mike if anything ever went south, I'd look after his family. And if things had gone the other way two years ago, he'd be your second-in-command at Renaissance right now."

Again, Scott couldn't help but be struck by how empty that sounded. The only people who would shed a tear if he suddenly wound up under a headstone were his coworkers in the department and the volunteers with Renaissance. Maybe the kids there, too. The members of Poughkeepsie's gangs would probably throw a block party. It was something, he guessed, but nothing like what he'd watched the Angelica family go through.

Or Riley.

The memory of the way she felt in his arms tore through him. And the chief just sat there, fingers steepled in front of him, gaze never wavering as if he was seeing so much more than he'd been meant to see.

"You done yet?" he asked casually.

Scott scowled.

"I understand, Scott. Believe me. I like to think that if I go down, you all will keep your eyes on Deb. But I also know how tough this is on you. Unlike your new partner, though, I also know you're a one-man circus. You're not alone with this. I'd have thought you'd gotten that with the party on Riley's front lawn the other day."

"A one-man circus?" God, could this get any worse? Not only did he have to deal with the fallout from his stupidity with Riley earlier, but now the chief was starting up this crap again.

"Liked that, did you?" A smile played on the chief's mouth. He was impressed with himself, no question.

Scott wasn't going to contradict a man who'd just blown off the mayor. "Okay, I'm not alone. Appreciate that. So, got any thoughts about who—"

"No, no thoughts. Told you, that's why I like working with you. The mayor would have had me jumping through hoops right now. You…" He shoved the chair back and stretched his legs out before him. "Well, it's damn peaceful in here."

"Thanks…I think."

"You're welcome. So what do you have in mind?"

"Work. What else is there?"

The chief frowned. "She's only been back, what…three weeks at best?"

Scott nodded.

"Hardly seems like enough time to start pissing people off with her articles."

"I agree. But after what happened last week in Hazard Creek..." Scott let his words trail off. The memory of her sitting in that ambulance made his stomach clench with almost brutal force. "She jumped right back in the thick of it. She covered Lundquist's press conference."

"I thought you said you hadn't interrogated her yet?"

"I haven't. I was at the house when she left this morning."

"Really?"

"Babysitting."

That got a reaction. "You *babysit?* What was she thinking?"

"She wasn't," Scott admitted, not in the least offended. "Camille got sick. I happened by at the right time."

An answer to a prayer.

"Kid still alive?"

"One-man circus yourself."

The chief chuckled wryly. Then they fell silent again, scanning through the rest of the reports, looking for something that wasn't there.

"I'll have to talk with her," Scott finally said.

"Yup." The chief agreed. "Keep me in the loop. That's an order. I don't want you alone on this, and I know what a pain in the ass you can be."

"You're hurting my feelings."

"If I thought you had any feelings, I'd apologize."

"Damned barrel of laughs."

The chief got to his feet. He gazed down and asked, "Do you know why I made you Mike's partner?"

"You always said it was because we were the same shade of green."

"Yeah, well, you both were that." He gave a gruff laugh.

"I put you two together because I knew you'd be good detectives. Damned good. There was only one difference between you."

"What was that?"

"Mike believed it. You didn't. You're never convinced you're doing enough."

There was so much truth in that statement Scott didn't know what to say. "And the reason for this trip down memory lane?"

The chief nodded. "Mike considered you a damned good friend. I know because he told me. And you've always done right by him. When he was alive. While you were investigating his death. You're still being a good friend."

"Yeah, and…"

"I thought you needed a reminder."

"I have no idea what you're talking about." But he did. A weight was settling on his chest, making it hard to breathe, almost impossible.

"Then you need to make some time to think about it." The chief gave a huff as if he didn't think Scott capable. "Mike made you a part of the family the minute he decided you were good people, Scott, someone he wanted around. You're the one who doesn't play well with others. I understand why, but it's time to learn. Stop tearing yourself up. You care about Riley and the kids, and that's okay." He pulled open the door, but paused, glancing over his shoulder with a narrowed gaze. "Remember what I said. And good luck."

The closing door echoed with a finality that jarred Scott's already fried nerves. His few hours' sleep after the night from hell was wearing off in a big way, evidenced by his inability to accept what the chief had said.

"You care about Riley and the kids, and that's okay."

Scott stared at the stacks of folders on his desk. He'd

known he wouldn't find anything about who might be stalking Riley. But he'd spent the afternoon going through them anyway, to be thorough, to investigate all the possibilities because he wouldn't take chances with Riley's or the kids' safety.

"You care about Riley and the kids, and that's okay."

He did care. He didn't want to dump this on her when she was so clearly struggling to get back on her feet. But he couldn't figure out what she might have stepped into without her help.

So why was he still sitting here? Why was there a vise crushing his chest, cutting off his air until he could barely think? Why did he hesitate to pick up the phone and call her when he knew the next step was to delve into her work, into what had been on her stolen equipment?

Then Scott knew. With a sickening certainty, he knew.

And there was no more running from the truth. No more hiding. So he sat there, hands stretched before him on the desk, lifeless, as if they belonged to someone else. Someone who hadn't been so disconnected from his feelings that he'd managed to deny the obvious. He'd been telling himself he had his feelings under control. He'd made the choice to act honorably, the only choice he could make and still look in the mirror.

The very silence in the office mocked him. How long? A day? Three weeks? Or had he been denying the truth even longer, burying feelings he didn't know what to do with for *years?*

How long had he been in love with Riley?

The truth. Undeniable. He'd have known by the sheer absence of anything like this in his life before. He'd simply never felt this way.

But it was there, had always been there. He'd noticed

her from the day Mike had introduced them. He'd lived with that truth, dodged it at every turn. Only a scumbag would have feelings for his friend's wife, and Scott had chosen not to live life as a scumbag. Simple. So he'd never allowed himself to get too close, had sidestepped her invitations time and time again. But he couldn't let go even after she went to Florida. He'd stayed connected through phone calls, had let himself get sucked into Sundays at Joe and Rosie's.

Helping Brian with the horses. Bringing a crew to maintain the lawn. Fixing the truck. All stupid little things that had meant so much to him. He told himself he was being a good friend to Mike, watching over his family, but he was a liar.

That didn't surprise him.

What kind of friend fell in love with another man's wife? The mother of his partner's kids?

Scott knew that answer, too—the diseased kind, the kind who'd inherited poison instead of blood running through his veins. The kind of man *he* was, the reason he hadn't allowed himself to get in deep with anyone, not once in all these years.

"You care about Riley and the kids, and that's okay."

No, it wasn't.

CHAPTER FOURTEEN

JASON STEPPED OUT OF his unmarked cruiser when the familiar motorcycle roared into view, pulling into the parking lot. Jason had chosen this long-abandoned tire plant as the meet point for a reason. The place was so remote this meeting with Tyrese should go unnoticed, and there were several access roads. They could go their separate ways, eliminating any connection between them should anyone take notice. Not that there was anyone around. This parcel of industrial acreage tucked away on the outskirts of town had been on the market so long, Jason wasn't even sure the owner—or the Realtor for that matter—was still alive.

Tyrese maneuvered the bike up close to the cruiser, cut the engine and removed his helmet. His expression was solemn. "You just used up your Get out of Jail Free card, Jason."

Through all the years of their acquaintance, Tyrese had called Jason a lot of things, starting with Buster and winding up with Brother in Christ. But Jason could never remember Tyrese ever using his first name. Not once.

"I don't know what kind of trouble you're in." Tyrese began unraveling the bungee cords that held a bulging laptop bag to the back rail of his bike. "But I'm praying for you, and I'm going to keep praying. I want you to know that."

Jason inclined his head but didn't say anything. He honestly didn't know what to say.

"I want to help you." Tyrese set the laptop bag at Jason's feet. "But I'm not doing any more of your dirty work. My account is closed. Paid in full." He fixed his dark eyes on Jason, eyes so dark they seemed almost black, eyes that suddenly saw through him to the quick. "You know what was with all that stuff you had me steal?" Emphasis on the *steal*. "Kids' stuff. Fishing poles. Roller-blades. And dolls, man. Little girl dolls. I had to dig through it all to get to that bag because your mark hid it under that stuff to protect it from thieves."

Thieves.

There was irony here. A mouthy hood with a rap sheet as long as his arm lecturing a police chief on ethics. There was definitely irony here. The kind that made him itch to defend himself, to explain to Tyrese exactly what was going down, so he'd understand why Jason had become a thief, had turned Tyrese into one again.

But there wasn't any defense. How could he defend turning Riley Angelica into a *mark?*

So Jason stood there in his neatly pressed suit that Callie had picked up from the cleaners just last night, a suit that had probably cost more than Tyrese grossed for six months of work at the church.

Tyrese, on the other hand, wore one of those casual shirts old men liked to wear. Neat-looking and light-weight, comfortable in the summer heat. The short sleeves didn't cover the elaborate tattoo adorning his left arm to the wrist, a jumble of thick black mathematical symbols that was a souvenir of his days as a member of 16 Squared. He'd have had to wear gloves to cover the prime numbers etched on the backs of his fingers in black ink, more souvenirs that marked him for exactly what he'd once been.

If Riley Angelica or any other soccer mom had spotted Tyrese in a grocery store parking lot, she'd have steered her cart in the opposite direction.

Jason knew better than anyone there was a lot more to Tyrese nowadays. He was getting through community college one class at a time. Yet, he'd used Tyrese's past against him because he had specialized skills. Skills that Jason needed because now he was the thief.

"We're square, Tyrese. You have my word." As if that counted for much anymore. "You head back to your life and forget that any of this ever happened."

Tyrese inclined his head. "I hope what you need is in that bag because I'm for real. I found the CD under a seat. It's in the bag, too."

"Thank you. Ditch the phone. We're square." On a debt that hadn't needed to be repaid. Jason had never once in all these years thought of what he'd done for Tyrese as a debt. Until now.

"Listen, brother. I'm going to tell you something someone told me back when I needed to hear it." Leveling that inky black gaze at Jason, he said simply, "'Own up, take the heat, then get on with your life.'"

At first Jason could see nothing but images of what he'd look like on the news when production ran clips of *that* video, of him having the time of his life with four hookers.

"Today, the Hazard Creek police chief was indicted on charges of criminal obstruction...."

Jason just stood there until Tyrese's voice broke in, all too real and surprisingly self-assured, a man with a message.

"It was good advice when you gave it to me all those years ago," he was saying. "It's still good advice."

Shoving the helmet onto his head, he kick-started the bike. "Good luck, man. I'll be praying for you."

Then he wheeled around and drove off, leaving Jason staring at his receding figure, the dust kicking up in his wake as the powerful engine growled through the buzzing, late-afternoon quiet. Jason stood there in his crisp suit, wondering what had happened to the man who'd cared enough about a mouthy street punk to give him a chance when no one else would.

RILEY KNEW SOMETHING WAS WRONG the instant she opened the door to find Scott on her doorstep, looking much the same as he had when he'd left earlier. Same rumpled shirt. Same faded jeans. Same hiking boots. His hair looked as if he'd shoved his fingers through it a few dozen more times.

"What's wrong?" she asked without preamble.

"Nothing. I need to talk with you about today."

Their gazes met.

Today?

Did he mean her stolen equipment and the time she'd spent in his arms?

"Come on in." She stepped aside and held the door wide.

He passed with a long-legged stride, gaze averted, tension all over him. While she might not know what part of today he wanted to discuss, their earlier exchange was between them in a big way. She was aware of him in every cell, the feel of his arms around her so much more than a memory.

"Any luck with getting the glass replaced?" he asked. "Your van isn't out front."

"I parked it in the garage. Gene from Abb's Auto Glass came this afternoon to install it. Popped it right in. Took a grand total of ten minutes."

"I'm glad it wasn't a hassle."

She forced herself to stand her ground, to meet his eyes, to get a grip, willing a sense of normalcy she didn't feel. "Not at all. But at this rate, I'm going to be on a first-name basis with every glass guy in town."

"I hope not."

"You're not the only one."

"How's Camille feeling?"

Scott moved through the front porch, and Riley pulled the door shut and locked it. "Much better, thanks. After a good night's sleep, she'll be good to go."

"I had no idea kids even got migraines."

She exhaled hard, trying to get hold of her breathing. Honestly. "Me, either. Not until she started getting them, anyway. It's a family thing from Joe's side. He got them when he was a kid. Caroline still gets them."

Scott stepped aside to allow her to enter the house before him. "Nothing they can do?"

"Medication once one starts. That's about it unless I'm willing to keep her medicated. I'm not. She doesn't get them all that often. And there are triggers—whenever she gets overexcited or eats too much sugar. Or spends too much time in the pool. The chlorine, I think. We can usually control that."

Scott didn't get a chance to reply before Camille's shriek echoed across the living room. "Mo-om. Jakie won't give me the dental rinse."

Riley seized the moment to catch her breath and regain her composure. "Everyone's ready for bed around here. Beyond ready. If you have a few minutes—"

"Go do what you need to do. No rush."

She motioned him toward the kitchen. "I won't be long. Brian's here. Why don't you—"

"Yo, man," Brian said around a mouthful of pizza when he appeared in the hall holding a massive slice. "Aunt Riley cooked. It's awesome."

"Scott, if you're hungry, help yourself. There's plenty." She did a double take at the pizza stone, where her ravenous young nephew had been eating his fill. "Brian, grab a plate for him, please."

Then she beat a hasty retreat, allowing the routine of tucking in the kids to calm her runaway nerves. Camille was down for the count the minute her head hit the pillow. Jake, on the other hand, was still wound tight from his first day of school without his sister. He got chatty, and Riley didn't have the heart to rush him, so she let him talk himself out while she talked herself down from her own racing thoughts about Scott.

Friends supported each other. Scott was a friend, and she'd needed support this morning. No reason to obsess over the exchange or read more into one hug than was there.

Except that she'd been aware of him as more than a friend. She'd been aware of him as a man.

Enough!

She finally kissed Jake and arrived back in the kitchen to find Scott washing the dinner dishes and Brian drying.

"Thank you so much," she forced herself to say lightly. "But you could have put them in the dishwasher."

"I told Scott." Brian scowled. "He wouldn't listen."

Scott didn't say a word, but Riley didn't miss the smile playing around his mouth. She knew exactly what he was doing and liked the influence he had on Brian. He knew teenagers, which shouldn't be a surprise with all his work at Renaissance.

"Well, less work for me, and I appreciate the help. I haven't gotten the kids trained to load the dishwasher yet.

Well, they're trained," she corrected. "Let's just say I don't trust them completely. Anyone want coffee?"

Another diversionary tactic.

Brian tossed the dish towel onto the counter. "No thanks. I'm out of here. Got an assignment due in the morning."

"Get going then, sweetheart," she said. "Jake already put in his request for French toast in the morning if you find yourself hungry again before class."

Brian bent down and kissed the top of Riley's head as he passed. "Glad you're home, Aunt Riley. Take it easy, dude."

Then he disappeared down the hallway.

Leaving Riley and Scott alone.

She wasn't sure why the sound of the front door seemed to echo as if in a cavern or why her insanely large kitchen suddenly seemed to be shrinking, but that's exactly how it felt.

Maybe the dark night from beyond all the windows was closing in. The kitchen had actually sold her on the house when Mike had brought her to see the place. It was the hub, wide open to a dining room that had a dozen windows looking out over the duck pond and the stables. A gorgeous view no matter what the time of day or the season.

Except on moonless nights. Like right now when the darkness pressed in until the big room felt like a closet with Scott only mere feet away.

"Scott, would you like coffee?"

"Only if you were going to make some for yourself. Otherwise, I'm good."

Very diplomatic, but not a no. "Let me ask you a question. Am I going to need coffee for whatever you want to discuss? I have to admit that it's been a pretty long day."

"Make the coffee."

She nodded and headed toward the pot. He went to stand in front of the windows, restless for a man who hadn't slept in a while. She could feel every inch of the silence stretch between them, not sure why. But, coward that she was, she was in no hurry to end it. Scott appeared to be so deeply in thought, his back to her as he stared out into the night. Things were changing between them, and she wasn't sure how she felt about that. Let alone what *he* might think.

His shoulders were so broad he appeared showcased by the window frame. His glossy black hair, longer than she was used to seeing it, curled around his neck. His hair was really wavy, and she wondered why she'd never noticed before.

"Did you get your article written?" he asked without turning around.

"Yes, believe it or not. E-mailed it off not long after I picked up Jake from school."

"How'd that go? Did you take Camille with you?"

She was surprised he'd thought of that. Then again, the man was a detective. Details were his business. "Thankfully Brian came home. He kept an eye on her. Don't know what I'd have done without all the men in my life today." She gave a light laugh. "Even Jake was a trouper this morning. He headed off to class without a peep. I was so proud of him."

"So he's settling in?"

Scott was making conversation, and she sensed that he was as unnerved by the quiet as she was.

"I think that will take some time for all of us. We'll be okay."

Scott inclined his head but didn't reply. He looked thoughtful standing there.

She brought two mugs to the table and sat down. He finally turned to face her, glanced absently at the table before pulling out a chair and sitting across from her.

"Thanks," he said.

"So, are you going to keep me in suspense any longer?"

"I need to know what was on your laptop and your camera."

An interrogation. Okay, she could handle this. "I use my laptop mainly for work because the kids play games on the desktop. The camera had both personal and work-related photos."

"By any chance did you have backups? I need to know as much as I can about the events you're covering."

"You don't think today was a random theft, do you?"

He leveled his gaze at her, and there was so much in his expression, so much she'd never noticed before. She just had to look past the vice cop persona, past the familiar seriousness, to see a man who was paying attention to the details, to her details. She saw a man who cared.

"I'm sorry, Riley," he said quietly. "The last thing I want to do is alarm you, but things aren't adding up. You wound up being treated by paramedics in Hazard Creek. Then you had a break-in. Now a car theft. We need to pinpoint what's going on."

She sank back in the chair. She'd nearly melted down over a migraine this morning. Where was she going to find the energy to deal with the frightening reality that someone wanted something from her, enough to break into the house and the car?

"Mommy died. Mommy died like Daddy…"

Riley inhaled deeply to dispel the voices in her head. She wasn't alone. The entire Poughkeepsie Police Department had her back, as Mike used to say.

But knowing that didn't feel so important right now. It was the man sitting across from her. The man who'd cared enough to drive by the house to make sure she and the twins were okay. The man who'd easily stepped in to babysit her sick daughter. The man who'd wrapped her in his strong embrace to make her feel better.

"Okay." She pushed away from the table and stood. "Come into the office so we can figure this out."

CHAPTER FIFTEEN

SCOTT WATCHED AS Riley sat on a blue exercise ball in front of her office computer.

"Why don't you take the chair," he suggested. "I'll grab one from the kitchen."

"I'm good, thanks. Strengthens the core muscles." She sat even straighter, sucking in her stomach a little for effect.

He shook his head. "And limits the amount of time you spend in front of the computer, I'll bet."

That got a small smile. "Saves me from dragging my children away from their games. They usually get up on their own after a reasonable amount of time."

"Smart."

"Desperate." She rocked forward on the ball and gave a little sigh. "I'm outnumbered around here."

If Scott hadn't appreciated what that meant, he'd seen the results firsthand earlier. "You've got it under control."

She shot him a surprised look. "Yeah, when tired vice cops ride in to save the day."

He hadn't thought of what he'd done in that way, but suddenly the morning was square between them. He braced his hands on the back of the chair while the computer blipped and beeped through the start-up menu.

He couldn't miss the flush of pink suddenly staining her

cheeks beneath the fading tan. "There's nothing easy about this situation."

For her or for him. But at least her situation wasn't self-inflicted torture.

Mike would never have asked Scott to watch over his family if he'd known how his best friend had felt about his wife. But he hadn't known. Scott thought he'd had a grip on his emotions, but he hadn't.

He'd been lying to himself all these years about how much he cared. And that said a lot about his capacity for self-denial. An ability he wasn't going to complain about. Not when he'd go right back to ignoring the way he felt about her. His feelings didn't matter. What mattered was Riley's safety. And the kids'.

Even if he couldn't get back to the blissful ignorance he'd been living in for all these years, he still had the single most important tool in his arsenal.

Free will.

The ability to make the right choice was his and his alone. No one could take that away. No person. No life circumstance. He'd learned that lesson the hard way. That's why he worked so hard to convince the kids at Renaissance that they had everything they needed to break away from the lives they'd been living. Free will might not seem like much, but it was everything. And for the kids he worked with, it was a start down the path to a new life.

Just as it had once been for him.

That's why he was here with Riley tonight, making the right choice and doing right by his friend. He was going to scan her backup files and assess what story had made her a target.

Scott sat down.

He wasn't going to notice how close they were, so close

JEANIE LONDON   151

his knee almost brushed hers. He wasn't going to remember the way she'd felt in his arms or the way her slender body had lined up against his in all the right places. Instead, he fixed his gaze on the monitor and watched windows flash open as Riley maneuvered the system.

"So, what have you got?" he asked, sounding impressively controlled.

"I've got so much stuff here," she said. "I really need to sort through my files instead of uploading everything and forgetting about it."

Scott scanned the thumbnails. "This is all stuff you've been working on since you got back?"

She nodded. "It's a mess, I know, but that's only because I don't work on the server. I have to attach everything to e-mail and send it to the paper, so things aren't organized the way they are on my hard drive."

He snorted. "I meant because there's so much. You've barely been home a month."

"Oh. Well, yeah. Every article requires a fair amount of research and fact-checking. It's time-consuming." She waved a hand at the monitor. "That's what most of this is. I open files and dump research inside from the various wire services. Then I use it to pull an article together when I sit down to write."

He'd read her articles before, knew she was good. "I understand. Do you have any completed articles here?"

She nodded.

"That's what I want to see first."

"You got it." She moved a few thumbnails around then brought up the word processing program and tilted the monitor his way. "How's that?"

"Perfect." He scanned the story about a prominent money laundering case where two local businessmen had been using offshore trusts to launder millions of dollars for U.S. citizens to help them avoid paying taxes.

Scott nodded, and Riley moved him on to another story. He found himself skimming the leads on stories he'd either read about or heard on the news. He forced his attention to the display, refused to notice the cool scent of Riley's hair or the way the lamplight played over the curls, making them look as if they'd be soft to the touch.

There were only two stories she considered hard news. The resignation of the chief executive that she'd started covering today, and what she called a "takeout" on a pharmaceutical company that had been offering free training and some other over-the-top benefits to doctors who prescribed its drug.

"What's a takeout?" he asked.

"Basically it's a running story. I write about the developments as they come up and put the news into context."

"Got it. That seems the more likely of the two. What are the chances you've inadvertently uncovered something that might implicate someone who doesn't want to be implicated?"

She leaned forward on the ball, and he refused to react when their fingers brushed as they both reached for the mouse at the same time. He would simply ignore the warmth radiating through his fingertips, ignore the blush of color in her cheeks, which suggested she'd noticed their touch, too.

He waited while she opened file after file and skimmed through the text with a frown. "If I'd uncovered anything that was news, I'd be writing about it, trust me. I'm trying to earn my keep at the paper. But I don't see anything here."

"I need to review those files and do some digging of my own."

"There's a lot of information here, Scott. Can I organize it for you? I'm serious. I cut and paste. I don't even reformat. Takes too much time for something I typically use only once."

Scott took the opportunity to take a breather. Shoving the chair back, he stood. "I've got a flash drive in my jacket. You can copy those files onto it. Want more coffee while I'm up?"

She nodded absently, attention still on the information she'd culled for that article. Scott took both their cups and headed out of the office, appreciating the quiet stillness of the house, the way the temperature had dropped enough so the cool air cleansed Riley's delicate scent that still lingered in his senses.

Grabbing his jacket from the coat rack in the foyer, he threw it over an arm before heading into the kitchen to refill the coffee mugs. He glanced at the refrigerator, where a magnetized frame that read World's Greatest Dad hung.

Glancing at the photo of Mike, a photo from way back, probably not long after the twins had been born, Scott anchored himself to his purpose.

Keeping Riley and the kids safe.

This was a job he was trained for. He needed to remember that. He needed to put his imagination on lockdown. He needed to shut away any and all unworthy thoughts and be the friend that he'd always claimed to be.

With that renewed resolve, he followed the warm glow of the light spilling from the office into the hallway.

"Here you go." He placed the cup in front of her. Then he produced the flash drive. "Will you copy those files onto this? I know it's late. Not too much longer, I promise."

"No worries, Scott. I'm much better off busy. Nothing worse than lying in bed having an anxiety attack."

She tossed that out so casually he knew she must be intimately acquainted with late-night anxiety. And that was exactly why he was here. To figure out what was going on so she could get back to her life.

And he could get back to being a sometimes visitor. He couldn't seem to handle any more than that.

"Take a look at these, will you?" Displaying two stories at once, she plugged the flash drive into a USB port.

He recognized the first. The failed DEA bust had turned into a news bit hardly worth the gas it had taken for her to drive to Hazard Creek. Or the risk to her safety.

The second was a longer piece on the painful unraveling of a criminal identity theft case, where a gang thug was arrested for a break-in and gave the victim's information to the police instead of his own. The criminal record and an outstanding warrant was attached to the innocent victim and not discovered until months later, long after the thug had done a ghost.

"What's Max doing assigning you all these gang-related stories?" Scott hadn't meant to sound annoyed. It really wasn't his business what Riley covered, but gangs...

"It's not Max's fault." She stared at the display, giving him a view of her delicate profile backlit in the golden glow of the lamp. She looked tired, worried, and the need to reassure her hit him again. Unbidden. Hard.

"The schedule's flexible," she explained. "Which is really helpful while I get the kids settled at school. After that, well, I've been giving that some thought. Maybe it's time for a career change."

"You're considering leaving the *Herald?*"

She turned to face him, met his gaze above the rim of the mug. "Let's just say I've been researching options. Between you and me, Scott, ever since that day in Hazard Creek, I'm not entirely sure this job is in all our best interests."

She cocked her head to the side and tried to look casual, a gesture he saw right through. She'd been as spooked as he'd known she'd been that day. As spooked as he'd been.

"I'm thinking life is dangerous enough without me placing myself in situations where I have to outrun drug dealers on foot. I don't want my kids to be orphans if I can help it." She didn't give him a chance to react, just forged on. "I'm looking into what it will take to get a teaching certificate. I've got my master's. So far it seems to be a realistic option."

"You want to work with kids?"

"I like them, and I could take mine to school with me. We'd have the same schedule and summers off together. Solves a lot of problems." She gave a smile that seemed a little strained. "Then if one gets sick, I can call a sub instead of recruiting the first nice guy who happens along."

He hated that she felt pressured to make these kinds of choices because she was scared for her safety. "Listen, Riley. The chief and I talked today. We'd feel better if you had protection until we figure out what's going on." He hadn't intended to put the chief's name in there, but he wanted her to know he hadn't been the one to come up with the idea.

She inhaled deeply, the sound of inevitability. "What do you have in mind?"

"Nothing crazy." But it was crazy. More crazy than she would ever know. "Just me. You can stand a few days of seeing my face, can't you?"

"You don't mind, Scott? It seems like an awful lot to ask."

That wasn't the argument he'd expected, which told him she was a lot more worried than she was letting on.

"No. I don't mind. Just like I didn't mind being recruited today. I'm not going to get any sleep anyway until we figure out what's going on. You don't want me lying in bed awake having anxiety attacks."

She only nodded. "Camille's got a trundle bed, I can put Jake in with her—"

"If you don't mind, I'll bunk on the couch."

She searched his face as if trying to determine how worried she should be. "I'll make you a nest, then."

A nest. A loving gesture that epitomized the sort of care and concern he'd always associated with this family, a family that was stretching its arms to include him with no clue how much he wanted to be included.

VETERANOS GOT IT DOWN. Ace cool in the game. The Busters hooked up. For a piece of curb service.

Jason finally clicked off the CD player after realizing he'd looped around to this same track for the third time. Or was it the fourth? He didn't know. He only knew he felt incredible relief.

He couldn't think, didn't want to move, didn't want to do anything to disrupt this stunned sense of hope. He just needed to catch a break. One break to help him crawl out from under the mess he'd made of everything.

Had he finally gotten it?

Pulling off the earphones, Jason let them fall to the desk. He could only stare at the portable CD player until his brain started working enough to process more stimuli. The desk where he'd been poring over his appointment book, figuring out how to schedule necessary meetings when his life had been taken entirely out of his control.

The moonless night, inky beyond the open plantation shutters that Callie had had installed last spring. A jaw-dropping expense, but a deal she simply couldn't pass on with the window treatment place going out of business. She'd wanted to upgrade from the stock blinds for so long.

The quiet that had settled over the house meant the kids were asleep. Callie would be puttering around, working on some project or another. She'd mentioned something at dinner, but he couldn't remember what she'd said.

Jason couldn't focus on anything but that CD.

He'd been expecting to hear a detailed and documented account of the "services" he'd been forced to provide Barry Mannis and his team. He'd expected to learn that the drug dealers who'd been picking up and delivering their poison at prearranged drops had known exactly who'd been providing the protection. He'd been expecting to learn that his unmarked cruiser hadn't fooled anyone.

Drug dealers were supposed to be afraid of the police— not looking to them for help. But that's exactly what had been happening since Agent Asshole had sunk his claws into Jason.

He'd been turning a blind eye to the local residences and businesses where powder cocaine was being transformed into the crack that went into the streets. He knew where the vessels and chemicals that were used to prepare the crack were being stored.

He knew where the new cookhouse had sprung up to replace the one cleared out for a fake bust. He'd even helped equip the place with a sophisticated surveillance system so the drug dealers wouldn't be surprised by the law. The "real" law. Not the bought-and-paid for kind he'd been providing.

He knew Agent Asshole and his team had been abusing federal resources to run drugs and get rich, but he had no way of knowing how deep their operation went or how long they'd been operating in the area.

But now, compliments of Riley's CD, Jason had a better picture of what was going on.

And it had never once occurred to him that he wasn't the only poor Joe on Agent Asshole's hook. The power-hungry bastard had been running his scam, getting bolder and greedier and including more people than was smart. It was only a matter of time until Mannis screwed up.

Jason knew that from personal experience.

CHAPTER SIXTEEN

RILEY DUG THROUGH the drawers of Jake's dresser, through the stacks of neatly folded clothes. Should she pack him an extra pair of jeans? It was September, and the temperature dropped at night. Would he be inside most of the weekend or outside? She couldn't be sure, so she grabbed a pair.

"Are you sure you want Camille and Jake to go with Rosie and Joe this weekend?" Scott appeared in the bedroom doorway.

"It's probably not necessary." She kept her voice light, didn't want Scott to know the idea of sending the kids away was rattling her in places she hadn't realized could still be rattled. They'd never been apart. Not since before Mike...

"I'm a big believer in going with the flow. Rosie and Joe have an unexpected chance to see Lily Susan, and the kids haven't seen her since we've come home. They'll only be two and a half hours away at Lily Susan's place in the city, and until we figure out what's going on...." She shrugged, another gesture to make her appear casual. Or maybe she hoped by acting that way, she might begin to feel that way, too. "The kids don't remember Lily Susan except from photos. And some time with Rosie and Joe will be a good thing, too. Everyone will have a chance to bond."

Scott eyed her with that dark gaze as if he didn't quite

believe her. Detectives. She inwardly sighed. Always looking for what was below the surface, regardless of whether or not she wanted to share. And she didn't. She needed to figure out how she felt about the way things were changing between her and Scott. She'd never expected this. Not once.

"Just so you understand we don't have much to go on here," he said. "Both attempts seemed directed at theft. Whoever wanted your equipment has it now. I don't want you to feel pressured or scared."

She felt both but wouldn't admit it. Not when Scott was being so sweet by addressing the issue, and by dropping everything to play her bodyguard. Again. She layered the new additions neatly into the duffel bag. "What time do you expect the lawn crew to be here?"

"Soon. They'll stay outside though. You won't have to see them."

"I should thank them for all their hard work, don't you think?"

He looked surprised. "I don't want you uncomfortable."

"Uncomfortable?" Her turn to be surprised. "Is there something about these kids you haven't told me?"

He frowned. "They're from Renaissance."

"I know that."

He frowned. "Gang kids. Well, *former* gang kids. I hope."

"I know that, too." She was surprised by Scott's perception and his thoughtfulness.

How had she missed so much about this man?

He stood inside the doorway, arms folded across his chest, radiating a quiet strength that made her smile.

"I'm okay with former gang kids, Scott. I appreciate the work they've been doing and would like to tell them that."

His eyes traveled over her, and she knew that slow,

searching gaze took stock of what she wasn't saying. "They'll appreciate the chance to thank you, too. It's tough for these kids to get honest work. You're a steady gig that pays well."

She knew it must be hard to get a chance to make different choices with their lives. "It all worked out, then. I really hated to put any more on Brian's shoulders."

Scott scoffed. "I haven't seen him straining himself."

"Is that Scott the Renaissance coordinator talking or Scott the cop?"

He gave a short laugh. "Both, I guess. He's a good kid, don't get me wrong, but he's got such a sweet deal here. I don't think he appreciates it as much as he should."

"Fair enough. He's barely twenty."

"I'll keep that in mind."

Whether or not he agreed, and she suspected he didn't, which said something about Scott the man she didn't know. Had he been the kind of kid who'd had to grow up fast? One with a lot of responsibility thrust upon him at an early age? As a parent she knew there was such a fine line to walk, balancing enough with too much. Had someone loved him enough to find that balance?

Riley knew nothing about his family. Mike had always said Scott didn't have any, but he must have some. Rosie had managed to drum up more about him than anyone, and Riley was surprised by how much she wanted to know about the events that had shaped this man before her, an honorable, dependable man, who bore the weight of her family's trouble with such ease and concern. Adding pajamas into the duffel bag, she zipped it shut. "I'm glad you suggested the Renaissance kids."

"That's generous."

"Not really. I have more understanding than most about

why kids wind up in gangs. Because of my work and yours. I don't blame them for their life circumstances. And I certainly don't blame all gang kids for what happened to Mike."

His expression softened. He didn't say anything, just kept watching her thoughtfully.

"Don't look at me like that. It's not anything special," she said. "Just healthy. I do try, and in some ways I'm actually surprising myself."

"Really? How's that?" He sounded amused.

"The grief counselors and the other folks in the support groups all said time would make the difference. I don't think I ever actually believed them. Now sometimes I surprise myself by how healed I am. I don't miss Mike any less, but I don't hurt so much. Instead of always seeing how he's not here, I remember when he was here. I feel…well, grateful. We had so much to be thankful for. I can't help thinking that time was so perfect because we weren't going to get a lot of it."

He was silent so long that Riley wondered if she'd made him uncomfortable, and felt uncertain by this intimacy of their changing relationship. In some ways she felt so at ease around him. But in other ways…

"May I ask you a question?"

She was grateful for the distraction, didn't want to overthink how much things had changed between them. "Of course."

"Are you glad you came home?"

She considered that for a moment, considered him, knew she would be honest. "In some ways. I liked our life in Florida. It was all shiny and fresh. We were making new memories, and trust me when I say you can't beat year-round sunshine and the beach. But I don't think I would have known how much I'd healed if we'd stayed. I needed to test myself. I needed to be healthy about the situation because the kids are taking their cues from me."

"You're doing a good job, Riley."

His comment seemed so random she could only glance up at him, found him watching her with an expression of quiet appreciation, one she found surprisingly intimate.

One that made her notice his dark, dark hair. And how he might be almost too thin if not for those broad shoulders, those long, strong legs that left no doubt that he was an active man. Even if she hadn't known how many team sports he was involved in through the department and Renaissance, she knew he was physical by the way he'd always helped out Mike, then Brian, with cars, tractors, trucks and the four thousand other things that could go wrong around here.

She wasn't sure what surprised her most—that he was even thinking about her parenting skills or that he thought she'd needed to hear that she was doing a good job. It occurred to her that it might have nothing at all to do with her and everything to do with his appreciation of family. He seemed to have fullness and balance in all the other areas of his life. Strong relationships with people he respected at the department. Through his volunteer work. On all the team sports he participated in. He was a good man. And if she hadn't fully appreciated how good before, she'd been getting an education the past two years.

It was such a surprising moment, one where Riley seemed to see him as she never had before, a stranger, not someone who'd been a part of her life for so long.

Perhaps because *this* Scott was different.

This Scott was a man, who'd been carving a place for

himself in her life. A man, she was coming to realize, she wanted in her life.

"May I ask you a question?" she said.

He didn't hesitate. "Sure, shoot."

"You and Mike discussed the possibility of him being hurt at work, didn't you?" *Hurt.* Not dying. She couldn't get that word out of her mouth.

He held her gaze steadily. "Yes."

That one word righted their equilibrium and put Mike between them where he'd always been. And it felt so comfortable to have him there.

But there was a part of Riley, a part that she wasn't sure how she felt about yet, that liked this new direction her relationship with Scott was taking, that liked the man she was getting to know.

ON A NORMAL FRIDAY, Jason would have been long gone by the time his son was heading to school, but he'd spent the night going through every file on Riley's notebook computer. File after file after file until his eyes had crossed.

But he hadn't found anything to make him suspect she had a clue he'd been working with the DEA on that bogus bust, nothing to hint she had any idea what was on that CD. He'd read her every article, every shred of research, which all seemed neatly tied to her articles.

He'd scanned photos of her kids, who were just a year younger than Kyle. Cute kids who looked more like Riley than Mike with that blond hair. They'd been pictures of the first day at school. Jason knew because he'd lived through the whole scene just a year ago himself.

Photos and video files that Riley must have uploaded from her camcorder. He wondered if she'd deleted them from her hard drive yet. If she had then she'd lost everything because he had her camera, too. He'd stolen more than equipment; he'd stolen memories. She wouldn't be able to replace those.

He'd finally passed out while sitting upright at his desk, his eyes scratchy and unfocused, his thoughts tortured with questions of how he could get this equipment back to Riley without leaving a trail of breadcrumbs back to himself or Tyrese.

Callie had found him like that, slumped, still dressed, in his office chair.

He'd lied, of course. Told her he was bypassing the office this morning to head straight to a meeting. She'd seized the opportunity to let Jessica sleep in, taking Kyle to school while Jason was in the shower.

That was the only reason why he was still home when the doorbell rang. He opened the door to find the FedEx guy with a package addressed to Callie.

Jason glanced at the sender's name then did a double take, his blood running icy through his veins.

Chola Party Babes
Maharaja Hotel
Atlantic City, NJ

Signing for the package with trembling fingers, Jason stared blankly at the courier before slamming the door in his face. Maharaja Hotel in Atlantic City was the name of the place where he'd screwed up his whole life. He didn't need to ask who the Chola Party Babes were. Just like he didn't need to ask who'd sent this package.

The man who'd set him up.

He had the envelope opened by the time he got to his office and, sure enough, there was a DVD inside a jewel case. He wondered what Callie would have thought had she opened the package. There was no accompanying documentation, nothing to give a hint what the DVD contained. Would she have popped it into the television or the computer, curious?

Jason had the overwhelming urge to check it out for himself to see if Agent Asshole was bluffing. He didn't. He scooped the cell phone off his desk and dialed.

Agent Asshole answered on the second ring.

"What in hell are you doing sending that...that *garbage* to my wife?"

"I told you to keep me informed," he replied in a cool voice.

"And I told you I would," Jason exploded into the phone. "I've been taking care of it. I haven't informed you of anything because there's nothing to tell you."

His words echoed sharply off the walls. He took a deep breath, tried to control the rush of blood behind his ears.

"Y'know, you're really a dumb-ass, Kenney. What part have you been taking care of? I must have missed it. Your busted attempt to get into that reporter's house ended up with the PPD on her doorstep. Now that cop's guarding her around the clock."

Jason froze where he stood, the anger draining away as fast as it had come. "You're tailing her?"

"I told you I didn't want any mistakes. You're a mistake. I'm just cleaning up your mess."

"Jesus, Mannis. What did you do?"

That cool chuckle bounced over the satellite signals with the force of a comet. "That problem isn't yours to worry about anymore, so put it out of your head. You just worry about doing what I ask you to do because the next time you might not be so lucky. Your wife might get the mail."

It took Jason a minute to realize the line had gone dead.

"Daddy," Jessica screeched so loudly that Jason jumped. He dropped the cell phone and it skittered loudly across the wood floor just as his daughter tore into the office on bare feet, her Dora the Explorer nightgown tangling around her knees.

"Daddy." She launched herself at him with complete abandon, arms outstretched, silky dark hair flying behind her.

She never once questioned whether or not he'd catch her. Jason hoisted her barely forty-pound body into the air, her giggles piercing his shame, anchoring him in the present.

When she finally stopped squirming, she threw her arms around his neck and hugged him tightly. For one heart-stopping moment, he felt like a man worthy of so much love.

"Good morning, my Jessie," he whispered into her hair.

"Morning, Daddy." She leaned back in his arms, would have landed on her pretty head had he not held her securely. Then she planted a big kiss on his cheek.

But Jason wasn't worthy.

In that instant, all the running, all the lying, all the hiding from the ugly reality of this situation reached a zenith. He'd betrayed his beautiful daughter's trust. He'd betrayed his wife. And the men in his department. And Tyrese, who'd proven himself to be a much better man. And Riley, who wasn't guilty of anything except running into him.

He was toxic, poison to everyone he came in contact with, people who should have never been dragged along for this ride.

All for a weekend of high-stakes poker and sex. No. Even worse. The gambling and the sex had merely been side effects of his ego. His greed. He'd wanted to be one of the guys with high-powered connections. He'd wanted more of that power for himself.

How had he gotten so far away from what was important? He'd never once thought about his responsibility to the power he already held, to the people who counted on him.

Pulling his daughter closely against him, he buried his face in her sweet-smelling hair.

CHAPTER SEVENTEEN

SCOTT COULD HANDLE THIS. All he needed to focus on was keeping Riley safe. Doing a job. Honoring a promise. *How* he felt didn't matter. He didn't always feel like getting out of bed to go to work. Or leaving a good basketball game at the Center to take some phone call that would send him to a crime scene where a drug deal had gone balls-up and left body parts everywhere.

Then again, Scott hadn't actually bargained on spending so much time with Riley. He didn't blame her. The situation had just been throwing them together. And one thing was for sure—talking to her from up the Eastern seaboard hadn't exactly tested him the way watching her walk down to the barn, carrying a pitcher of iced tea for the crew, the sun glinting off her hair did.

He'd never actually had to stand around and see a half-dozen kids vie for her attention. They'd been charmed by Riley, by her goodness—who wasn't? And these kids were nothing if not savvy about spotting the sun through cracks under the doors.

How had Mike handled it?

That didn't take too much thought. Mike had been secure in Riley's love. He'd never minded men ogling his wife, in fact, he'd been amused by it. Proud, too, Scott thought. He would have been if he'd been a family kind of man.

That reminder helped steel his resolve, helped keep him focused on the job at hand. Leaving the cool recesses of the barn, where he'd been returning some tools, he took stock of where each member of the crew was with the work.

Cakes was almost done bundling the shrub and tree limbs to stack beside the road for the trash pickup.

Mateo and Do-Wap were still on their knees weeding in the back bed. Wouldn't be much longer and all this work wouldn't make a difference. The weeds would soon be dead, along with the flowers they'd planted at the start of summer.

General E. was driving the lawn mower. Week after week his age and experience gave him his pick of jobs. The one he chose usually involved being in the driver's seat of the riding mower.

"Hey, Scott," Joe's familiar voice called out.

Scott shielded his gaze and turned into the sun. Joe was coming down the slope from the house.

"How are you holding up?" Joe asked. "Tired of farm life yet?"

"What's to get tired of when all the kids do the work?"

Joe laughed, his gaze darting around to see the kids attending to their various tasks, taking casual notice of this newcomer. "Sounds like a plan. Maybe I should get them over to my place."

Scott nodded. "You bring the kids from school?"

"Yeah. Figured it would be easier than making you pack things up here. Riley didn't think you'd want her to go alone."

Scott didn't reply, although Riley had been right. He would have left the kids here alone before allowing her to go off anywhere without him.

"Listen, Scott. I really appreciate all you're doing. Rosie and I both do. But talk to me. How worried should we be?"

"Don't worry—"

"Cut me a break." He frowned. "When Riley agreed to let us take the kids, we knew there was trouble. How much?"

In Scott's opinion, there were only two kinds of fathers—the ones who cared about their kids and the ones who kids were better off without. Joe was one of the good ones.

"I'm trying to figure out why someone would want her equipment," Scott said. "Some story she's covered. Some evidence she's come across. I haven't found anything solid to point me in a specific direction. Kevin's running a few leads. Hopefully something will turn up."

"What about what happened in Hazard Creek?"

"Looks random as far as I can tell. Like she was just in the wrong place at the wrong time."

"She was the only press there. You don't think that's suspicious?"

Joe was just trying to help. He'd already lost his son. He didn't want to lose a daughter-in-law he loved, too.

"It's suspicious, no question," Scott admitted. "But I don't have anything to tie it to the other incidents. If someone wanted to hurt her, they wouldn't go from trying to run her down to breaking into her house and car. And I could think of much better places to go after her than in front of the DEA and the whole Hazard Creek PD."

Joe snorted. "Got a point there."

"We'll figure it out. Most likely she came across something while researching one of her stories that someone doesn't want to get out. If that's the case, it'll just take time to make the connections." He tried to look reassuring. "You know the PPD. We'll be on red alert until we get this sorted out."

"I know you will. My son was fortunate in his friends."

"Your son was a good friend."

Joe just inclined his head, letting the words linger.

"Taking the kids away this weekend is a big help," Scott

said. "Riley's really worried about them, even though she's not saying as much. I wish she'd go with you. A break would probably do her good, but she's determined to be here while I go through her work files until I find something solid."

"And you will." Joe rocked back on his heels to meet Scott's gaze. "She couldn't be in better hands. Both Rosie and I feel that way. We appreciate everything you've done since Mike passed. Don't you forget that."

Scott felt uncomfortable with such a blatant vote of confidence. Joe was a good one definitely.

"You got my cell number. Call if you need anything. I mean it, Scott, anything at all."

"I will, but don't worry. And don't let Rosie worry, either. Have a good weekend."

"We will. Lily Susan's excited about seeing the kids. She's been making plans all day. Lots to do in the city for young people."

Didn't take much to envision visits to parks and toy stores and Broadway shows. A real family that enjoyed being together. Scott knew what a family should be like, even if he hadn't lived the reality himself; he'd seen it up close with the Angelicas.

Joe clamped a hand on Scott's back. "I'm out of here, then. Good luck."

"I'll come say goodbye to Rosie." Scott walked with him back to the house, found everyone all packed with the bags waiting on the front porch.

"Didn't want to put the kids' stuff in the car until you got here," Rosie said with a twinkle in her eyes. "Figured you'd want everything in a special way."

"Of course." Joe glanced at the two duffel bags sitting side by side, identical except for the colors—one blue, the other pink. "Jeez, Riley. Look at the size of these. They're only going away for two nights. What do you have in here?"

Riley seemed ready. "Only the essentials. I promise."

"Grandpa, we have to take Franny," Camille explained.

"And Gentle Ben," Jake added. "And my special pillow."

"Important stuff, Joe." Scott reached for the duffel bags and hoisted them over his shoulder. "And not nearly as heavy as they look. The kids could even carry them."

Riley cast him a grateful glance before she said, "They *should* be carrying their bags."

Both kids only laughed and cut off Scott as they ran out the door. Scott followed, not minding his turn as pack mule for the few short steps to Joe's Cadillac. As Rosie predicted, he made a production of stowing everything in the trunk.

But Scott was more interested in watching Riley in his periphery, the way she'd knelt down in front of the kids and talked to each of them in hushed tones.

He strained to hear and, with effort, could make out her whispering voice. Telling them what to do if they wanted to talk to her, reminding them how they should behave, promising that she wasn't so far away if they needed her.

She couldn't seem to keep her hands off them. Adjusting Jake's belt. Brushing strands of hair from Camille's neck. Finally taking their hands in hers, a routine they'd all obviously played time and time again.

Then she was kissing and hugging them and telling them how much she loved them before letting them loose. They raced to the car as if they'd been fired from a gun.

"Have fun, you guys," she said while Joe held the door for Rosie. "Stay in touch and kiss Aunt Lily Susan for me."

Joe rolled the windows down and reached for Riley's hand. "Don't you worry. We'll take good care of them."

"I know." Riley squeezed his hand. "Have a great time."

Then she let go and stepped back from the car, blowing kisses to the kids, both of whom had stuck their arms out the windows on either side as if trying to make the car fly.

"Bye, Mommy. Love you, Mom," came the excited voices as the car pulled out of the driveway.

Even Scott gave a wave, smiling as the Cadillac took off with a gleam of red taillights. That was until he heard a strange gulp of breath and glanced at Riley. She stood beside him, still waving, her smile collapsing.

"Riley?"

She wouldn't look at him, just waved him off.

"Riley, they'll be fine."

She nodded, but didn't say a word as she visibly fought to control her expression.

Scott knew she trusted Rosie and Joe to care for the kids. Was this some sort of mom thing? Could she miss them already? Or was this about all the pressure that had been on her lately, all the responsibilities of parenting alone and going back to work and facing the past and outrunning drug dealers on foot and break-ins at the house and in the car and her equipment stolen...

"Riley." He reached for her like he had only days before, without thought, just wanting to take away her pain.

The instant she was in his arms, Scott knew that touching Riley was playing with fire. She melted against him with a breathy sigh and pressed her cheek to his chest. He could feel her shudder, feel every curve of her slim body as if she was some missing piece of him.

He had no business feeling this way, imagined Mike up *there* somewhere, that place his grandmother claimed existed when he'd been a kid, the place where his mother watched over him, always loving him, no matter how shitty life got. And it had gotten really shitty after his grand-mother had died and he'd gone to live with the old man. Scott had always kept that thought close. But in this moment, with Riley in his arms, he hoped his grandmother had been wrong. He didn't want Mike to look down and see his friend taking advantage of his wife's need.

Because that's what he was doing.

He didn't let her go. He only held her close, a man without the will to resist temptation, a man who savored this time, knowing he'd never get another chance.

He couldn't stop from running his hands over her hair, down her back—simple, forbidden touches. He'd never felt this way, wouldn't have allowed himself to feel this way if he could help it. But he couldn't. Need left him helpless. He just wanted to hold her close. To soothe away her pain. Riley didn't stop him, though he wished with every shred of reason he had left that she would.

And still he couldn't let her go.

He stood with his cheek pressed to the top of her head, the breath trapped in his chest as he fought his desire to keep touching her.

RILEY STOOD IN THE DRIVEWAY long after the kids, Rosie and Joe had driven away, surrounded by Scott's strong arms. His hard body blocked the fall breeze as the sun began its late-afternoon descent.

She should move. She should say something, do some-thing, *anything* to end a silence filled with a desire that she could no longer deny.

She could hear his steady heartbeat throbbing beneath her cheek, feel the softness of his T-shirt and the warm strength of the man beneath it. With every breath, she inhaled the smell of him, musky and almost overpowering, the smell of a man who'd been doing yard work all afternoon. It was a new smell, Scott's smell, not unpleasant.

His body was hard with the muscular strength of an active man, a man whose arms held her so close her breasts pressed against him, her stomach lightly grazed his, their thighs brushed together. She could feel everywhere they touched as if a current ran between them.

What was this? She only knew what *this* wasn't—the grateful reaction to the comfort of a friend. *This* was something so completely different, something so unexpected that she simply stood there unmoving. Something so much more.

This was a feeling she hadn't felt in so long…a feeling she'd never expected to feel again. Not since Mike, the man she'd loved with her heart and soul.

Arousal.

For Scott.

Every nerve ending in her body tingled, and she could only tighten her grip around his waist, an instinctive move to feed the pleasure. He shuddered, a full-bodied motion as he anchored her even closer, one big hand trapped in her hair, the other securing her around the shoulders, molding their bodies together intimately.

Bringing their bodies to life in an unexpected way.

His breath came in a ragged burst. Riley's caught in her throat, a sigh of surprised pleasure, an exhalation of profound relief to rediscover such a forgotten part of her.

A sound that echoed between them.

And jolted Scott from the moment. His entire body went rigid, and he sprang away as if he'd been detonated, leaving her staring up at him in surprise.

She felt trapped beneath his dark gaze, every tingle that shouldn't be happening, every raw breath that lifted her chest and drew attention to breasts that felt full, show-cased beneath eyes that saw everything.

"Riley—" The voice broke from his lips, a plea.

Still, she could only stare, overcome by the need pouring through her. She tried to make sense of what was happening, of what she felt…of Scott's broken expression. Then, in the wake of the need, came panic.

She hadn't misread his reaction to her, but what if he hadn't wanted to react? What if he'd only wanted to comfort her?

"I'm not normally such a wimp." The words erupted from her, a desperate bid to fill the silence to distract them from what had just happened.

"I don't think you're a wimp." His reply sounded just as raw, just as grateful.

"I can't imagine why. I've been totally acting like one."

"We could argue that I smell like a goat. I've been outside all day working on the yard."

She laughed stupidly. "I honestly didn't notice. Shows you how far gone I was."

It was the most stupid exchange ever between a man and a woman in the history of mankind. There was no question at all about whether he was as sideswiped as she. Not when they kept staring at each other like deer caught in headlights, nonsense pouring from their mouths.

Scott came to his senses first. "I need to check on the crew."

"I've got to start dinner. The least I can do is feed you." But she was staring at his broad back before the words were all out of her mouth because he took off so fast, long strides chewing up the ground and putting distance between them.

The instant she could no longer see him around the side of the house, Riley waved her hands in front of her as if she might shake off the crushing wave of embarrassment. She headed straight for the house to get as far away from the scene of her humiliation as possible.

CHAPTER EIGHTEEN

THE PHONE IN JASON'S POCKET vibrated. Not his personal cell phone, but the untraceable one that Agent Asshole had provided to tell Jason when to jump. He flipped it open by the fourth ring to find out how high.

"Yeah."

"Got details for you." The harsh voice shot over the line. "Going to need a few more men for protective detail. You can handle that."

Jason stared at the highway unwinding in front of him, faded yellow lines anchoring him to the reality of his world. He willed himself to reply normally, when he felt anything but normal. "When?"

"Tomorrow night. Late."

"No problem."

Agent Asshole didn't reply. He didn't have to. Jason knew he'd expected no other answer, not when Mannis had already bought and paid for services rendered.

"Where?" Jason asked, impressed by how businesslike he sounded when his stomach roiled violently. His pulse pounded so hard behind his ears he had to strain to hear the details of this all-important drop.

Agent Asshole relayed the coordinates of a private airfield in the northern part of Jason's jurisdiction, an airfield where the high profiles who did business and vacationed in the area were afforded the sort of privacy they needed to come and go without fanfare. They paid for that privilege.

The fact that this DEA team gone bad was shelling out the price for this added protection confirmed what Jason had suspected all along.

This drug shipment wasn't coming through the same channels as the others. This must be coming straight out of Mexico from one of the more well-known cartels. This posh private airstrip would be the perfect place to enter the area unobtrusively, a place where they'd be able to unload the drugs then disperse them in every direction—upstate, into the city, local stash houses and into the prison system if the information on that CD was correct. If Jason had had any doubt before, he didn't now. Agent Asshole was uptight. That's why he sent the DVD to Jason's house and stepped in to deal with Riley. He'd known he needed extra protection, and wanted to make sure he'd taken care of any wild cards and had Jason well under his thumb.

Jason hadn't thought Barry Mannis possessed any conscience and found it somewhat reassuring to know the man did care about something—if only his three-quarters of a million-dollar shipment and his reputation with the bad guys.

"You got that?" Agent Asshole asked.

"No problem."

"Keep me informed. This needs to go off nice and neat. Trust me, you won't be sorry."

But he was. About this whole mess. "Got it."

The line disconnected.

Jason flipped the phone shut and tossed it onto the passenger seat as he passed a sign marking an approaching Poughkeepsie exit.

He wanted to know what Agent Asshole planned to do

about Riley, but he hadn't asked, hadn't wanted to give the guy one whiff of suspicion that would cause him to question Jason's loyalty when he probably wouldn't get a straight answer anyway. But Jason knew that with the drop scheduled to go down tomorrow night, Agent Asshole wouldn't leave any loose ends. Riley was exactly that.

Funny that his moment of truth had come while sitting behind the wheel of his cruiser, heading south on a highway that could take him away from this nightmare.

The only sane thing to do was arrange for the extra security and show up for tomorrow night's drop. Agent Asshole would expect him to bring his men. He could simply tell them they were assisting the DEA like they had in that bogus sting. No one would question that. Jason would safeguard himself from another copy of the DVD showing up at his house. Worse yet, Agent Asshole might send the DVD to the media, where everyone in the world would be treated to his downfall. If he stuck with the program, he might even get tossed a bone for good behavior. Agent Asshole had said as much.

The trouble with this was two-fold. Compliance left an innocent woman at risk and gave Agent Asshole license to continue the blackmail. Jason would like to think eventually this DEA unit from hell would leave the area, but this could go on forever. Or until something went wrong and the situation blew up in his face. Jason wasn't stupid. Blackmailers would keep blackmailing as long as their victims let them.

That left him only two choices. He could keep driving and forget this nightmare had ever happened. He could lose himself and start up someplace new, where no one knew him, or what he'd done. Canada, maybe. Or South America. He could give up his life. Callie. His kids. His parents.

The very thought should have killed him. Giving up all the people he loved, who loved him…he was numb. He'd unloaded all over his confused wife this morning, leaving her worried and scared and without answers. Such a selfish bastard.

"Own up, take the heat then get on with your life."

Tyrese's words had been replaying in his head. *His* words. From back when he'd known there was more to life than believing his own press. Honor. Something he'd forgotten along the way.

Jason could come clean, but he wouldn't have a life to get on with. His career would be over—even if he managed to avoid jail time. His marriage, too, most likely. How could Callie ever forgive him? How could he forgive himself?

"Own up, take the heat then get on with your life."

Jason hadn't had any clue the kind of courage it would take to follow that advice when he'd given it to Tyrese. But could he live with himself if something happened to an innocent woman? Could he look himself in the mirror every day, knowing he'd been too much of a coward to do the right thing?

He saw the exit sign ahead, wondered if he'd take the turnoff ramp toward Poughkeepsie or hit the gas and keep driving.

RILEY PROWLED THE ROOMS of the house, thoughts racing. She washed her hands and brushed her teeth. She arranged the kids' stuffed animals on their pillows, marking the spot where those sweet little heads would lay once they returned home from their trip. She emptied the dryer of a load of whites, folded and put them away before finally remembering she really did need to start dinner.

With a goal to ground her, Riley headed into the kitchen and willed herself to focus. She opened the fridge and took stock of what she had available. Sauce, mozzarella and a chunk of parmesan left over from the pizza. Several pounds of frozen chicken breasts that wouldn't take long to defrost. Without a great deal of work, she could put together chicken parmesan that should satisfy a hungry man.

Satisfy a hungry man.

Those few innocent words conjured up memories that sent another wave of heat flooding through her and started the whole sorry process of obsessing all over again.

She tossed the chicken onto the counter, where it landed with a solid thunk, and headed toward the coffeepot. No, she didn't need any caffeine when adrenaline was spiking her anxiety quite nicely, thank you very much, but coffee always made everything better. And with any luck the caffeine would constrict her blood vessels so she could focus for two minutes to make sense of…*that.*

She got the coffee brewing then arranged the chicken in the microwave to defrost, willing herself to calm down, to think clearly. She was an adult with some problems that needed resolutions. She couldn't afford the luxury of freaking out because she'd responded in Scott's arms, had been taken by surprise by her reaction to him.

And Scott's reaction to her. A shiver coursed through her as she remembered the expression on his face. Shocked. Stricken. And as embarrassed as she'd been. That much she hadn't imagined.

And aroused?

Yes. She hadn't imagined that, either.

Definitely aroused whether or not he'd wanted to be.

Pulling a skillet from the cabinet, Riley assembled everything she needed to bread the cutlets. Spear a cutlet.

Roll it in flour. Submerge it in egg. Coat it with seasoned bread crumbs. Then place it in the skillet.

She caught sight of a glossy black head in her periphery and glanced up from her task to see him crossing the yard toward the barn with a boy who was even taller than he was.

Flour. Egg. Bread crumbs. Skillet.

She willed the repetitive action to keep her attention and calm her jangled nerves. Once she got a few swigs of coffee in her, she'd be able to think more clearly.

Scott was an attractive man, a gorgeous man. Riley had always known that. Anyone with eyes would know that. Admittedly, she had to wonder why someone hadn't scarfed him up long ago. He'd dated some really nice women. Most hadn't been around long, but there'd been a few who'd hung around so she'd remembered their names from one police function to the next. Jennifer. Stephanie. Who was the one with the exquisite taste in shoes? *Dana.*

Mike had always told her not to worry about Scott. He'd said that Scott had some issues to sort through before he could commit to a woman. And then finding one might be a problem because he'd set his sights extraordinarily high.

That instantly recognizable black head caught her attention again. This time, Scott left the barn with two young men, probably Brian's age or close to it, in tow. The one who was taller than Scott—what was his name again? Eric. And the Hispanic boy, Mateo. She speared a cutlet from the skillet, accidentally spattering oil when she didn't drain it long enough.

What idiot had thought shutters would only detract from the view of the farm through all these windows? The idiot standing here with a fork in her hand, catching glimpses of a man she didn't want to see. Every single time she caught sight of him, those broad, broad shoulders, Riley found her thoughts circling right back around to *that*.

True, their relationship had been changing lately, but she'd gone from zero to sixty in his arms. There was no other way to describe it.

Riley had to get a grip. She wasn't a sixteen-year-old with moody hormones, and Scott wasn't someone with whom she had the luxury of losing control. He was involved with her family. He was a friend. She couldn't damage their relationship over some…she still didn't have a clue what *that* had been.

Flour. Egg. Bread crumbs. Skillet.

Darn it. What was wrong with her? Was she so emotionally vulnerable that she physically reacted to the first attractive man she felt comfortable with? And here she'd been telling Scott how healthy she was.

But that didn't ring true. Not really. No question they'd been growing closer. No question that she liked the man she was getting to know. But she was honestly surprised *that* part of her hadn't died along with Mike. Of course the grief counselors and people at the support groups had all said time would eventually help her get back to living. She was young. Her kids were young. They had a future meant to be lived. Riley hadn't believed them.

"Riley?"

She spun around, almost upending the bowl of flour. Scott stood in the doorway of the kitchen, and she'd been so pre-occupied with her thoughts she hadn't heard him come in.

"Crew took off and I have good news." He sounded normal.

"I'm all ears." She sounded normal, too.

He leaned against the doorjamb, still not meeting her gaze. "Kevin found a possible answer—he just called to tell me. A local drug rep from one of the companies under investigation has a connection to someone we've gotten to know pretty well down at the department the past few years. Someone who'd know to bring along a radio to a cop's house."

"The pharmaceutical case?"

Scott nodded. "It's weak at best, so don't get your hopes up. But it's something. Kevin's on it."

"Thanks, I—"

"Listen, Riley," Scott cut her off. "I'm sorry about today. I was totally out of line."

"Scott, I—"

"I don't know what happened." He shoved his hand through his hair, upending the thick waves almost comically. "I shouldn't have invaded your personal space. I...well, I wanted to make you feel better."

He was taking the responsibility for what had happened? "But, Scott, you weren't—"

"I'm going to put the security on." He was already turning, ready to bolt. "I really need to shower. Do you mind?"

Whether she minded or not didn't seem to be at issue because he was gone before she could reply. Again she stood there staring after him as she heard the rapid beeping of the security panel as he set it, then the door to the kids' bathroom slamming firmly shut across the house. And some rapid-fire sputtering it took a moment to identify.

"Oh, no." She spun toward the skillet to find two cutlets burning.

She rescued them with a fork, shaking her head. What kind of conversation had that been? Why was Scott assuming the blame? She'd been the one to ignite like a spark to kindling in his arms. Could he have possibly misinterpreted her reaction?

Replaying the exchange over and over in her head, she finished assembling the meal and put it in the oven to bake. Then she washed the dishes. All she knew was that had been the second stupidest exchange between a man and woman in the history of mankind. Only this time she hadn't been the one with the stupidity pouring out of her mouth. She hadn't been able to get a complete sentence out thanks to Mr. Noble Gentleman.

So what was she supposed to do now? Just accept his apology and pretend nothing had happened? That didn't even make sense. Normal people discussed situations that needed discussion. But if he wasn't willing, then maybe she should figure out what was going on with her before addressing the issue with him or trying to.

He didn't seem to mind having conversations all by himself. Or assuming all the responsibility for something that had clearly happened between the two of them.

It was nearly five o'clock when Scott resurfaced. She intended to sit him down at the dinner table and try to revisit the subject, but the sight of him looking so freshly scrubbed from the shower derailed her.

There it was again. That *awareness*. Of how shiny and black his hair was with the waves still damp from the shower. How pink his cheeks were where he'd shaved. His jeans were clean. His shirt was fresh and neatly pressed. She could remember exactly how his hard chest would feel beneath that crisp white shirt.

"Smells good in here." He met her gaze this time, seemed to have collected himself. Apparently he intended to follow through with his pretend-nothing-ever-happened strategy.

"Hungry?" she asked. "Or is it too early for you? I'm on kid time myself."

"I'm starving, but don't go to any trouble for me."

Hadn't she said she would cook for him? Hadn't he even noticed that she'd been cooking for the past hour and a half since the kids had left? "No trouble. The least I can do is feed you—"

His phone rang. He reached for it with an apologetic expression, and she decided she wasn't going to catch a break right now. Not to talk with him.

Scott was frowning, so she asked, "Kevin again?"

He shook his head, sending a damp wave curling over his forehead. "I don't recognize the number." Flipping open the phone, he said, "Emerson."

He went utterly still while listening to his end of the conversation, and Riley, too, went on red alert. She knew the look, knew this call involved something he was invested in. His mouth compressed into a tight line, his jaw clenched as he responded in monosyllables. She noticed his knuckles grow steadily whiter as his grip tightened on the phone.

"I'll get him there," Scott said. "Chick's. Forty minutes?"

Chick's in the Valley was a tavern that had been around a lot longer than Riley had, a total hole in the wall that had become a Pleasant Valley institution.

Scott ended the call and for a moment was silent, as if he still hadn't transitioned from the call back to reality. He finally met her gaze. "I've got to leave for a little while. There will be a unit parked outside until I get back. Just a precaution. I won't be long."

"Is everything all right? I assume that call didn't have anything to do with me or you wouldn't be leaving."

His dark gaze bored into her with such intensity that Riley's pulse kicked up a notch. "I'll know more soon, but I've got to make some calls myself."

Then he left the room, leaving her staring after him again. What was this man's problem?

CHAPTER NINETEEN

JASON FOUND A PARKING SPOT beside the back door that led upstairs to the apartments above the tavern. He still wasn't sure if he'd made a mistake by agreeing to this meet at the height of Friday-night rush-hour traffic. He'd thought about waiting until after dark, but decided it would be easier to hide his movements in the traffic rather than try to slip away from home at night.

He wasn't worried about Callie. She was used to the demands of his job and wouldn't think anything strange, but he didn't trust Agent Asshole not to have put a tail on him. For precisely that reason, he'd asked Tyrese for another favor—borrowing the man's motorcycle, a favor much more to Tyrese's liking. That's why he'd jumped on board the "reform Jason" train with more than prayers. But Jason appreciated the prayers. He needed a miracle.

Once inside the back entrance, he pulled off the helmet.

Jason made his way down the narrow hall, finally pushing through swinging doors to the bar. Chick was behind it, where he'd been for the past forty years, maybe longer.

"Bud." He slapped down a ten, waited until he had the icy longneck in his hand before saying, "I'm meeting—"

"Private room." Chick cocked his balding head toward the swinging doors. "They're waiting for you."

Jason tipped his bottle in salute, then took a deep drink as he went to meet his fate.

Scott and Chief Levering were both inside the small dining room. The chief was sitting, nursing his own beer, while Scott prowled the perimeter. Jason closed the door.

"Chief." Chief Levering saluted Jason in a greeting that was a joke between them ever since Jason had left the PPD to lead Hazard Creek's department.

"Chief." Jason made his way to the table and extended his hand. "Thanks for coming on such short notice."

"What do you have?" Scott asked.

The moment of truth.

Jason set down the beer. He cocked his hip against the table and folded his arms across his chest. Taking a deep, fortifying breath, he felt the silence stretch, knowing the time had come to commit to the decision he'd made.

To do the right thing.

"I stepped in a pile of shit and need your help getting out."

To Jason's surprise that admission didn't get as tangled up with his pride as he'd expected. His voice sounded almost normal as he detailed the situation from the setup in Atlantic City to his appointment on the Narcotics Commission to Agent Asshole blackmailing him to provide law enforcement protection at various drug drops into the area.

When he finished, there was more of that silence.

"Shit, Jason?" Chief Levering shook his head, looking disgusted. "You're not kidding. What the hell do you think we can do for you?"

"Help me bring this asshole down," Jason said simply, all the humiliation, all the tension, all the goddamn months of sick pressure lessening with every word. "I'll give you everything you need and then some to set this guy up. I've got details on three-quarters of a million in drugs coming in. I want to go in with your best men undercover and bring every one of these hoods down."

"You'll be going down with them," Scott said, scowling.

It took effort to get the words out. "I know, man. I screwed up. But I don't want the media wiping the floors with my family. If you help me bring these assholes down, I'll have something to offer the D.A. We can keep this reasonably quiet."

Chief Levering's gaze narrowed. "You know the way this works, Jason. You're well-known around here. Do you think swinging a deal is even possible? What else do you have?"

Jason wasn't going to dwell on where basking in the local limelight had gotten him or the irony that all he wanted now was to disappear into a hole. "Enough to blow open something that's going to solve problems you didn't even know you had."

"You mentioned Riley on the phone," Scott said.

Jason nodded. He took a step away from the table, that feeling of relief getting lost somewhere beneath the sober admission he needed to make.

"I'm responsible." He met Chief Levering's gaze. "I sent someone to break into her house and car. I needed to find—"

He'd been too busy battling down guilt and pride as he faced his old boss to notice the powerful right hook coming at him. Then the side of his head exploded and he was tripping backward over a chair. He crash-landed against the wall with a thud that rocked the door in its frame. He had time to register Scott bearing down on him when Chief Levering's command rang out, "Knock it off."

Scott stopped short when Chief Levering caught a hand in his collar. "Don't make me say it again."

"Son of a bitch," Scott growled, visibly shaking.

Jason rubbed his jaw. He couldn't meet either man's gaze. Not when he hadn't even gotten to the good parts yet.

"Get up," Chief Levering said to Jason just as the door opened and Chick stuck his bald head into the room.

"You want me to call the cops?" He gave a short laugh.

"Aren't you a comedian." Chief Levering scowled. "Bring us another round, would you?"

Chick disappeared again, and Chief Levering pointed to the table. "Both of you sit and get a grip. Now."

Chick returned a few minutes later with three beers on a tray and left with a muttered, "Do not tear up my place or I'll kick all your asses, cops or not."

"You got it, buddy. No problem." Chief Levering glared down at the table as the door slammed shut. "You finish talking," he charged Jason. Then he directed Scott, "And you don't open your mouth again until he does."

Jason gulped down half a beer before explaining how the CD in Riley's van had begun a chain reaction.

"Damn it." Scott swore, clearly forgetting the part where he was supposed to keep his mouth shut. "I heard something when she cranked up the radio in the car that day, but I never gave it another thought. Just figured one of the kids had been pushing buttons."

"I didn't think you'd heard, but with everything going on I couldn't be sure if you were setting me up or not. I needed to get hold of that CD to find out exactly what was on it."

Scott sank back in the chair, glaring. "That was what you were after."

Jason nodded.

"Well, you got it," Chief Levering said dryly. "Don't keep us in suspense."

"The CD wasn't what I expected." Coming across that CD and learning what it contained were the luckiest breaks he'd had lately. Jason reached inside the inner pocket of his jacket and pulled out an envelope. "Turns out it had nothing to do with me and everything to do with the assholes blackmailing me. Details about operations that went down when they first got into this area nearly three years ago."

That got a reaction. Both Chief Levering and Scott stared at him as he withdrew two burned copies of the CD and slid them across the table. "Here you go."

Scott took it. "Riley had this?"

Jason nodded. "When you hear what's on it, you'll draw the same conclusions I did."

"Cut to the chase," Chief Levering ground out harshly, and Jason didn't miss the way his face had drained of all color, making him look old and tired.

"It had to be Mike's. That's the only way to explain why it surfaced now. Riley must have come across it after she got home. I'm willing to bet money she doesn't have a clue what it is because she'd have never left this sort of incriminating evidence lying around under the car seat. She's a reporter. She's not stupid."

"Incriminating evidence about this DEA agent," Chief Levering repeated.

"And about the people responsible for gunning down Mike."

The sudden silence seemed alive. Then Scott was shaking his head. "No way, man. We brought down everyone. Every damn one."

"That you knew about. Because if you'd have known about the DEA, you'd have fried them like you fried everyone else involved in Mike's murder, and saved me a boatload of trouble."

Jason snorted. "My guess is you didn't know Agent

Asshole was blackmailing a parole officer. But those hoods who recorded this CD did. They detailed everything they might need to make sure they weren't nailed if any shit went down. If you'd known about that parole officer, you'd have blown open this whole thing. I'm thinking Mike must have come across this CD. I'm thinking that's what got him killed."

That silence again. Jason wanted to tell Chief Levering to sit down before he fell down, just as the older man dropped heavily into a chair.

Scott slammed a hand down on the table. "The CD that went missing from the evidence room."

"You knew about it?" Now it was Jason's turn to be surprised.

Scott nodded. "It was the only loose end we had after the investigation. A CD that was picked up in a bust and logged in as evidence. We never could find it."

"What happened?" Jason asked.

"I'm thinking Mike must have taken it home," Chief Levering said.

"Mike would never have taken anything from the property room without signing. He was by the book." Scott scowled. "That CD was never checked out. I know because I went through every damn entry myself."

"It wouldn't have been Mike's job to log it out, but the officer on duty in the property room," Chief Levering pointed out. "We questioned everyone about that CD. Maybe no one could remember anything because someone screwed up. We don't have any clue when Mike might have taken it. And we've got a couple of cops who aren't even with the department anymore. Maybe someone was covering his ass because he screwed up and forgot to log that entry and was afraid to say something."

It happened, Jason knew. Just like he knew if that CD

had been logged out of the property room the way it should have been, Mike Angelica might still be alive and Jason himself wouldn't be staring at the end of his own life as he'd known it.

"And you're willing to testify about all this if I help you set up the DEA?" Chief Levering eyed him levelly.

"I want to cut a deal." There was only one way he stood a chance with Callie. That was by owning up and taking the heat. "I'm not one of these assholes, no matter what you think. I have to try to salvage something from the wreckage. I've got details about the biggest shipment he's brought into the area that I know of. A well-known drug distribution ring operating out of Mexico. Your department will be shining stars."

"Why?" Scott said.

"Why what?"

"Why are you coming to us now? You've known this DEA agent and his team went bad ever since they set you up. Why the change of heart now? Why not *before* you involved Riley—" Scott turned to stare at Jason, understanding all over his face.

Jason didn't have to say a word. He half expected Scott to come after him again, but Scott was already on his feet, cell phone at his ear, voice raw as he barked into the receiver, "Charlie, talk to me. Everything okay there?"

Jason just sat there, feeling sick all over again when Chief Levering's gaze swiveled to him. "Tell me that agent didn't make you target Riley."

He was saved from replying when Scott demanded, "What delivery? Did you check out the driver? What about the flowers?"

Scott shot Jason a gaze that made him marvel at the man's self-control.

"Are you inside yet?" Scott hissed into the receiver. "Is she okay?"

As Scott waited, he covered the receiver and told Chief Levering, "I got a bad feeling. I'm heading back. We can brief for the operation—"

A shock of sound emitted from the phone so loud that even Jason could hear. The phone flew from Scott's hand as he instinctively jerked it from his ear. It hit the table and skittered hard, but Scott caught it in a fast lunge.

"Charlie?" He yelled into the receiver. "Charlie, are you there?" Scott snapped the phone shut, cursing, then jammed a few buttons. He dragged the phone back to his ear. "Come on, Sal."

Chief Levering was already on his feet when Scott announced, "He's not answering, either."

CHAPTER TWENTY

RILEY SET the extravagant basket of flowers on the kitchen table, then stepped back to view the result. She wasn't sure why the *Herald* had sent them. Max had been pleased she'd made her deadline despite stolen equipment, but she didn't think he'd been responsible. It was more likely Shirley Henderson, his assistant.

The card read, *So you know the Herald cares.*

This sweet show of support only added to her conflict about the job. She liked the familiarity and flexibility but didn't want to cover the action anymore. It just wasn't safe. Maybe, like so many areas of her life, the time had come for a new challenge.

She stared outside at her freshly mowed yard shadowed in oncoming dusk and remembered the kids from Renaissance she'd met earlier. They'd worked so hard, had spent hours and hours hacking away brush and weeding beds. They might have looked like hoods that she would have avoided on the street, but they'd been very polite when Scott had introduced them, so appreciative of her efforts when she'd brought them iced tea. Just kids.

They hadn't had the breaks her own kids were getting. Even though losing Mike had unexpectedly and irrevocably altered their family, her kids still had a parent to help them make sense of the tragedy of losing their dad. They had extended family who loved them. They had stability.

Not the kids Riley had met today. She didn't know their individual circumstances the way Scott did, but she knew those kids had been forced to face the hard side of life at too young an age, might not have had parents who loved them or who could take the time to teach them how to live purposeful lives.

That didn't make them bad people. Scott knew that. She liked that about him. And he was right about something else, too. Whatever she decided about her job ultimately, she shouldn't decide because she was scared.

Setting a good example for her kids was the most important thing. She didn't want to teach them to run away from life's difficulties. Move on, yes—sometimes they wouldn't get a choice—but never run because they were scared.

"Riley?" A sharp knock echoed down the hallway. "Open up."

She recognized Charlie's voice. Smiling at that bright floral arrangement, she spun on her heel and headed out of the kitchen. She'd give the circulation desk a call while she was folding the laundry. Shirley would already be gone for the weekend, but Riley would leave a message.

Then the house literally shook beneath her feet. The walls vibrated around her, and a rush of heat filled the hallway as the security alarm, wired to sense fire, shrieked a warning. But Riley didn't need the alarm to know what was happening. She could hear the roar of flames, and froze for an instant, her muscles utterly rigid as panic and reason collided.

Get out. Call 9-1-1.

Her cell phone was in the bedroom. She didn't need it. Charlie or Sal would radio emergency if they hadn't already.

Launching herself into motion again, she covered the distance to the front door in a few bounding steps. She flipped the dead bolt and yanked the door wide.

She expected to find Charlie, but not lying in a heap on the floor. For another stunned instant she stared down at the collapsed officer on her front porch. How had the explosion harmed him here when she hadn't been hurt inside the house?

She noticed the cell phone discarded beside him, and the ajar porch door just as it swung wide, slamming into her with such force that she rocked backward. Staggering to catch her balance, her feet tangled in Charlie's inert form, and she yelped, bracing herself as she fell.

"Sorry, ma'am." Strong hands grabbed her arm, dragged her upright with enough force to nearly yank her shoulder from its socket. Riley cried out again, glancing up to find a muscular man in a paramedic uniform hanging on to her.

He pulled her through the open doorway, then let the door swing shut again. Charlie disappeared from sight.

"I'm okay," she insisted over the steady shriek of the security alarm. "But Charlie—"

"Don't worry, ma'am. He'll be taken care of," the paramedic said coolly. "Right now we need to assess your condition."

Don't worry? Her house was burning down and there was a family friend lying unconscious on her porch floor. *Don't worry?*

Riley glanced around, the panic tightening like a vise around her chest. She struggled to draw in a good breath, to make sense of the sight before her.

An ambulance idled beside the police cruiser in the driveway, but she didn't see any sign of Sal, who'd ridden with Charlie. Had he radioed in the explosion? Was that how the ambulance had gotten here so quickly?

"The fire department—?"

"Already on its way," the paramedic said, steering her around the cruiser and toward the ambulance.

She noticed another man behind the wheel of the emergency vehicle, but something wasn't right. Riley didn't know what it was, only that panic was well and truly taking hold of her.

Something wasn't right.

That thought lodged in her brain as she stumbled along on clumsy feet as the paramedic rushed her toward the ambulance, keeping up a steady stream of chatter. How had it gotten here so quickly? Even if Charlie had radioed the instant he'd heard the explosion…

Charlie was unconscious. Unconscious? Or dead?

The thought finally pierced Riley's confusion, and she pulled away. The man's grip was a vise around her upper arm. When she resisted, he simply tightened his grip and lent his considerable bulk to the cause, shoving her toward the waiting ambulance.

"Come on, ma'am. We need to check you out."

"Let me go." She fought with every ounce of her strength, kicking out as the certainty that something was terribly wrong drove away all thoughts of the man on her porch and the fire raging in her kitchen.

"Sal," she screamed, relieved by the power of her voice. If he didn't hear her, someone else might. "Sal. Help me."

As quickly as she started fighting, Riley stopped, becoming a dead weight against the man's grip, drawing on every ounce of defense training Mike had ever taught her. The paramedic staggered, caught by surprise, his balance uncertain. Riley slammed the heel of her hand into his face while pulling away. She heard a sickening crunch, and the man grunted loudly. This time she broke free.

Lunging into motion, she managed to get almost to the cruiser when the sound of a blaring horn startled her. But she didn't even flinch, just kept running.

Until the paramedic tackled her.

The breath fled her lungs with a whoosh as his muscular frame slammed into her, knocked her to the ground. She hit the concrete hard enough to make her see stars, and for a stunned instant she didn't move, didn't fight back.

That was all he needed to drag her upright by the hair. In one skilled move, he locked his arm around her throat and half dragged, half carried her to the ambulance.

He hefted her up and tossed her inside without a word. She landed in a heap, her chest still seized around a breath. She couldn't expel any air, couldn't drag any in.

He slammed the doors shut, sealing her in darkness. Then the vehicle accelerated with the screech of tires, and Riley was slammed backward, hitting something—a gurney, she thought. With her feet, she anchored herself upright, fighting unconsciousness, refusing to leave herself so vulnerable. She needed to remain alert, to look for the opportunity to escape, or at the very least signal help.

Scott.

Just the thought of him helped focus her, and she fought for that breath, to control her panic and fear, to relax her chest enough to breathe, breathe, *breathe*.

In slow degrees, the vise eased. Oxygen flooded back into her lungs, sharpened her vision, or maybe she was just growing accustomed to the darkness. She willed herself to think, though her brain didn't seem to be working yet. The lack of oxygen or the fear, she didn't know.

She just knew she couldn't panic. Who had her and why? The medical scam she'd been investigating? The ambulance. Made sense. Her abductors were professional.

That much she knew. This was no random abduction but a well-planned attack.

The ambulance skidded around a curve so hard Riley flung an arm out to brace herself. The gurney rattled noisily. Equipment, wires and hoses and belts, swung wildly until the ambulance righted itself. They were probably taking the curve near Mrs. Haslam's place.

She tried to focus, but disjointed thoughts kept racing through her head. Thank God the kids were away. If they had been inside the house, that explosion... She hadn't been able to protect herself. Thank God the kids were with Rosie and Joe. They were the only things that mattered. She could live without the house, without her mementoes of life with Mike. As long as she had her kids and her memories.

An emergency siren screeched, and for a heart-stopping second, Riley felt a wave of hope so strong, she gasped aloud. Help had arrived. Scott had come.

She knew he would find her.

Then she realized the sound was coming from *this* ambulance, a diversion that would give her abductors the advantage.

With a cry, she flung herself at the doors, hoping to unlock them. It didn't matter how fast they drove. She'd throw herself into the path of oncoming traffic if it would get her out of this ambulance before they merged onto Mountain Road, which would lead them to the Taconic Parkway where her abductors could drive eighty miles an hour to anywhere they wanted.

She pulled on the door latches, tears springing to her eyes when they levered ineffectually against her grip.

Locked.

She pounded her fists against the door, drawing a laugh

from one of the men in the cab, a laugh she could hear over the blaring siren and the sounds of two sweet little voices.

"Mommy died. Mommy died like Daddy."

CHAPTER TWENTY-ONE

"CAN'T YOU GET THEM on the radio yet?" Scott demanded.

"Damn it." The chief braced himself against the dashboard as the cruiser's wheels lifted off the ground, then landed again with a jarring thump. "No wonder you can't keep a partner when you drive like this."

Scott didn't comment. He was too focused on keeping the car on the road after his left wheel caught the shoulder, kicking up gravel and dirt and practically ripping the steering wheel from his grasp. From Chick's in the Valley to Riley's house was barely a five-minute drive, but all of Traver Road wound through a mixture of hilly woods and farmland. Not an easy road to travel at high speed, especially when it was getting dark.

The chief's answer was to radio through to dispatch again.

"Still no contact with Charlie's unit, but we've got our first report of a fire at Riley's address," the chief said grimly. "A neighbor. She wanted to know why the ambulance took off before the fire truck got there."

"How the hell did the paramedics get there when they're still two minutes behind us?" Scott glanced away from the road and found the chief staring back, gaze narrowing.

Strangely, Scott had Jason to thank for being with the chief right now. And he couldn't think of anyone he'd rather have sitting beside him. Except for Mike. Not when his heart was pounding the rapid-fire rhythm of an automatic weapon. Not when only long years of training kept him focused with the roar of that explosion looping in his memory. The sound of Charlie cursing. Then the awful silence.

Having the chief beside him took some of the pressure off. Scott didn't have to think of everything. He didn't have to explain himself. He didn't have to battle through this unfamiliar panic. Together he and the chief wouldn't miss any detail with Riley at risk.

"Sheriff's got units on the way," the chief said.

Scott nodded and slowed enough to take the switchback turn, the last turn before the farm.

He spotted the smoke coiling from the back of the house before turning into the driveway. He hissed in relief that the entire house wasn't up in flames. Charlie's cruiser sat unmanned. Beside it was a dark stain he couldn't quite make out in the fading light. Blood?

His heart thudded a single hard beat, but he didn't get a chance to put his gearshift into Park before the porch door burst wide and Sal appeared, one side of his face angry and swollen.

But no blood.

"We were sandbagged," he called out. "Two men disguised as paramedics. Armed and dangerous. Professional. She's gone. They took her in an ambulance. Toward Freedom Road."

"Was she hurt in the explosion?" Scott asked.

"I'm sorry. I didn't see her. I came around when the ambulance was pulling out."

"Charlie?" the chief called through the open window.

"Unconscious. Got a pulse. I'll get him out." Sal waved them toward the road. "They're not two, maybe three minutes ahead of you. Go, go, go."

"Fire department is right behind us. Sheriff, too."

With a scowl Sal waved them off again, and Scott shoved the gearshift into Reverse and gunned the engine. He corrected the wheel and spun back onto Traver Road. He could hear the wail of sirens in the distance.

The fire department, most likely.

He didn't think, just drove while the chief put an APB out on the ambulance. Three minutes could mean the difference between Riley's life and death.

Scott gained time on the open stretch that ran alongside a dairy farm on approach to the turn at Freedom Road. No sight of the ambulance, but a choice of three different roads.

"Taconic?" the chief asked.

"They're not going far in an ambulance," Scott said. "They'll have to make a switch somewhere. The nearest medical facility is an urgent care on Route 55."

The chief placed the emergency light on the dash as Scott slowed to maneuver the intersection. He was about to gun the engine and speed toward LaGrange when he caught sight of fresh tire tracks in the field off the shoulder, as if someone had pulled off the road in a hurry.

"Get an ID on that ambulance," he ground between clenched teeth. He didn't want to be responsible for running down a legitimate emergency vehicle and possibly killing someone.

Instinct had him making a wide turn down Mountain Road, which led straight toward the Taconic Parkway. The back of his neck prickled as he scanned the area, taking in the rising and rolling hills that blocked the distance from view. The sprawling barns that dotted those slopes.

Kondas Brothers' Dairy Farm.

The perfect place to make a switch?

"Vassar Hospital is missing an emergency unit." The

chief grabbed the overhead handle when Scott turned off the road into the field. The car's suspension bucked wildly as he descended the first slope, but while the ruts faded, he could easily follow the indentations in the grass.

There were houses in the distance, likely the folks who owned the farm. But an ambulance could have easily hidden behind either, especially the ranch-style house on the highest rise before the forested slope of the mountain began.

Scott circled the first of the two barns and just as he made the curve, a vehicle cut him off.

"Shit." He jammed his foot on the brake as a pricey four-wheel-drive with tinted windows narrowly missed his quarter panel.

It must have been lying in wait, watching their approach, and now it circled around and bore down on them, keeping them occupied as an ambulance started bouncing wildly down the hill to get away.

"There she is," the chief said, on the radio again, this time calling for backup.

Scott's pulse slammed against his inner ears, the rush of blood throbbing so loud he could barely hear the roar of the engine as he spun the wheel again, tires grinding through dirt and grass as the car spun in a three-sixty. He managed to avoid taking a hit by the taller vehicle.

But as he jammed his foot on the gas, intent upon shooting out of the 4X4's way, he heard the chief issue a stream of curses. Scott glanced out of the corner of his eye…just as the ambulance sent dirt spewing upward as tires skidded along the ground, vainly spinning for purchase.

His heart stopped beating as the back of the ambulance pitched over the lip of a small gulley and went straight down.

"Shit," the chief ground out as the crash resounded through the field, and all they could see of the ambulance was the underbelly of the cab pointing straight toward the sky and the tires spinning in the air.

Riley.

Scott was so focused on the ambulance that he didn't see the 4X4 spin out in reverse. He gunned the engine to get out of the way, but several gunshots rang out, distracting him. The steering wheel bucked in his hands, and he fought to stop the car as the 4X4 rear-ended him hard. Once. Twice. Each crash resounding louder than the last as it finally pushed his front end through the fence and into the side of the barn.

Wood splintered around them. Glass shattered when some sort of shelving collapsed, spewing glass all over the hood of the cruiser. Scott slammed the car into Reverse and glanced in his rearview mirror simultaneously.

Sure enough, the 4X4 had bought enough time to speed to the ambulance. It stopped in front of the wreck, blocking it from view.

"Go, go, go," the chief yelled as Scott gunned the engine. More wood splintered. Something was trapping the front bumper, and Scott had to rock the car to break free.

He cleared the fence, but not before the 4X4 circled the gulley, its back door slamming shut as it took off with a shuddering jolt and began a speeding ascent toward the houses.

"Riley?" Scott followed the 4X4 automatically, but had no way of knowing if they'd taken her or left her in the ambulance.

"I don't know," the chief said. "Give me the wheel."

Scott pulled the cruiser in front of the crash site and ground to a halt. He jumped out, and the chief took his place in the driver's seat. The entire exchange had taken only seconds, but already the 4X4 was disappearing up the slope. If it headed into the woods, the chief might lose them completely.

"Riley," he yelled. His entire body started to shake when he glanced down to see how tightly the ambulance was wedged in the gulley, the clearance so compressed it would take heavy machinery to remove it.

The only luck had been the backward descent. Had it gone in cab first, the ambulance would have likely exploded on impact.

"Riley?" Scott called again as he yanked back the door of the cab. "Riley, are you here?"

Silence.

"Riley." He tried to gauge the stability of the vehicle, but with the darkness descending, he could only see shadows. He scrambled gingerly into the cab, relieved when the vehicle seemed solid, shoving aside radio equipment that hung from the instrument panel. He sprawled across the front seat and peered down into the darkness.

"Riley."

No reply. Then, after a breathless instant, Scott heard movement. A metallic clatter. The thud of some smaller items hitting the back door. Then a moan.

"Riley." No longer a question, but a sigh. "Riley, are you injured? We have to get you out of here. Can you move?"

"Scott?" She sounded a little dazed but alive.

Alive.

"Yeah, it's me," he choked out, the words lodging in his throat. "Are you hurt? Talk to me."

"No, no. I'm okay."

His eyes shuttered instinctively, a prayer of thanksgiving.

"You're here."

"I'm here." Those words tangled with a breath in his

throat, threatened to choke him. Or was that relief because she was alive? "I'm here. I'll help you climb out. Or do you need me to come down to you?"

"No. No. I'm okay."

"Is there anything on top of you? Anything I need to move?"

He heard her grunt of effort then the sound of something heavy being shoved aside. "If I can swing my legs around…" Her words trailed off.

"Just go slowly. Make sure you're okay."

The shuffling sounds of her maneuvering. He prayed the doors underneath her were solidly locked or crushed shut against the gulley bottom. There was no way to know.

"Got it. I'm okay. Just a little banged up."

Thank God. "Okay, good. Can you see my hands?"

He forced himself to remain calm, to keep his voice steady when his heart was pounding too hard and his throat was tight. Anchoring his thighs against the backrest of the seat, he leaned down into the darkness, stretching his arms out before him.

Her hair was a pale blur in the shadows, a beacon that drew him toward her. "I want you to grab on to me. I'll pull you out."

His lungs compressed against another crushing wave of emotion, making it so hard to breathe as he waited.

Then her fingers were brushing his, soft, warm, and he was threading his hands firmly around her wrists as if his life depended on it.

"Riley." His voice was a whisper in the darkness as he pulled her up inch by inch. She used her feet to find footholds, to steady herself against the equipment that shifted with their movements, impeded the speed of their progress.

But she came to him. Slowly, ever so slowly she

emerged until he was forced to slide out of the cab to bring her the rest of the way.

"You got her, Scott?" The chief's voice called out and a flashlight beam slashed through the darkness.

"Yeah, I got her. I guess that means you didn't find them."

The chief gave a grunt and didn't bother replying. He just shone the flashlight into the cab. "Need a hand?"

"Yeah. If you could hang on to me while I pull her out."

A few solid moves and they had Riley seated in the grass, looking unsteady but alive.

"You need medical attention." The chief sliced his light across her.

"No, no. I'm okay. I'm okay. The house. And Charlie."

She could barely get the words out. She was going into shock if she wasn't there already. Scott knelt beside her and shoved hair from her face, running his fingers along her temples, her cheeks, down her neck, over her shoulders. He could feel nothing but the smooth curves of this beautiful woman, this beautiful, breathing woman.

"Anything hurt?"

"No. Really, I'm okay."

"What about the explosion at the house?"

She shook her head. "Charlie called me. I was out of the kitchen when the fire started. He was…hurt."

"He's fine," the chief reassured her. "In a real ambulance on the way to a real hospital, but he'll be okay. His head's as hard as a rock. Trust me. And your house…well, from what I hear, the only damage is in the kitchen. And the smoke. Don't worry. We'll lock it up tight."

"Lock it up," she repeated. "No. I need to go home. Brian will be coming home to deal with the horses."

"You need to be checked out, Riley," the chief said sternly, glancing at the ambulance. "You may be concussed—"

"Chief, I didn't hit my head. Honestly, you two, I'm okay. Just banged up a bit. I'll go see my doctor tomorrow."

"Tomorrow's Saturday."

"Then I'll have my brother-in-law check me out if something doesn't feel right. All I want to do is go home."

The chief cut a meaningful glance at Scott, who said, "Listen, Riley. You and I are going to take a ride. I'll give Brian a call on the way. Sound good?"

She turned those sparkling eyes to his, and even in the darkness he could see the shock taking hold. She was running on adrenaline at the moment, but he needed to get her someplace safe, where he could assess her before she crashed.

"Backup on the way?" he asked the chief, who nodded.

"Go. Trooper's pulling off the Taconic. Two minutes max."

Scott slipped an arm beneath Riley's and helped her stand.

The chief came at her from the other side and they guided her back to his cruiser. She quickly strapped herself into the passenger seat.

The chief shut the door on her and met Scott's gaze. "This cruiser took a beating tonight. Is it still going to get you where you need to go, or do I need to call in—"

"It'll be fine. I don't want to wait."

"Then let me know where you wind up."

Scott circled the car. He slipped behind the wheel, then headed out of the dark field and back onto the road. He saw the trooper's visibar flashing in his rearview mirror as he sped toward Overlook Road, wanting to avoid Riley's place, which would still be surrounded with emergency vehicles.

She didn't need any more surprises tonight.

He gave Brian a synopsis of the situation and worked out an arrangement for the kid to deal with the horses and pick up some things while a patrol unit stayed tonight. He told Brian to go to his parents' or a friend's to sleep, then meet up with another patrol in the morning. Just until they had a lock on the men who'd abducted Riley.

That wouldn't happen until they rounded up everyone at Jason's bust.

"Okay, Brian's all set," he told her.

"The kids, Scott," she said, voice shaky. "They're going to call so I can tell them good-night."

He held up his phone. "Want me to call Joe?"

She shook her head. "I need to talk to them."

He handed her the phone, frowning when her hand shook. "You're still feeling okay? Not dizzy or anything, are you?"

"No. I'm okay. Really."

But she struggled to dial. He knew what was happening—the adrenaline was wearing off. He knew because his was on the way out, too.

Yet she was so determined. Cradling the phone against her ear, she rested her head against the window and closed her eyes. "Hi, sweet pea. It's Mommy," she spoke softly, looking so relieved. "You and Camille okay?"

Scott drove through the city, listening to her as she mothered her kids long distance, talking to them in turns, getting excited as they related their stories of the day, loving them, all while her hands trembled and her breath came in ragged bursts. They had no clue about what had happened tonight. How close they came to losing their only remaining parent. She bore that burden right now. Alone.

"I love you so much," she finally said. "Call me if you need me. But call me at Uncle Scott's number, okay? I misplaced my phone. I know, silly Mommy. I love you. Tell Jake I love him, too. Sweet dreams, pretty. I'll talk with you in the morning."

Then she flipped the phone shut. She just held it in her

lap as if it were a solid connection to her kids. She never opened her eyes.

"Joe and Rosie?" he asked.

"I'll tell them when I talk with them next. No need to stress them out just yet."

Scott wasn't surprised she was thinking about others, even when she was coming apart herself. But she was so still as he drove through the city to the outskirts of town.

The silence was complete, as if someone had pressed a mute function. The blue and red blasts of the emergency light sliced through the darkness at rhythmic intervals, the only sign of life except for the sound of Riley's shallow breathing.

He wanted her safe. He thought about taking her straight to a hospital, but didn't want her exposed until the chief had a lock on the situation. He compromised. Putting a call in to Brian's father, Scott made arrangements for Alex to check Riley out in his office at the hospital. She argued, but Scott didn't want to find out that she was more banged up than he could handle without assistance.

After a perfunctory examination, Alex declared Riley in the clear of any major trauma and let Scott take her. Then he drove to the only safe place he could think of. Wheeling off Salt Point Turnpike, he headed down a dirt road. The path followed a creek that wound through the parcel of wooded acreage, not too far from the Clinton townline.

He pulled up in front of the stone bungalow that overlooked the creek, a place that had once been a guesthouse for the larger residence on these acres.

Riley never asked where they were, and he understood why the minute he opened her door.

She was shaking, a lot.

"Come on. It's just mild shock. Alex said to expect that, so don't worry." He hoped. "We'll get you feeling better."

With his arm tightly around her, he helped her climb the front steps. He unlocked the door, flipped on a light then led her straight into the living room.

"Sit. I'll be right back." Scott headed into the kitchen, turned on the stove light and pulled open the refrigerator. Where was it… There. He withdrew a cardboard container, remnants of takeout dinner from the Canton, his favorite Chinese place in downtown Poughkeepsie.

Pouring the broth into a mug, he withheld the wontons then shoved the mug in the microwave to nuke for a few minutes.

He went to the bedroom and yanked the comforter off the bed, then brought it to Riley, who gazed up at him, plaintive eyes gleaming in the darkness.

"I c-can't s-stop shaking."

"You need a nest." With a hand on her shoulder, he helped her lean forward so he could wrap the comforter around her. Then he slipped off her shoes. "Pull up your legs."

He tucked her feet beneath the heavy comforter, too, then went to retrieve the broth when the microwave beeped.

"Drink some of this."

She shook her head, tangled blond hair coiling around her neck. "N-not h-hungry."

"I know. Trust me. It'll help."

She couldn't hold the mug, so Scott sank down beside her and pulled her onto his lap. Slipping his hands over hers, he helped her steady the mug as she brought it to her lips.

"Just take small sips."

The glow from the kitchen barely penetrated the living room, and he willed the dark quiet to calm her, calm *him*. The adrenaline was wearing off too fast, leaving him wired and overwhelmed by how close he'd come to losing her.

The memory of that ambulance… It was a miracle she was alive, unharmed.

"It's okay," he crooned in a whisper against her hair, as much to himself as to her. "Everything is okay now."

He tried to block out the memory of staring down into the darkness of the ambulance, not knowing if he would find her, and if he did whether she'd be alive or dead. He just focused on the way she folded into the curve of his body, fitting neatly against him as if she belonged there.

"N-no m-more," she said weakly, pushing the mug away after only a few sips.

He didn't try to convince her otherwise, even though her tremors were growing more violent rather than less. He set the broth down on the coffee table and ran his hands over her shoulders, down her arms. He tried to warm her, wanted to soothe her fears away.

"Shh. Everything is okay now," he whispered over and over.

But it wasn't. Tremors became spasms. Her teeth chattered.

"F-freezing."

Had he made the wrong choice by bringing her here? For an instant of blinding uncertainty, Scott froze with his arms around her. Should he call 9-1-1 or take her to the emergency room?

No. Alex would never have let Riley leave the hospital if she wasn't okay. Until the chief called, she was safest here. If the DEA was responsible for her abduction—and who else would be so skilled as to make use of emergency equipment for a kidnapping?—Scott had no way of knowing how ambitious they would be. If that CD was the reason Mike had been killed, then Scott couldn't take any chances with Riley's safety.

But once this was done, he would kill Jason Kenney himself.

Riley's spasms and chattering teeth gave way to dry, heaving breaths, and Scott shifted out from under her, reached down and lifted her into his arms.

"It's okay," he crooned, over and over, willing her to believe him, willing her to calm in his arms.

The need to do something finally spurred him to his feet and he carried her into the bathroom, cradled her against him as he shoved open the shower door so hard the glass rattled in its frame, and turned on the water one-handed. Soon clouds of steam billowed from the stall, and he shoved the comforter off her, kicked it away, along with his shoes.

"Close your eyes." He stepped under the spray, and she buried her face against his chest.

Hot water pounded, quickly soaking their clothes, the fluid heat blasting through fabric and skin, a heat to sink bone deep.

Riley's hair plastered against her head, the water turning natural curls into dark, unfamiliar waves that twined around her cheeks and neck and made her skin seem unnaturally pale. Her thick lashes formed dark crescents beneath her eyes, and she nestled closer against him as though they might actually fuse into one so she could share his warmth.

And she trembled.

Scott had no clue how long they stood there, him crooning nonsense, his hands never ceasing their travels over the smooth curves of her back, her arms, anywhere he could reach while still holding her tight. He couldn't stop touching her.

He'd never known such powerful relief, a sensation that robbed him of reason, of speech, of everything but the knowledge that she was *alive,* here in his arms, and for this moment, this forbidden moment, he could touch her. He could inhale the scent of her hair, caress the slick wetness of her neck. Pretend that he had every right to feel the way he did.

Scott was so caught up in his own thoughts he didn't notice her trembling had eased until it stopped completely. He was so caught up in the feel of her body that he didn't notice when her hands had joined his, traveling over his wet clothes, trailing along his shoulders and down his back, mirroring his strokes.

He only came fully to his senses when she started to move, pushing out of his arms and stretching her legs underneath her. She slid down the length of his body, ready to stand on her own. And he steadied her during the descent when their sodden clothes dragged together, her shirt pulling up to reveal flashes of her smooth stomach, the strap of her bra. He stood transfixed by the long, sensuous unfolding of sleek curves and firm muscles. But Scott knew exactly when Riley came back to herself.

She tilted her face up and kissed him.

CHAPTER TWENTY-TWO

THE EVENTS OF THE NIGHT FADED. Her racing thoughts. The anxiety. The fear. All gone beneath the steady pounding of the hot water.

Riley was tired, so tired, but the heat and the feel of Scott's strong arms around her anchored her to the moment. A moment where she was safe and standing in the only place in the world she wanted to be.

The feeling didn't make sense. Not if she started picking it apart with her head, but Riley knew her body. And just as she'd been certain she hadn't sustained any hidden injuries from the night's events, she knew that being in Scott's arms was exactly where she should be.

She couldn't think beyond that. Wouldn't. She had only this second. Didn't want reason. Didn't want any more fear or worry. She wanted to feel the way she felt right now.

Good.

She never dreamed her body would ever awaken, would ever feel alive this way again. But the water warmed her until the heat became so much more, a fire that pulsed thickly through her veins, until all she was aware of was the strength of Scott's arms around her, the way he held her close.

She might come up with a thousand reasons why she shouldn't feel this way. Scott might refuse to discuss the awareness that had flared between them so unexpectedly. But she recognized this feeling on a purely instinctive level.

This wasn't fear. This wasn't weakness. This wasn't grief.

This was *want*.

She wouldn't resist. Not now. Not after tonight. Not after the twists and turns her life had taken the past few years. She'd learned one valuable lesson at least, and she wouldn't waste a second because she might not get another.

So she stretched languidly against him, forced him to let her down, greedy to feel him against her, to discover the hard contours of his body, to test this awareness and learn if he was as aware of her as she of him.

She hoped. The intensity surprised her.

Her feet touched the floor of the shower stall, but his arms still held her steady, so she rose up on her tiptoes and pressed her mouth to his.

He tasted wet with the water that sluiced over them, so unfamiliar yet so male. And for a stunning instant, Riley simply stood there, waiting for him to react. Her breath trapped in her lungs. Her heartbeats throbbed hard between them.

Then he sucked in a sharp breath that stole hers. And his mouth came against hers with such unmistakable need that a memory of the hurricane chamber at the Florida science museum flashed in her head, of hundred-mile-an-hour winds whipping around with fierce intensity. The way Scott seemed to explode around her as if his need had been so tightly contained one touch was all it took to shatter his control.

Suddenly his hands were everywhere, one banding around her waist, the other spearing into her wet hair, and he brought her up against him with a force that dragged another gasp from her, a crazy exhalation that burst against his lips. His body was a solid wall of muscle, wholly unfamiliar with its long contours. Tall, lean strength. So much contained power.

He kissed her with a possession that surprised her. Their tongues tangled as their lips glided silkily beneath the steady stream of water. Until Riley could taste this kiss in the pit of her stomach, in the wild heat pooling even lower, in the way her legs grew molten and heavy beneath her.

She could only sink against him for support, suddenly unsteady, but she found no respite because he leaned back to brace himself against the wall, an action that crushed her breasts to his chest. Her stomach cradled the hardness of his growing desire. Her thighs stretched out against him with an intimacy that was intensely physical.

Riley couldn't think, only feel, knew a need to touch him that drowned out everything else. Her breath fluttered in her throat, and with a forbidden thrill as she slid her hands between them, coaxed her fingers beneath the dripping hem of his shirt and brought her hands in contact with his bare skin.

His stomach contracted at her touch, a hard expanse of muscle that invited exploration. She skimmed her hands upward, felt the crisp ruffling of hair beneath her palms, the hollows of definition, the supple skin that barely masked the throbbing heartbeat and told Riley he felt her touch the way she felt his. She dragged her palms slowly over his nipples, shivered when his low moan burst against her lips.

Suddenly his hands were on her face, dragging her mouth more deeply into their kiss, and the force of his need sparked her own until she gasped, the ache inside suddenly overwhelming.

Slipping her arms around his waist, she let her hands glide over his butt, tightly encased in wet jeans. She pressed him close, rocking her hips to ease the need within.

Scott followed her lead because his hands began a traveling descent, raking down her throat with firm strokes, over her shoulders and down her back. They mirrored each other stroke for stroke, drank in the long-forgotten feel of arousal.

Scott sighed against her lips, and then his hands were everywhere. Reaching for the hem of her shirt and tugging it upward. She raised her arms into the air to assist, and he broke their kiss to drag her sodden shirt over her head. It hit the floor with a wet thud. Her bra followed. She worked the buttons on his shirt until she could shove the whole wet mess over his shoulders and down his arms, baring the expanse of his chest.

Then, as if they'd been magnetized, they came together, their bodies drawing close, the tips of her breasts pressed against his warm, wet skin.

Now it was her turn to gasp. His hands contained such unleashed strength as he caressed her back, her waist, her ribs. He stroked the undersides of her breasts and she trembled, such a blatant admission of her desire.

She wanted him. He wanted her. That much she knew.

There were no questions, no indecision.

Only too many clothes.

Popping the button at her waist, she worked her dress slacks over her hips. They were so weighted with water they slipped down her legs with little effort. Scott's jeans proved much more of a challenge, and Riley sank to her knees to peel away the stubborn fabric, freeing his maleness with an intimate touch that made her heart beat so hard it actually hurt.

His groan carried over the sound of the pulsing water, and she glanced up, startled, aware of this desire. She wasn't the only one. His eyes fluttered shut, as if he was too overwhelmed, too caught up to resist.

She didn't want him to. She wanted him to give way to

this pleasure. Didn't want to think, didn't want to be re-minded that anything but the two of them existed right now, and the unexpected surprise of what burned between them.

She couldn't resist trailing her mouth down the length of his thigh, entertaining herself with this slow task, smiling when a shiver rocked his entire body.

Impatiently, he kicked away the jeans, then dragged her up against him. His breathing grew ragged, his chest heaving as their slick skin came together in a fluid glide. Riley could feel him everywhere, feel his whipcord arms bracing her closer, ever closer. His eager hands exploring her with greedy abandon. The heavy length of his need branding her with its heat.

She just melted against him, so caught up in the moment, in the feel of him. What else could she do in the face of such unexpected, powerful need? Only give in. She had no fight left. Not tonight.

Pressing kisses along his shoulder, she tasted the pulse at the hollow of this throat. Her body was alive with desire, awakened to a need she hadn't known existed. She'd for-gotten that she was a living, breathing woman.

A woman who wanted this man.

Riley wasn't the only one who wanted. With an abrupt-ness that startled her, Scott broke away. She heard the faucet snap shut. The water stopped its flow and the shower door shot open. He stepped through, dripping everywhere and not seeming to care. He didn't grab towels. He didn't say a word. He simply reached for her hand to lead her from the stall, then lifted her into his arms.

The cool air assaulted her. Burying her face against his neck, Riley tried to contain the trembling that had begun again, a trembling so different from the physical reaction that had rocked her earlier.

This time she felt only eager.

There was no question. No need for discussion. There was no past between them. No worries about the future. There was only right here and right now. The soft bed beneath her. And then Scott's warm, wet body surrounding her, so hard and heavy in all the right places.

SCOTT STARED INTO his dark bedroom. Not morning yet, which bought him a little more time. Stolen time. Time to imprint in his memory the way Riley felt in his arms. Her sleek curves pressed against him. Her thigh casually tossed over his. Her cheek pressed to his shoulder. Her arm draped across his waist. The shiny hair that had dried into wild disarray.

He smiled into the darkness. Her hair was everywhere. Draped over the pillow. Trapped behind her shoulder. Tucked around his neck. Even in his face. Whenever she moved those spun silk curls would go into his mouth and up his nose. He kept trying to blow them away so he wouldn't sneeze and wake her.

He didn't want to do anything to bring an end to this night any faster than it was already coming.

He had no justification for his actions. No excuse that would wash. He'd been so affected by his fear for her that when she'd kissed him, he'd flat-out lost it.

How could he resist Riley?

He couldn't. He'd lost control, plain and simple.

Scott's eyes squeezed shut against the emotion, a brutal combination of relief and awe and gratitude and an unavoidable truth. A truth he wanted to block out for a little longer.

The night would only complicate things between them. Try though he might, he'd been projecting his feelings for

Riley ever since he'd realized how he felt about her. It was only natural she'd react. His need for her was so powerful.

And that's where the guilt was coming from. It wasn't about Mike, which surprised Scott. It was all about Riley. She deserved someone so much better. A man from a normal family, not someone who would only open the door to a world she'd been lucky enough to avoid.

She shifted again, this time nestling her face into the crook of his shoulder. After she was comfortable again, she exhaled a sigh that warmed his skin. Scott held her. Just held her. Tried to burn the feel of her silky curves into his brain. The way she stretched out against him, all sleek, toned skin. The arm that draped across his stomach, hand outstretched, fingers curled ever so slightly. The slim foot she rested on his ankle. The annoying little curls that kept tickling his nose.

The darkness began to fade beyond the blinds. Morning had finally come. Scott pressed his lips to her head, smiled when she sighed. Then he untangled himself from her and slid from the bed. He had a job to do.

To protect the woman he loved.

Scott made coffee and started with the phone calls. He needed to get a grip on himself, to get his head back in the real world before tackling the shower with its memories of Riley. Trembling from shock. Trembling from desire.

She was still sleeping when he finally emerged and dressed quietly, hoping not to disturb her, and he'd have left her that way, except this time when his cell rang the call was for her.

"Riley." He knelt beside the bed, not trusting himself near her, not when he still ached to touch her. "Kids on the phone."

Though she'd been dead asleep, she instantly blinked to awareness. Scott placed the phone in her hand, unable to take his eyes off her.

She was gorgeous with a drowsy-soft expression, mouth still full and pink from his kisses, bare shoulders peeping through the wild mass of her hair, which had dried into a shape not unlike that of the pillow.

He put some distance between them, half sitting against the dresser while she talked with each kid in turn, gave reminders about their plans for the day.

And loved them so completely.

It was in everything she said, the look on her face, the tone of her voice. Such a loving woman, so willing and passionate in his arms.

And she finally sat up, looking like a fantasy that had parked square in the middle of his bed. She wrapped the comforter around her, and it drooped in places that gave him choice views of bare curves and tan skin.

He left the room and poured coffee, which he brought to her. Lifting her gaze to his, eyes sparkling, she smiled a smile of such welcome that his heart gave a single hard beat.

She took a sip, then another, looking grateful. Then she was kissing the kids goodbye and flipping the phone shut.

"Good morning," she said huskily.

"Good morning." He folded his arms over his chest and filled her in on the news. He didn't give her a chance to address the night, interjected reality between them as a distraction—for her and for him. "Charlie's home. Concussed but completely fine. So no worries there."

"You've been working this morning?"

He nodded.

"Do you have any idea who those men were last night?"

Given his way, Scott would have let Riley believe the pharmaceutical story she'd been working on had invited the trouble. He didn't want to reopen old wounds about Mike based on Jason Kenney's word. At least until after the bust when Scott and the chief could break open Mike's case again and go through everything until they figured out exactly what had gone on.

But Riley was a reporter. And a good one at that. She wanted answers. As much as he wanted to spare her the uncertainties, he wouldn't outright lie to her.

"It's a long story, Riley. The chief and I don't have all the pieces in place, and a lot of what we do have I can't tell you yet. Not until after tonight."

"What happens tonight?"

"Undercover bust with Hazard Creek PD."

"You're going?"

He nodded. "The chief needs a strong team. We'll be dealing with some skilled criminals. We don't want any gunplay."

She sank back against the pillows and took a swig of coffee. "Hazard Creek, hmm. Did I step into something the day I showed up to cover that DEA bust?"

"Yes and no. I'm sorry to be cryptic, but I don't have all the answers. Let's just say it wasn't all about the bust."

"So it wasn't the pharmaceutical story I was working on?"

"No. Doesn't look like a story you were working on at all."

She was silent for a moment, staring down into her coffee mug, looking thoughtful. Then she said, "What about me? If you're working tonight, does that mean no one's after me?"

He forced himself to meet her gaze, felt her hope deep down in his gut. He wanted to sit next to her, take her in his arms and reassure her. He gripped the edge of the dresser to keep himself from going to her. "I've made arrangements for you to catch up with Joe and Rosie in the city."

"You told them what's going on?"

He shook his head. "They already knew. Alex told Caroline after we left last night—"

"Got it." She held up a hand to stop his explanation.

"I gave Joe a call this morning to fill him in. Sal and Janet are going to pick you up at noon and drive you into the city. You'll catch up with everyone and stay there until we get the situation under control. How does that sound?"

"Sal and Janet are staying, too?"

He nodded, watching the understanding dawn on her beautiful face. "The chief sent a disaster recovery company to your house this morning to assess the damage. They met up with Brian when he came over to feed the horses. Your insurance will handle it. You'll get a new kitchen and a clean house out of the deal. The bomb was meant more as a diversion than anything else."

"Good to know that no one wanted me dead."

Scott didn't point out that if they had, they'd have had ample opportunity to kill her yesterday. Not when the thought made him grip the dresser even harder.

"Please tell him thanks for me when you next talk to him."

"I will."

"And Janet and Sal are coming for me at noon?"

He nodded. "Are you hungry? I can fix you something to eat while you get ready."

"No thanks." She set the mug aside and glanced around. "Is this your place?"

He nodded again.

"Mike told me about it. It's beautiful." She gave a shrug. "What I saw of it in the dark, anyway."

"Not big. Grand tour will take all of five minutes. Feel free to look around." He glanced at her mug. "Want more coffee?"

A tiny frown creased her brow. "Scott, we made love last night. We slept together in this bed. Are you really going to stand there and act like it never happened?"

He met her gaze then, surprised by both her candor and

his own stupidity. His head flooded with a thousand things he wanted to say, but not one he could actually admit aloud.

"Why won't you talk with me about this?" she said. "Please tell me. I want to understand. You shut me down yesterday, too."

"Riley, I—" He what? He loved her, but couldn't bring himself to tell her when it meant revealing that he wasn't the man she thought she knew, but a man who'd come from a dark past.

She swung her legs around and stood up, dragging the comforter with her. It revealed more than it concealed, but she didn't seem to notice. He did. A gut-deep ache started inside, and he had to fight the urge to cover the distance between them, to admit he'd loved her forever, that he wanted nothing more than to continue loving her forever.

"Are you intentionally trying to make this weird?" she asked in a clipped tone he'd never heard before. "You care about me. You wanted me last night as much as I wanted you. I'm not imagining any of that."

"No," he admitted, forcing the words out. "You're not."

"Then what's the problem, Scott? Just talk to me."

He stared at her. At the confusion and anger on her beautiful face. What could he say? She was a strong woman. A woman who believed in people. She wanted to believe the best in him, too. And knowing that made him feel more powerless, more toxic than he'd ever felt before.

"Riley, I'm not who you think I am."

She shook her head, trying to shake off her confusion, as if she wasn't sure she'd heard him right. "I don't understand."

"No. You don't," he agreed. "You've been through so much. There's no happy ending with me. I'm no good for you."

Scott didn't give her a chance to reply. He left the room.

He could protect Riley from the men who'd killed Mike, but he didn't know how to protect her from himself. A man who didn't know the first thing about healthy, loving relationships.

CHAPTER TWENTY-THREE

JASON STOOD UNNOTICED in a side room, peering through the ajar door, for once out of the glare of the spotlight of news crews that had been assembled for this press conference.

"Last night's operation dismantled an organization that has abused its power and connections for the past several years by importing powder cocaine from Mexico, converting this material into street drugs and distributing it throughout our city and surrounding communities," Chief Levering told the reporters. "The D.A. will bring charges against the individuals involved. The success of tonight's operation is thanks to the cooperation of the FBI, Poughkeepsie and Hazard Creek Police Departments. Federal and state authorities will continue working together to attack public corruption and the sale of illegal drugs."

Jason waited through the ensuing question-and-answer period, didn't come out until the room had cleared of the media and Chief Levering was gathering items into his briefcase, looking as if he was about to head out himself.

"Chief," Jason said. "You treated me better than I deserved tonight. I wanted to say thanks."

The bust had gone down with the help of the FBI, and they'd rounded up a total of thirty-two drug dealers and six DEA agents under the command of Barry Mannis. The drug dealers were with a well-known cartel out of Juarez,

Mexico, and Chief Levering had directed Scott to book Jason privately. The chief had already worked out an arrangement with the D.A. and a judge to release Jason on his own recognizance until Internal Affairs began their investigation and decided whether or not to bring charges against him.

It had been much, much better than Jason deserved.

Chief Levering leveled a no-nonsense stare from beneath grizzled brows. "I know you're facing a tough road ahead, but I also know you did the right thing tonight. We shut down an operation that has been pumping drugs into our neighborhoods and the prisons for too long. And you've helped us to get the person responsible for Mike's murder. I appreciate that personally. I know you made some poor choices recently, but it looks like you've got company."

"Are you talking about the parole officer?"

"And a prosecutor with the D.A.'s office and correctional officers at Downstate and Green Haven. That's so far."

"Jesus," he blurted. "That many?"

Chief Levering nodded. "Seems Agent Mannis has been running quite the tight operation, which might explain why he tried to eat his gun when his drug deal went south."

"I missed that."

"Thought you might have. You and your men looked pretty busy with the feds on that plane."

No argument there.

"You came clean. That wasn't easy. It was right. Remember that when you're looking in the mirror." Chief Levering extended his hand. "Good luck, Chief."

Jason shook his hand, surprised that he didn't feel like a hypocrite for the first time in a long, long time.

The sun was coming up by the time he left the police

station by the back exit. He walked out the door into a day that looked like it might turn out to be one of those rare Indian summer days. He wasn't exactly a free man, but he was outside and not locked in a cell.

It was a start.

"Damn it," he swore as he reached into his pocket. The booking sergeant had returned his keys, but his cruiser was still at the airfield. Scott had driven him into Poughkeepsie to be booked.

Jason could have gone back inside to ask someone for a ride, but he pulled out his cell instead. He'd used up a lot more than his fair share of luck with the PPD and didn't want to push it any further.

He was about to call directory assistance for the number to a cab company, but to his surprise, he caught sight of a familiar figure at the edge of the fenced parking lot. A casually dressed black man who leaned against a motorcycle with his tattooed arms folded across his chest. Jason was surprised by the strength of the emotion he felt and headed straight toward this unexpected visitor.

"It's Sunday morning, Tyrese. Shouldn't you be at church or something?"

"Services don't start until ten. But I heard how things went down last night and thought you might need a ride."

Jason didn't ask how Tyrese had heard. The media had only just gotten hold of the story, and they wouldn't be implicating the Hazard Creek police chief, anyway. He could only assume Tyrese still had street connections. "You have a divine vision or something?"

Tyrese flashed a toothy grin and his grill gleamed. "I know how it works around here. Just glad you're walking out the door without cuffs."

"Me, too, man. Me, too."

"Then hop on, boss." Tyrese motioned to the helmet on the bike's back rail. "You're in for the ride of your life."

That was the damned truth. Jason wished he had one-tenth of Tyrese's faith that everything would turn out okay. But the sick feeling he had in the pit in his stomach promised that facing Internal Affairs and the FBI wasn't going to be pretty. And even worse would be facing his family, especially Callie. He was going to break her heart. He might find himself alone for the first time since he'd met his oh-so-competent wife.

Well, not entirely alone thanks to Chief Levering and Tyrese, he reminded himself while climbing onto the bike. And Callie did love him. He didn't doubt that. If his luck held a little while longer, he might convince her to give him a chance to earn her forgiveness, too.

"I DON'T UNDERSTAND," Riley told Chief Levering when he called to tell her and her entourage, which included her kids, in-laws and two police escorts, that the coast was clear and they could come home. "I haven't been able to reach Scott by phone ever since I left his house Saturday."

"I told you, Riley," the chief said. "He's fine. There's nothing to worry about. The sting went down better than we had a right to hope. I didn't want you coming back to town until the FBI rounded up everyone. Just a precaution."

"You're not answering my question."

"You haven't answered mine, either. Did Jake tell you where he found that CD?"

"Yes," she said, chagrined. "Behind the desk in Mike's office."

"Behind the desk?"

"Mike kept his laptop bag on the floor beside the desk.

If he put the CD in an outer pocket, it could have fallen out. Unless he had it on the desk and accidentally knocked it off himself. I don't know. Except that my inquisitive son found it."

"Which turned out to be a good thing."

"Yes, mostly," she admitted. Finding out that a corrupt DEA agent had been responsible for taking her husband's life still didn't bring him back. And considering the break-ins and the abduction and the explosion in the middle of her kitchen… "Now back to Scott. If he wasn't hurt in the sting, then why aren't you telling me where he is?"

"He got a phone call about some personal business he had to deal with out of town."

She glared at the phone, plastered a smile on her face while crossing the living room, where Rosie, Lily Susan and the kids sat poring over old photo albums. She pulled open the door and slipped onto the patio.

"Out of town is a big place, Chief. Anywhere in particular?"

"I understand you're annoyed, but I can't tell you what you want to know."

To say she was annoyed was a dramatic understatement. She simply didn't believe the man had made love to her then disappeared off the planet without a word.

"Chief, my house and minivan were broken into. My equipment was stolen. I'm so scared for my children's safety that I have to send them away and get around-the-clock police protection, which didn't do the trick, I might add. My kitchen blew up. I'm abducted in an ambulance that winds up in a ditch. You find the people responsible for my husband's murder and bring down a drug organization that involves public corruption on local, state and federal levels." Her voice rose in a crescendo despite her best efforts at remaining rational. "After all I've been through, you won't tell me where Scott is?"

"Riley, please, I can't tell you." The chief sounded as helpless as she felt, and guilt pricked her conscience.

It passed quickly. She wasn't going to accept this. She wanted answers. Scott wasn't giving them to her, so the chief was her next best option.

Before he got a chance to make another excuse or hang up, Riley launched into her plea. Not the gory intimate details, of course, but the broad strokes.

"I know Scott cares about me," she told him. "but he has totally shut down. He refuses to discuss what's going on between us, and I don't know if he's flipping out because of Mike. I didn't expect this any more than he did, but we can't pretend it isn't happening. He said he wasn't good for me, and now he's AWOL. Do you understand why I'm worried? You know him better than anyone. Can't you give me something to work with here?"

To her surprise Chief Levering chuckled. "Having cops is more trouble than having kids."

"What does that mean?"

"It means you've convinced me to betray his confidence."

"I did?" She frowned, afraid to believe winning him over had been that easy.

"You did. How much do you know about Scott's up-bringing?"

Sinking onto the edge of a planter, Riley stared out at the street with its traffic rushing in all directions. "I know he comes from New Jersey. Caroline told me his mother died when he was young and his grandmother raised him for a while. Mike only said his past had been somehow…difficult."

"*Difficult* doesn't describe it, Riley, but that's Scott's story. Right now all you need to know is where he is."

"Why are you telling me now?"

"Because I know Scott. I don't want him to let a good thing pass by because he's a stubborn pain in the ass."

"And…" She couldn't get out another word around the lump in her throat.

"*And* I hate that he's alone right now. His father died, Riley. He got the call a few hours after the sting."

"Oh, no."

The chief snorted. "Don't get me wrong. He hated the son of a bitch. If he'd had any choice, he wouldn't be dealing with this at all. But he's next of kin. And given the circumstances, there wasn't anyone else."

"What circumstances?"

The chief's sigh made Riley brace herself. "His father was a lifer. Tri-State Correctional Facility in Jersey. Murder one. That's all I'm going to say. You want to know more, then talk to Scott. He went to sign papers and make arrangements. I offered to go with him, but he wouldn't let me. He knows this place is a zoo with the Feds here."

Still clutching the phone, Riley stared into the street, consumed by the idea of Scott alone. Thoughtful, kind Scott, the man who made nests and babysat sick little girls, who helped teens fix cars and get their lives on track. The man who'd always been there for her, who'd held her, who'd listened to her rant, who'd rescued her from an ambulance in a ditch. The man who'd reawakened her ability to feel and brought her back to life with his kindness and kisses.

Had Mike been alive, he'd have been with Scott right now. There wasn't a doubt in Riley's mind.

"I'm on my way, Chief."

"Good girl." He gave a laugh. "Just give me a call when you get close. I'll find out exactly where he is. If he's still at the correctional facility, I'll make some calls to get you in."

"Got it."

"Good luck, Riley."

She laughed. "Sounds like I'm going to need it."

After disconnecting the call, she remained outside, taking time to collect her thoughts and whisper a silent plea to Mike for some idea of how best to be there for Scott.

And Riley knew as surely as if he'd spoken to her directly from heaven what Mike would have done—he would have offered unconditional support and love just as he always had.

That was one of the things she'd always loved and admired about her husband.

But Riley wasn't the only one who loved Scott, and as far as she was concerned things always worked out for a reason. At the moment, she had a whole living room filled with people who considered Scott one of the family.

With an utter certainty she hadn't enjoyed in a long time, Riley headed back inside the apartment and called her kids. "Hey, guys, want to help me make somebody feel better?"

"Who?" Camille asked.

"Uncle Scott. His dad died, so I'm thinking we should try to make him feel better. What do you think?"

Those two sweet little faces reflected so much concern that Riley could only marvel at how mature they were becoming. They understood what it meant to lose a dad.

"I still feel sad," Jake admitted. "Hugs make me feel better."

"And pizza," Camille suggested. "We can bring Uncle Scott pizza. That will make him feel better."

Riley could not have possibly been more proud. Laughing, she met Joe's gaze above the kids' heads. "Those are great ideas. Now go make sure you've got everything in your duffel bags, okay? We don't want to leave Aunt Lily Susan's house trashed or she won't invite us back."

The kids took off for the guest bedroom, leaving Riley to relay the adult version of the situation to Rosie and Joe.

Then she was sitting between her kids in the back seat of Joe's Cadillac heading south on the Jersey turnpike.

The correctional facility turned out to be barely more than an hour outside of the city. She called the chief when they arrived in town to find that Scott had already gone to the funeral home to finalize burial arrangements. When Joe wheeled into the parking lot, Riley spotted his car immediately.

"Why don't you all wait here for a few minutes," she suggested. "Give me a chance to find him."

"You got it," Joe said. "Wouldn't mind getting out and stretching a bit."

Riley kissed his cheek. "Just a few minutes."

"Take your time."

Steeling herself with a few deep breaths, Riley hurried inside. The foyer had been decorated in standard upscale funeral home style, and she couldn't help but remember the last time she'd been inside one—when life as she'd known it had ended. Ironic she'd be back inside one today, hoping that her life as she'd come to know it would change again.

Fortunately she didn't walk in on any services, but a gentleman in a suit emerged from an office to greet her.

"Good afternoon," he said. "May I help you?"

"I'm looking for Scott Emerson. I was told he's here."

"Right this way." The man extended an arm toward a long hallway, and Riley followed him. She found Scott seated at a conference table with paperwork spread out in front of him.

Riley drank in the sight of him, glossy dark hair, broad shoulders, cheeks drawn and tight in a carefully blank expression that revealed nothing and everything all at once.

She knew that look, could visibly see what it cost him to keep detached from the task at hand.

"Mr. Emerson," the funeral director said. "Someone here to see you."

Scott glanced up absently, then did a double take. "Riley?"

"Will you give us a few moments?" she asked the funeral director, who was already retreating from the room. He closed the door behind him.

"What are you doing here?" Scott rose slowly to his feet, clearly rattled.

"I came so you wouldn't be alone."

He stood there, hands hanging helplessly before him, the pain in his expression practically breaking her heart. "Riley, you don't understand."

"No," she admitted. "But I want to."

"You shouldn't have come."

"Can't it be enough that I didn't want you to be alone right now? That I wanted you to know how much you mean to me? Not only to me but to all the people who love you."

He scowled, and she came face-to-face with that stubborn pain in the ass the chief had mentioned.

"I appreciate what you're trying to do," he said. "But you shouldn't be here."

"Tell me why not? You're burying your father, Scott. That's difficult under the best of circumstances. From what I understand, these don't even come close."

He looked stricken, and Riley ached for his pain, pain she was causing him. Stepping forward, she took his hands in hers, felt the warm strength she'd only just gotten to know.

"I want to be here for you," she said. "The way you're always there for me." She meant it. She wasn't sure how it had happened, but she'd come to care so deeply about this man.

He pulled his hands away. "You shouldn't—"

"Yes, I should. You care about me, too. Don't bother denying it. I'm not stupid. I can't explain why this is happening between us. And I don't have any answers about where it might lead. But I do know how I feel."

"Not here. Not for *this*." There was a broken boy inside that gruff plea, and Riley recognized him, couldn't resist the need to comfort and love him.

Slipping her arms around his waist, she pressed close, rested her cheek against his chest. Then she held him. He didn't move, stood so still he might have been carved from stone.

She held her breath, refusing to let him frighten her off, only wanting to help, only wanting him to accept her help.

"When I was in that ambulance," she whispered, "the only thing that kept me from going to pieces was knowing you wouldn't stop looking until you found me. Don't ask me to stop looking for you."

He responded then, arms anchoring her tight, his whole body contouring to hers, such a perfect fit. They stood there, holding each other in the silence, proving without words how much they cared.

And when Scott pressed soft kisses into her hair, down her cheek and finally caught her mouth with his, Riley knew they'd weathered this storm, knew they'd be okay.

"Thank you," he whispered against her mouth.

She had no words, only had emotion to guide her. Rising up on tiptoes, she kissed him until there could be no doubt she meant everything she'd said. Then she stood behind him, with her hand on his shoulder as he finished signing the papers. He set the pen on top of the stack and pushed away from the table.

"Done?" she asked.

He met her gaze and didn't try to shield the emotion there. "No viewing. No service. There's no one to come."

She placed her hand in his and held on while the funeral director reviewed the formalities.

Then they left hand in hand, Riley smiling at Scott's surprise when he recognized who awaited him in the parking lot.

Two generations of Angelicas descended on him. Joe shook his hand and said all the right words, and Rosie hugged him fiercely. Jake must have thought Scott didn't need another hug because he mimicked his grandpa, shaking Scott's hand so stoically that Scott's expression twitched with suppressed laughter.

But Camille sealed the deal when she circled Scott on her wheeled sneakers and asked, "Pizza will make you feel better, won't it, Uncle Scott?"

Scott's smile broke free then, and he ruffled her blond head fondly. "You know. I think pizza's just the thing."

Camille wheeled around her brother with her hands outstretched in an I-told-you-so-gesture. And as they walked to the cars, working out seating arrangements for the ride to the nearest pizza place, Riley found herself beside Joe.

He took her hand and whispered, "Mike would be very proud of his family today."

Riley felt that familiar emotion well in her throat, but today it was a full, good feeling. She knew Joe was right. Mike had always understood what she was now just accepting.

Life was meant to be lived.

And her beloved husband would have wanted nothing less than that for the people he loved.

She kissed Joe's cheek. "I think you're right. He would be very proud of his family. All of them."

EPILOGUE

Two years later

SCOTT SWUNG DOWN from the tree, where he'd been string-ing streamers in the branches the way kids toilet-papered houses at Halloween. He stepped back to survey his handiwork. "What do you think, guys? This what you had in mind?"

"It's perfect, Uncle Scott." Camille breathed an excited sigh, eyes sparkling like her mother's when she gazed around the scene at the fishing hole with undisguised delight. "Mommy's going to love it."

"Too much pink, Camille." Her brother screwed up his face in distaste. "It looks like someone puked strawberry Kool-Aid. I told you to get blue balloons."

"Mommy doesn't like blue, Jakie."

Camille was the only one nowadays who could get away with calling her brother by that name. To the rest of the world, this eight-almost-nine-year-old man wanted to be known as Jacob.

"We're never going to catch any fish," Jacob lamented.

Scott wasn't sure the decorations would scare off any fish, but he did have a point. "We need to tie the horses farther downstream just in case the balloons pop. They'll spook."

Two impish faces spun around to stare, clearly curious

about what spooked horses involved, and Scott realized he might have made a mistake giving them any ideas. "Come on, guys. Give me a hand. Jacob, you lead Shadow. Camille, take Baby."

He led Charger downstream himself, until they found a place where the horses could graze and drink while the rest of them got about this day. They'd been planning this for weeks now, and Scott didn't want the kids to forget anything important to them.

Riley knew something was going on—how could she not when they'd abandoned her with the picnic basket at the house? She didn't know what and played along anyway, telling them she would check the picnic basket again to make sure they had everything for their afternoon of fishing.

That had been an hour ago.

"Are we ready to call your mom?" Scott asked. "Can you think of anything we missed?"

"Call Mom, Uncle Scott," Jacob said. "I'm starving."

No news there. "You ready, too, Camille?"

"Ready."

Scott flipped open the cell phone and hit speed dial.

Riley picked up on the first ring. "Hey, you. I was getting worried."

"Just a few logistical things to work out."

"I can't imagine what you're doing. I'm excited."

"Me, too," he admitted.

"Not one hint?" she coaxed in a voice that made him smile.

"Not even one. We want you to be surprised."

"Okay then." She strung the words out, but he could hear the amusement in her voice. "Ready for me?"

"Always ready for you, gorgeous."

She laughed, and the sound spiked his growing anticipation, a feeling of contentment he'd never known before and welcomed fiercely. Life had been so good, in fact, that he was determined never to take one second for granted. "See you in a few, then. And don't go straight to the fishing hole—meet us downstream. We'll be waiting."

"Will do." She blew him a kiss over the line, and Scott disconnected, turning to the kids. "She's on her way."

"Got the blindfold, Jakie?" Camille asked.

"Check." Jacob produced the bandanna he'd rolled up for just this occasion.

"Got the ring, Uncle Scott?"

"Check." Scott patted the pocket of his cargo pants, where not one but three jewelers' boxes were concealed.

"Decorations?"

"Check."

"Flowers."

"Check."

"Mom has the food, right?" Jacob asked uncertainly.

Scott inclined his head. "Check."

It wasn't long until Jacob cocked his head to the side, and his eyes widened. "I hear her. She's coming."

Sure enough, Riley rode into the clearing on Sugar, her eyes sparkling as she glanced around curiously. "Is this where we're picnicking today?"

Scott reached up to take the basket. "No, ma'am. This is the parking lot. Here you go, Jacob. One full picnic basket."

Jacob didn't have to be asked twice. He took the basket so Scott could help Riley dismount.

"Where is it?" Camille hissed to her brother. "The blindfold?"

Jacob wasn't relinquishing his hold on the picnic basket, not even to perform his prescribed part in this drama.

Camille snapped the bandanna out of his back pocket and told Riley, "Kneel down, Mommy."

"You're blindfolding me?" Riley gasped, but she did as asked and submitted to her daughter's ministrations, which turned out to be a fairly haphazard job at best.

"No peeking," Camille instructed. "Ready, Uncle Scott?"

"Ready. I'll grab one side and you grab the other."

With them acting as honor guard, they carefully escorted Riley back to the fishing hole and led her into the center of the clearing where she couldn't possibly miss the full effect of all their hard work.

"Ready?" Scott asked Camille, taking a step back and folding his arms over his chest so he could enjoy the scene.

She exchanged a glance with Jacob, then shook her head. "Okay, Mommy, you can look now."

Riley peeled away the blindfold then opened her eyes. She brought her hands to her mouth and twirled, taking in their carefully executed decorations.

"Ohmigosh," she exclaimed with exactly the perfect amount of surprise for the occasion. "This is amazing. Did it rain pink fairies today?"

Camille giggled.

"But it's not my birthday. It's not even any of your birthdays." She glanced suspiciously at them. "So what are we celebrating?"

Jacob, still hanging on to the picnic basket, glanced Scott's way. "Go on, Uncle Scott. Do it."

Scott made a great show of unfolding his arms and pushing away from the tree. He gave an exaggerated cough to clear his throat, ready to play his part. But he obviously wasn't moving quickly enough because Camille took his hand and led him to Riley.

"Go on," she said. "Do it right. Like we practiced."

Riley met his gaze above the kids' heads. He winked, knowing that in that instant, her surprise wasn't feigned.

Slipping his hand inside his pocket, he felt around for the appropriate box. Then he knelt in front of Riley. Her eyes grew wide and her mouth formed a delightful O at the exact time he flipped open the jeweler's box and held it out to her.

"Riley Angelica, I love you, and I love your kids. I want us to be a family."

"A *real* family," Camille said.

"A real family," he repeated. Then he removed the ring from the box and slipped it onto her finger.

The ring fit perfectly, as he'd known it would, and he pressed a kiss to her fingers and smiled up at her. Those gorgeous blue eyes were glinting suspiciously, and he knew she was too overcome to reply.

He bought her some time by motioning for the kids. "Come here, you two."

He pulled the remaining boxes from his pocket, and when they saw there were more gifts, they were flanking Riley before Scott could take his next breath.

"For us?" Camille gasped, a mini-version of Riley as she brought her hands to her mouth in surprise.

Scott nodded and knelt before them. "Camille, Jacob, I love you both, and I love your mom. I want us to be a real family."

He opened the other jeweler's box to reveal a little-girl-size ring with a pink pearl and two tiny diamonds. He slipped it onto Camille's finger.

"Oh, I do," she squealed, throwing her arms around his neck. He caught her delicate body in a big hug, laughing.

"You didn't get me a ring, did you, Uncle Scott?" Jacob slowly set down the picnic basket, clearly worried.

"Will you turn me down if I did?" Scott laughed.

"Uh, yeah." He sounded as if that should have been obvious.

"No ring. I didn't want to risk it." He handed Jacob the remaining box, waited while he opened it to find one top-of-the-line Swiss Army knife.

"Too cool." The box hit the ground at his feet and he started prying out the equipment for inspection. "Screw-driver. File. Whoa. Look at this knife."

Riley found her voice. "No missing fingers today, please."

"Mom, I have an axe, remember?" This blade was small by comparison.

Camille shifted around to sit on Scott's knee, and he looped his arm around her waist to hold her steady and asked, "So, what'll it be, Jacob?"

"Oh, yeah." He held up the knife with a gleam in his eye that would have made most folks nervous.

Scott wasn't entirely sure that yes had been for him, but he'd take it.

"Oh, no." Camille brought her hands to her mouth in horror. "You're the only one who didn't get a present, Uncle Scott."

"That's not true. I'm getting the best present of all. You guys as my family." He glanced up at Riley, whose eyes were sparkling. "That is if your mom accepts."

Camille hopped off his lap and went straight to Riley. "Mo-om, you're supposed to say yes."

Scott got to his feet, suddenly breathless. His future hung in the balance as he awaited an answer from this woman he loved more than life itself. The woman who loved him unconditionally in return and had helped him recognize that, though he'd loved her forever, he'd never betrayed Mike's trust with those feelings. An honorable choice worthy of the people he loved. He had nothing to be ashamed of and a life filled with love to look forward to.

"Yes," Riley said simply.

One word and his whole life changed, was suddenly complete. Then she was in his arms, her laughter breaking against his mouth as they kissed.

"Yes." She breathed the word again. "Yes."

"What are we going to call you, Uncle Scott?" Jacob asked. "You won't be our uncle anymore after you marry Mom."

"That's true." Scott abandoned his attempts to kiss his new fiancée—he should have known better by now—and twisted Riley in his arms so they could both face the kids. "I'll be your stepfather."

Jacob screwed up his face in that look that said more than words ever could. "That's not working for me."

"He's Lieutenant Emerson at the station," Camille said.

"That's stupid, Camille." Jacob earned a look from Riley that should have made his ears dry up and fall off. "We can't call him Lieutenant Emerson."

"How about we refrain from the name-calling and brainstorm," Scott suggested. "I could use some help here."

And he got his help from the beautiful young girl who looked so like her mother that he melted inside when she turned sparkly eyes up to his and said, "Daddy's Daddy, so you can be…" Her words trailed off as she cocked her head to the side, considering. "Pop. You'll be Pop, Uncle Scott. It's just right."

And it was.

* * * * *

Kay Young returned to woozy consciousness to find that she was lying on a soft sofa beneath a heap of quilts near a cheerfully burning fire. When she tried to move, however, everything hurt, and she groaned.

At once she heard a sound, then a stranger with a hard, harsh face was squatting beside her. "Shh," he said softly. "You're safe here. I promise."

"I have to go," she said weakly, struggling against pain. "He'll find me. He can't find me."

"Easy, lady," he said quietly. "You're hurt. No one's going to find you here."

"He will," she said desperately, terror clutching at her insides. "He always finds me!"

"Easy," he said again. "There's a blizzard outside. No one's getting here tonight, not even the doctor. I know, because I tried."

"Doctor? I don't need a doctor! I've got to get away."

"There's nowhere to go tonight," he said levelly. "And if I thought you could stand, I'd take you to a window and show you."

But even as she tried once more to pull away the quilts, she remembered something else: this man had been gentle when he'd found her beside the road, even when she had kicked and clawed. He hadn't hurt her.

Terror receded just a bit. She looked at him and detected signs of true concern there.

The terror eased another notch and she let her head sag on the pillow. "He always finds me," she whispered.

"Not here. Not tonight. That much I can guarantee."

Will Kay's mysterious rescuer protect her
from her worst fears?
Find out in HER HERO IN HIDING
by New York Times *bestselling author Rachel Lee.*
Available June 2010, only from
Silhouette® Romantic Suspense.

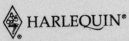

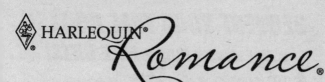

HARLEQUIN® *Romance*®

GIRLS' Weekend in VEGAS

Four friends, four dream weddings!

On a girly weekend in Las Vegas, best friends Alex, Molly,
Serena and Jayne are supposed to just have fun and forget
men, but they end up meeting their perfect matches!
Will the love they find in Vegas stay in Vegas?

Find out in this sassy, fun and wildly romantic miniseries
all about love and friendship!

www.eHarlequin.com

HR17663

REQUEST YOUR FREE BOOKS!

2 FREE NOVELS PLUS 2 FREE GIFTS!

HARLEQUIN®
Super Romance®

Exciting, emotional, unexpected!

YES! Please send me 2 FREE Harlequin® Superromance® novels and my 2 FREE gifts (gifts are worth about $10). After receiving them, if I don't wish to receive any more books, I can return the shipping statement marked "cancel." If I don't cancel, I will receive 6 brand-new novels every month and be billed just $4.69 per book in the U.S. or $5.24 per book in Canada. That's a saving of at least 15% off the cover price! It's quite a bargain! Shipping and handling is just 50¢ per book.* I understand that accepting the 2 free books and gifts places me under no obligation to buy anything. I can always return a shipment and cancel at any time. Even if I never buy another book from Harlequin, the two free books and gifts are mine to keep forever.

135/336 HDN E5P4

Name _____ (PLEASE PRINT)

Address _____ Apt. #

City _____ State/Prov. _____ Zip/Postal Code

Signature (if under 18, a parent or guardian must sign)

Mail to the Harlequin Reader Service:
IN U.S.A.: P.O. Box 1867, Buffalo, NY 14240-1867
IN CANADA: P.O. Box 609, Fort Erie, Ontario L2A 5X3

Not valid for current subscribers to Harlequin Superromance books.

Are you a current subscriber to Harlequin Superromance books and want to receive the larger-print edition?
Call 1-800-873-8635 today!

* Terms and prices subject to change without notice. Prices do not include applicable taxes. N.Y. residents add applicable sales tax. Canadian residents will be charged applicable provincial taxes and GST. Offer not valid in Quebec. This offer is limited to one order per household. All orders subject to approval. Credit or debit balances in a customer's account(s) may be offset by any other outstanding balance owed by or to the customer. Please allow 4 to 6 weeks for delivery. Offer available while quantities last.

Your Privacy: Harlequin Books is committed to protecting your privacy. Our Privacy Policy is available online at www.eHarlequin.com or upon request from the Reader Service. From time to time we make our lists of customers available to reputable third parties who may have a product or service of interest to you. If you would prefer we not share your name and address, please check here. ☐

Help us get it right—We strive for accurate, respectful and relevant communications. To clarify or modify your communication preferences, visit us at www.ReaderService.com/consumerschoice.

HSR10R

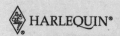

HARLEQUIN®

Showcase

Vicki Lewis Thompson

On sale May 11, 2010

Reader favorites from the most talented voices in romance

Save $1.00 on the purchase of 1 or more Harlequin® Showcase books.

SAVE $1.00 on the purchase of 1 or more Harlequin® Showcase books.

Coupon expires Oct 31, 2010. Redeemable at participating retail outlets.
Limit one coupon per purchase. Valid in the U.S.A. and Canada only.

52609015

Canadian Retailers: Harlequin Enterprises Limited will pay the face value of this coupon plus 10.25¢ if submitted by customer for this product only. Any other use constitutes fraud. Coupon is nonassignable. Void if taxed, prohibited or restricted by law. Consumer must pay any government taxes. Void if copied. Nielsen Clearing House ("NCH") customers submit coupons and proof of sales to Harlequin Enterprises Limited, P.O. Box 3000, Saint John, NB E2L 4L3, Canada. Non-NCH retailer—for reimbursement submit coupons and proof of sales directly to Harlequin Enterprises Limited, Retail Marketing Department, 225 Duncan Mill Rd., Don Mills, ON M3B 3K9, Canada.

U.S. Retailers: Harlequin Enterprises Limited will pay the face value of this coupon plus 8¢ if submitted by customer for this product only. Any other use constitutes fraud. Coupon is nonassignable. Void if taxed, prohibited or restricted by law. Consumer must pay any government taxes. Void if copied. For reimbursement submit coupons and proof of sales directly to Harlequin Enterprises Limited, P.O. Box 880478, El Paso, TX 88588-0478, U.S.A. Cash value 1/100 cents.

5 65373 00076 2   (8100)0 11651

® and TM are trademarks owned and used by the trademark owner and/or its licensee.
© 2009 Harlequin Enterprises Limited

HSCCOUP0410

COMING NEXT MONTH

Available June 8, 2010